W9-BFZ-028

 Frankston Library Service

Please return items by the date printed on your loans docket.
To renew loans by phone, quote your library card number or go to
http://library.frankston.vic.gov.au. Overdue items cannot be renewed
Fees are charged for items returned late.

FRANKSTON LIBRARY
60 Playne Street
Frankston 3199
Victoria Australia
Tel: (03) 9784 1020
Fax: (03) 9783 2616
TTY (03) 9784 1707

CARRUM DOWNS LIBRARY
203 Lyrebird Drive
Carrum Downs 3201
Victoria Australia
Tel: (03) 9782 0418
Fax: (03) 9782 0187
TTY (03) 9782 6871

The Year of the Ladybird

Also by Graham Joyce from Gollancz:

Leningrad Nights
Smoking Poppy
The Limits of Enchantment
The Facts of Life
The Tooth Fairy
Memoirs of a Master Forger (as William Heaney)
The Silent Land
Some Kind of Fairy Tale

The Year of the Ladybird

Graham Joyce

GOLLANCZ

LONDON

The right of Graham Joyce to be identified as the author
of this work has been asserted by him in accordance with the
Copyright, Designs and Patents Act 1988.

First published in Great Britain in 2013 by Gollancz
An imprint of the Orion Publishing Group
Orion House, 5 Upper St Martin's Lane, London WC2H 9EA
An Hachette UK Company

A CIP catalogue record for this book
is available from the British Library

ISBN 978 0 575 11531 6

1 3 5 7 9 10 8 6 4 2

Typeset by Deltatype Ltd, Birkenhead, Merseyside

Printed in Great Britain by
CPI Group (UK) Ltd, Croydon, CRO 4YY

The Orion Publishing Group's policy is to use papers that are natural,
renewable and recyclable products and made from wood grown in
sustainable forests. The logging and manufacturing processes are expected
to conform to the environmental regulations of the country of origin.

www.grahamjoyce.net
www.orionbooks.co.uk
www.gollancz.co.uk

To my son Joe, who inspires me to do better.

I

Lend them no money buy them no beer

It was 1976 and the hottest summer in living memory. The reservoirs were cracked and dry; some of the towns were restricted to water from standpipes; crops were failing in the fields. England was a country innocent of all such extremity. I was nineteen and I'd just finished my first year at college.

Broke and with time on my hands I needed a summer job. Looking for a way out from the plans my stepdad had made for me, I got an interview at a holiday camp on the East Coast. Skegness, celebrated for that jolly fisherman in gumboots and a sou'wester gamely making headway against a seaward gale: *It's so bracing*!

But when I arrived in Skegness there wasn't a breath of wind, not even a sigh. The train rumbled in on hot iron tracks, decanted me and a few others onto the platform and wheezed out again. The dirty Victorian red brick of the station seemed brittle, powdery. Flowers potted along the platform wilted and the grubby paintwork was cracked and peeled. I took a double-decker bus – mercifully open-topped – and I asked the driver to drop me at the camp. He forgot, and had to stop the bus and come up the stairs to tell me he'd passed it by. I had to backpack it a quarter of a mile, all in the shimmering heat. I followed the wire-mesh perimeter of the site with its neat rows of chalets and the seagull-like cries of the campers.

I thought I might get a job as a kitchen porter or as a white-jacketed waiter bowling soup-plates at the holidaymakers. Any job at all, just so long as I didn't have to go home. The manager in charge of recruitment – a dapper figure in a blue blazer and sporting a tiny pencil moustache – didn't seem too interested. He was preoccupied with sprinkling bread crumbs on the corner of his desk. As I waited to be interviewed, a sparrow fluttered in through the open window, picked up a crumb in its beak and flew out again.

'That's amazing,' I said.

No eye contact. 'Tell me a bit about yourself.'

I coloured. 'Well, I'm studying to be a teacher, so I'm good with children.'

One of his eyebrows raised a notch. Encouraged, I added, 'Actually I like children. And I can play a few chords. On the guitar.'

The first bit was true but the thing about the guitar was a good stretch. I mean I knew the rough finger positions for the E, the A and the C chords. Go and form a band, as they said at the time. The sparrow winged in again, picked up more breadcrumbs and fluttered out.

'What's your name again?'

'David Barwise.'

'David,' he said at last. 'Find your way over to the laundry room and tell Dot to kit you out as a Greencoat. Then report to Pinky. He's our Entertainments Manager, you know. He has an office behind the theatre. You know where the theatre is, don't you?'

I'd stuck in my thumb and pulled out a plumb. It

was early June and the temperature was already soaring into the high eighties. The kitchen was a sweat at any time. A Greencoat's job on the other hand had to be the prized option. I didn't know too much about it but I guessed you organised the Bathing Belle Parade around the swimming pool; you got to walk around in the fresh air and to fraternise with the holidaymakers.

To get to the laundry room I had to pass between a little white caravan and a beautifully kempt crown-bowling green. Despite the drought regulations a sprinkler ticked away, keeping the grass green for the bowling. Outside the caravan was a professionally-painted billboard with a picture of an open palm bearing occult lines and numbers. The billboard advertised the services of one Madame Rosa, *As Seen On TV*, palmist and fortune-teller to the stars. I didn't think I'd ever seen anyone called Madame Rosa on TV.

But the carnival stopped there, and the laundry room was a soulless breeze-block construction behind the offices where Dot, a stressed and rather grouchy woman with grey roots under her thinning bleached hair, toiled away in clouds of billowing steam. I interrupted her in the act of pressing shirts with an industrial iron. I smiled and let her know I needed kitting out as a Greencoat.

'You?' she said.

Maybe I blinked.

She seemed to be able to focus one eye on me while keeping the other eye on her work. 'You could cut your hair and smarten yourself up a bit.'

I bit my lip as she unearthed a set of whites for me – trousers and shirts – plus a green sweater and a loud blazer, candy-striped green, white and red. She dumped them on the counter.

3

The sizes were all hopelessly wrong, and I protested.

'Yeh, you tell 'em,' she said, turning back to her labours with the iron. The contraption made a huge hiss and she retreated into her cave behind a cloud of steam.

Clutching my new clothes, I was directed to the staff chalets. I say chalets, with its suggestion of delightful beachside cabins, but they were just a row of shaky, plaster-board rabbit-hutches with a communal shower and toilets. It was all pretty basic. Each 'room' had just enough space for two narrow cots, with a gap of about eighteen inches between them, and a pair of miraculously slim wardrobes.

But I was happy to be by the seaside. It meant I didn't have to work with my stepdad. It was a job. It paid cash, folding.

One of the beds was unmade and a couple of shirts hung on wire hangers in its frail partner-wardrobe. It seemed I had a room-mate, but aside from a whiff of stale tobacco there were few clues to give me any hint about his character. I unpacked my belongings and changed into the whites I'd been given.

The trousers were baggy at the waist and long in the leg; the shirts at least one collar size too big. I had a sewing kit in my bag, something I thought I'd never need, so I turned up the trouser cuffs to shorten them and though I didn't make a great job of the sewing, the cuffs stayed up. It left me baggy in the crotch but I had a good belt to keep my trousers aloft. At least the candy-striped blazer was a rough fit. I gave myself the once over in the mirror on the reverse of the door. I looked like a clown. I tried out a showbizzy greeting smile in the mirror. I scared myself with it.

4

I'd been told to meet Pinky in the theatre. I passed through an impressive front-of-house built to emulate a West End playhouse, with a plush foyer of red velvet fabrics and golden ropes. Billboards proclaimed a range of theatre acts with gilt-framed professional black-and-white head shots. One giant picture had a wild-eyed man called *Abdul-Shazam!* in a tasselled red fez pointing his fingers at the camera in mesmeric fashion. His eyes followed me as I passed though giant doors leading into a hushed auditorium. I made my way down past the shadowed rows of red velvet seats to the front of the stage where I could see a small light illuminating an old-style Wurlitzer organ. The organist was studying some music scores while a second man in a blue-and-yellow checked jacket looked on with a doleful expression.

The heyday of the British holiday camps had slipped. The age of cheap flights had arrived and holidays in the guaranteed sunshine of the Costa Brava had dented the industrial fortnight supremacy. It all felt time-locked. The doleful man glanced up at me as I proceeded down the aisle, and I felt he, too, was time locked, maybe in the 1950s. His hair was pressed into a permanent wave that had crawled to the top of his forehead before taking a look over the edge and deciding to go no further. He held an unlit cigar between his fingers and his eyebrows were perpetually arched, as if he were so often surprised by life that he had decided to save himself the energy of frequently raising and lowering them. 'Let's have a look at you then,' he said.

I stepped into the light shining from above the Wurlitzer.

He took a puff on his unlit cigar. 'Christ,' he said.

5

Pinky Pardew – real name Martin Pardew – was the Entertainments Manager. He governed the camp jollies: the Children's entertainment; the daily timetable of events; the Variety acts in the Theatre; the bingo, the darts and dominos; the singalong in the saloon; everything occupying the campers' time from 9.30 in the morning until 2 a.m. that didn't involve food and alcohol. It was a busy programme of enforced bonhomie. He was also boss to an Assistant Stage Manager, the Children's Entertainer and the team of six Greencoats – three boys and three girls. I'd arrived at the right moment to replace a Greencoat who'd quit. Good timing.

He stared at me glumly, cigar wedged deep between his fingers, his eyebrows still arched high like windows in a locked village church.

'I think whoever had these before me,' I said seriously, 'must have been a bit overweight.'

It got a snort from the man at the organ. He was of only a slightly more contemporary cut. He wore a black turtle neck shirt and his hair was trimmed pudding-bowl style, like one of the Beatles when they were still shocked at their own fame.

'All right,' Pinky said. 'We'll see if we can improve on that lot. Tomorrow. Meanwhile you're just in time for lunch at the canteen. Then at two o' clock you'll find a bunch of lads waiting for you on the football field. Referee a game, will you?' He rummaged around in the pocket of his chequered jacket and brought out a silver object on a string. 'Here's your whistle. Try not to use it. Who are you?'

'I'm David,' I said. I shot out a hand expecting him to shake it. It was a nervous gesture I instantly regretted.

Pinky looked at my hand as if he hadn't seen one before. To my relief he then conceded the handshake. But it was a brief gesture before he turned back to the man at the organ. The musician tapped out three quick rising notes on the keyboard. Pa-pa-pah! I took that to be theatre-speak for *thanks, right, g'bye*.

The staff canteen thrummed and clattered. A few faces glanced up to take in the new boy, but returned to their conversations without paying me much attention. I felt clumsy and I knew I looked uncomfortable in my ill-fitting 'uniform'. I slid my tray along the rail and two ample but deadpan ladies from behind the counter loaded my plate with leek soup and a dollop of cod in white sauce.

All the tables were occupied with chattering staff and the only empty chairs would have me crash some intimate group. Except for one table where a couple in white cleaners' overalls ate in sullen silence. The male hunched over a bowl of soup looked pretty rough, but two chairs stood empty at their table. I went for it.

'Mind if I sit down?'

They didn't even look up at me.

My cheeks flamed. The buzz of canteen conversation diminished. I got the strange sensation that everyone else eating there was suddenly interested in my progress. They all continued to talk but with less animation; they flickered glances in my direction but looked away just as quickly. The tension in the room had ratcheted up out of nowhere, but everyone was pretending nothing had changed.

The man bent on ignoring me had a close-crop of tinsel-grey-and-black hair that reminded me of the alpha-male silverback gorilla; and though he was still hunched over his soup bowl, he had frozen. His spoon, having ladled, was arrested mid-path between dish and lip. I switched my gaze to his partner, a much younger woman maybe in her late twenties. The palm of one delicate hand flew to her face, but then she too was immobilised. Her brown eyes were opened in alarm, though her gaze was tracked not on me but on her partner.

I looked back at the man. 'I didn't want to crowd you. There aren't any other seats.'

At last, at long last, he lifted his bony head and gazed up at me. His complexion was ruddy and weathered, all broken surface capillaries. The whites of his cold eyes were stained with spots of yellow. He blinked in frigid assessment. Finally he offered the briefest of nods which I took as permission to sit down. I unloaded my soup and my fish and leaned my empty tray precariously against the leg of my chair.

The man's wife – I took the wide gold band on her finger to mean that they were married – relaxed a little, but not completely. She glanced at me and then back at her husband. Meanwhile he put his head down and continued to eat, reaching all the way round to the far side of his dish, digging back into his soup before raising his spoon to his mouth. His sleeves were rolled. Naval tattoos, faded and discoloured on the pale skin beneath the dark hairs of his arms, flexed slightly as he ate. Between the lower finger knuckles of his fists were artlessly tattooed the words LOVE and HATE in washed out blue ink.

I started in on my leek soup.

'First day?' I heard him say, though he appeared to

growl right into his dish. His voice was a miraculous low throaty rasp. Southern.

His wife looked at me and nodded almost imperceptibly, encouraging me to respond.

'Yes,' I said brightly. 'Trying to work out where everything is. Get the hang of things. You know? Got lost three times already.' I laughed. I was a bag of nerves and I knew it and he knew it. I coloured again and I hated myself for it.

He lifted his head at last and looked from side to side as if an enemy might be listening. It was like we were in prison. Almost without moving his lips he croaked, 'Keep your head down. Be all right.'

His wife was looking at me now. Her beautiful brown eyes blazed at me. But behind them her expression seemed to be saying something else.

He pushed his empty soup bowl aside and sucked on his teeth before reaching for his plate of fish. His wife quickly buttered a slice of bread and set it before him. She had long elegant fingers. Her extreme delicacy and prettiness was a shocking contrast to the coarseness of her husband. He took the buttered bread and between strong fingertips coloured like acorns with nicotine he folded and squeezed it. After swallowing a mouthful of fish he leaned back in his chair and said, 'Don't give 'em nothing.'

I had no idea who he was talking about.

He shot a glance through the window and spoke out of the side of his mouth. 'Don't lend 'em any money. Don't buy 'em a beer.'

I was about to say something but his wife flared her eyes at me again. Very wide. She was warning me not to interrupt him.

'You can lend 'em a cigarette. A cigarette is all right. *One* cigarette. Not two. One cigarette is all right.' Then he looked back at me again. 'Don't tell 'em nothing they don't need to know. Nothing. Be all right.'

Then he bent his head over his cod in white sauce and ate the rest of his dinner. The conversation was over. His wife looked up at me briefly and this time her eyes said *there you are, then*.

Football I could do. When I got down to the bone-hard and dusty soccer pitch there were about twenty enthusiastic lads waiting to be organised so I divided them into teams and let them have at it. I lavished them with uncritical praise and if they fell over I picked them up. If they got roughed up I pulled them to their feet and told them what a great thing it was they were so hard and that good footballers needed to be tough.

When it was time to finish I noticed Pinky and another tall, slightly stooped man watching, both with folded arms, from the side of the pitch. I gave a blast on the whistle to end the game, collected the ball and walked over to them. Pinky introduced the man to me as Tony. I recognised him as the fez-wearing figure on the billboard in the foyer of the theatre. *Abdul-Shazam!* Though in real life he looked no more Arabic than do I.

Tony – or Abdul-Shazam – gave me a wide professional smile and pumped my hand. 'You'll do me, son. Pick 'em up, dust 'em down. Up you get and carry on. Like that. Like it. You, son, are now officially on the team. Come on. Coffee time.'

Pinky excused himself and Tony whisked me to the coffee bar. There he charmed a couple of free and frothy espressos out of the girl behind the counter. He introduced me to her and said something that made my face colour. When we sat down he proceeded to brief me.

'Everything son, you do everything. It's all in the programme. You get Saturday off every week, changeover day. Meet in the theatre each morning at 9.30 sharp. Check in, cover the bases. Can you sing? Dance? Tell a funny story? Just kidding son, just kidding. You check the bingo tickets, get everyone in the theatre, give the kids a stick of rock every five minutes. Been to college, haven't you? You can write, can't you? Write down the names of the winners of the Glamorous Grandmother comp and all that. A monkey could do it, no offence. If you're chasing skirt, make sure you share yourself round the ugly ones, because it's only fair. Smile all the way until October. That's all you have to do. A monkey could do it.'

'What happened to the last monkey?'

'What?'

'The one I replaced.'

Tony looked up and waved wildly at a family passing by our table. His face was like soft leather and it fell easily into a wreath of smiles, like it knew the lines into which it should flow. His skin was super-smoothed by remnants of stage make-up. 'Howdy kids!'

'Shazam Shazam!' the entire family shouted back at him. He looked pleased.

When they'd gone I reminded him of my question.

'Look, don't worry about a thing.' I don't know why he said that because I wasn't worried. 'Any problems, see me, except when there's a problem, see someone else.' Then he burst into song, crooner style, throwing his arms wide and turning to the campers seated at other tables. *The answer, my friend-a, is a-blowing in the wind-a, the answer is a-blowing in the wind.* He pulled a handkerchief from his pocket and blew his nose very loudly. Everyone laughed and I did, too, for reasons I didn't quite understand.

He drained his cup and stood up. 'You're back on duty in one hour. Bingo in the main hall. After that, theatre, front of house.'

Then he was gone.

2

And the white knight is talking backwards

I was an Alice in Wonderland. It was a world I knew nothing of, hyper-real, inflated, one where the colours seemed brighter, vivid, intense. I was excited to be working there, being a part of it, but the truth is I felt anxious, too. It wasn't just about being an outsider, it was the strangeness of it all. Many of the staff I met were odd fish. I had a crazy idea that they all had large heads and small bodies, like caricature figures on an old-style cigarette card.

Back in my tiny room on my first night I lay awake for hours. Of my room-mate there was still no sign and I was wondering what I'd done in signing up to this place. I was over-stimulated by the day's events and sleep didn't come. I lay in the darkness with my eyes wide open.

At some point I put the light on and got out of bed. The toilets and showers were at the end of the staff block. It was about 3 a.m. and I decided to take a shower to try to relax. When I got back to my room I dried myself off and decided to take my clothes – still in my backpack – and hang them in the slim wardrobe.

When I'd done that I sat down on the bed and took the photo from my leather wallet. It was a small black and white photo, maybe three inches square with a thin white margin. The photo-chemicals were either unfixing or the picture was over-exposed. Either way the shot was of a seaside scene. The subject was slightly blurred but a muscular man, maybe in his twenties, wore dark bathing trunks and smiled back at the camera. The wind whipped his hair across his eyes so you couldn't fully see his face. He stood with arms akimbo and behind him the sea frothed and foamed at the sand.

The man in the picture was my biological father. I turned the photo over in my hand. On the back of it someone had written one word in pencil. The pencil had faded just like the photo, but it was still easy to read what was written there: Skegness.

One word. It was a word I'd peered at many times, as if it were code or a mantra or a key of some kind. My father had taken me to Skegness when I was three years old – I don't know where my mother was at the time – and I was told he'd suffered a heart attack on the beach. I was with him at the time, though of course I had no memory of these events. Later my mother married my stepfather. This was the only photograph I had of my father. I'd stolen it. I don't even know whether Mum knew I had it, though she might have guessed.

I'd found the photograph when I was old enough to snoop. It was in a tin box kept at the foot of my mother's wardrobe. In the box were various documents like birth certificates and some old costume jewellery plus a series of postcards. There were photograph albums in the house so I knew instantly this one was rogue. I quickly figured out this was my natural father. At some point in my teens I took and kept the photograph for myself.

It was not as if we had never discussed my biological father. Any time I asked I would get some basic biographical details and the same account of a tragedy that took place on a beach. The account was always consistent and unvarying.

'Why on earth would you want to go there?' This was my stepfather, Ken, when I announced I was going to Skegness to look for seasonal work.

It's an extraordinary thing. If my mother had dropped the dishes on the floor or they had turned to gaze at each other meaningfully, I could have understood it. But when I said that I was going to Skegness they instantly announced their serious displeasure by not doing anything. Ken was eating his fried breakfast and Mum was at the sink. I'd been back from college for just two days. The fact that they made no movement – made no eye contact either with each other or with me – tipped me off to the fact that I'd just lobbed a grenade.

Ken gazed down at his breakfast, carefully sawing through his bacon and sausage with his knife. His blond eyebrows seemed to bristle over his red, weathered face. Mum rinsed a plate and shook the droplets from the plate as if they had to be counted.

Finally she spoke, but still without turning to face me. 'But Ken's got you good work with him.'

Ken was a builder. He usually had a number of projects going on different sites. I'd worked for him before, mostly as a ladder-monkey and errand boy. It was okay but unless you like running up and down a ladder and whistling at passing girls once every four hours it was dull. 'I know that, Dad,' I said. Sometimes I called him Ken and sometimes Dad, without particular intention. 'But I want to do something different.'

'How much are they paying you?' he wanted to know. 'It won't be much.'

'I haven't even got a job yet,' I said.

'Why there?' Mother said.

'I've got a friend who is working there.' This was a lie.

'I'd got it all set up for you,' said Ken. 'It doesn't make any sense.'

'I'm sorry,' I said.

My mother turned off the running tap and with agonising delicacy she set the plate on the draining rack, as if it were a fragile and rare piece of china.

The next day at the morning briefing I got to meet some of my fellow Greencoats. One was a rather sad and overweight sixty-year-old with a pale face and a rotten wig. The three girl Greencoats were professional dancers in the evening theatre, doubling on the entertainments programme in the day-time. They were all sweet-natured, leggy, tanned and beautiful, and seemed as unattainable as the planets in the night sky. The other male Greencoat was absent to no one's great surprise or concern.

Offered the choice between organising a Whist Drive or a kids' Sandcastle competition on the beach I plumped for the latter. I preferred the idea of outdoor work. I had little desire for the beer-and-smoke taverns in which I now knew a lot of the activities took place. One of the dancers, Nikki, felt the same and because her pirouetting colleagues preferred the indoor work, she was the one who showed me the ropes.

Which meant showing me the store-room where the gun-metal bins of pink candy-rock were kept under lock and key. I carried the bin to the beach. It felt ceremonial. Nikki meanwhile took with her an official-looking clipboard and pen.

Down on the beach about thirty tousle-haired kids had assembled. The sea in Skegness ebbs a long way out, exposing miles and miles of light golden sand backed by a dune system. The tide that morning had pulled the sea out and the waves were only a distant murmur, visible through a rippling heat haze. Nikki kicked off her sandals and, barefoot, she marked out a big square on the hot sand, telling the wide-eyed kids she was timing them and that they had exactly one hour, not a minute more, not a minute less. She told them they could start when she blew her whistle.

From her pocket she pulled a whistle on a string, exactly like the one I'd been given to referee the football game. She looked at me pointedly. 'Are we ready?' I guessed we were ready, so I nodded. Nikki produced a short blast on the whistle and the kids set to it.

'What do we do now?' I said, still cradling my tin of rock.

'We sit down ont' sand,' she said. 'Then after an hour you give everyone a big smile and a stick of rock.'

She rewarded me with a smile of her own. Nikki had jet-black hair and flashing dark eyes. With her skin like dark honey I suspected Mediterranean blood but her accent was as Mediterranean as the Ilkley Moor. She stripped off her candy-stripe blazer and sat back on the golden sand. I did the same. She hitched up her white skirt to let the sun to her lovely legs. I could see the white cotton of her knickers.

Nikki made a visor with the flat of her hand and looked at me. 'Student then, are you?' She made the word roll out on her tongue. *Stooooodunt.* Is it possible to fall in love with someone because of their accent? I think so.

'Yes.'

'I'd love to be a student, me.'

'Why don't you then?'

'Too thick.'

'I'm sure that's not true.'

'What do you study?'

'English literature.'

'Lots of books.' *Boooooks.*

'I'll say.'

'That's just it. I can't read a book to save my life. Can't settle to it. Too thick.'

I tried to tell her that she wasn't thick. I explained that only 50 per cent of any population anywhere read books, regardless of their occupation. It doesn't matter if you're a doctor or a lawyer or a factory worker, I told her, only half of them will read books. But in my earnestness I'd lost her attention already. Her eyes fluttered half closed and she gazed out to sea. She was away on some flight of imagination, or other life path, or dancing in a world with no books, only theatre lights. She lay back on the sand, folded her hands behind her head and closed her eyes.

After a while I got up: I had to do something to fight the temptation to look at Nikki's white cotton underwear. I don't like sand. I've never much liked the gritty feel of it between my fingers and toes but I knew I should just get on with it. So I moved among the sand-castles, making encouraging noises. I praised the good efforts and where I saw the kids were struggling, I got down on my hands and knees and helped them along a bit. With the very little ones I asked them their names and when they told me I pretended to mishear, saying, 'Fish and chips?' and they would say their name louder and I would say, 'Oh, I thought you said fish and chips: well, my name is David.'

You do that and kids turn their heads back and forth, trying to puzzle you out. Is he funny? Is he silly? Maybe he's both.

I looked up from this game and I saw a man and a boy standing by the water's edge. They were some way off and the sun was right behind them so I couldn't make out their faces, though I knew they were both staring at me intently. The man wore a blue suit and a tie.

There was something wrong. The man's suit was wholly inappropriate for the beach in such hot weather. I could tell the little boy was aching to come and join the sandcastle fun. Then the boy lifted his hand and gently waggled his fingers, waving at me. I felt a shiver of loneliness for them.

I figured that the man and the boy were not staying on the holiday camp, and were therefore not permitted to join in the organised programme. But I thought what the hell, so I beckoned the boy and his father to come and join us. What did it matter if the boy sat at the edge and joined in? They showed no sign of coming over so I smiled and beckoned them again. I couldn't tell for sure but I thought the man was carrying a rope looped over his shoulder. Then I felt a sharp tug at my sleeve and a little girl with white blond ringlets and a freckled face said, quite indignantly, 'My name isn't fish and chips.'

'Oh, so what is it?'

'Sally Laws.'

19

'Sausage Legs?'

'No! Sally Laws!'

Sally Laws wanted me to go and look at her sand-castle so I forgot about the little boy and the man in the blue suit. When I looked up they were already moving away. I felt sad for them so I stood up to go after them, but some sudden jolt, some squeeze in my gut prevented me. Instead I watched them go.

After a while I went back and sat down next to Nikki. I thought she'd fallen asleep, but with her eyes still closed, she said, 'You're good at working the parents.'

'The *parents*?'

'They love it, that. When you pay attention to their kids.'

I looked hard at her. She kept her eyes closed now but she must have been watching me as I'd made a circuit of the sandcastles. I guess I was a bit shocked at her cynicism. I just wanted to make sure these children were having a nice time. I hadn't done it to impress the parents. Then I remembered that Nikki was a profes-sional dancer, and that entertainment was her trade. It was showbiz. We were being paid to be nice. Like Abdul-Shazam in the cafe, serenading the punters. You were paid to smile.

The hot sun climbed a little in the sky and when the hour-point was reached Nikki gave an impressive blast on her whistle. The children were beautifully behaved, sitting in stiff attention, as together Nikki and I judged the results. We awarded first, second and third prize positions and, like a scribe in the temples of Egypt, Nikki with great ceremony wrote down the names of the winners on her clipboard. They were to be awarded prizes at a theatre gala event on the final day of their holidays. Meanwhile I saw to it that every child who had taken part got a stick of rock.

We were then left with a free hour before lunch at the canteen. Once again we resorted to a coffee bar to fill the gap, but this time the one with sky-blue parasols alongside the swimming pool. On the way there we passed, scurrying by in her white cleaning overalls, the woman whose table I had shared with her husband only the day before.

'Hello!' I called cheerily.

She dealt me the quickest of smiles I'd ever seen. She compressed her lips and seemed to scuttle on by even faster.

'Friendly,' I said to Nikki after the woman was out of earshot.

'I heard about that,' Nikki said, donning a pair of sunglasses. With her raven hair radiating an almost blue halo in the sun I thought she looked impossibly glamorous. Like a movie star. 'Didn't you sit at their table in the canteen?'

'News travels fast.'

'You were lucky.'

'Oh?'

We got coffees and took them to our table by the pool. She stirred a packet of sugar into her cup and as she spoke I noticed that she had two babyish fang-shaped canines either side of her front teeth. No, they didn't make her look like a vampire. They made her look girlish, cute, kissable. 'Last time someone tried to sit down at his table he grabbed their soup and flung it across the room, followed by their dinner, followed by their tray. He shouted *this is my fucking table and no one sits at my fucking table unless I fucking ask them to fucking sit at my fucking table.* Not for the first time either.'

'They don't fire him?'

'Easier to let sleeping dogs lie.'

There was a huge splash as someone belly-flopped into the deep end. She told me that the man's name was Colin and that his wife was called Terri. Nikki said Colin wouldn't allow her to talk with anyone. I made some remark about Terri being very pretty.

'Well, don't let Colin catch you even so much as glancing in her direction.'

'I won't,' I said. 'I never look at women I fancy.'

'So how would they know you fancy them?'

'I just don't let them see me looking.'

'What?' Nikki took off her sunglasses and stared at me hard. 'You're a strange boy.'

'Well, yes.'

That night through the thin plasterboard walls I heard someone snoring heartily on one side and someone grinding their teeth on the other side. From across the corridor came the sound of athletic coital grunting, even though I'd been told that we were not allowed to 'entertain' people in our rooms. Whoever was in there was getting a good entertainment. In the fitful snatches of sleep I did get, I dreamed unpleasant dreams. I woke in the night feeling that I should wash the sand off my hands.

So I was awake on my second full day at six in the morning. I got dressed in my whites and went for a walk along the beach. The sun was already up and throbbing as I crunched the pebbles underfoot. I got breakfast in the staff canteen as soon as it opened and, still way too early, I went into the theatre with a paperback book in my pocket, planning to relax on one of the plush velvet seats while waiting for the others to roll in for work.

I went round the back of the theatre, through the stage-door. It was a place where smokers went outside for a tab between stage calls and it led into the wings. You could squeeze between the scenery boards – theatre people call them 'flats' – on the stage and from there get down into the auditorium. But before I went into the wings I stopped dead.

I stopped because I heard a songbird.

It was a woman singing from the stage itself. Her voice was soaring in the empty auditorium above an audience of empty seats. I recognised the piece. It was an old Dusty Springfield number and it seemed to me this voice could even outshine ol' Dusters. No, it wasn't my cup of tea; I was listening to The Velvet Underground and Jimi Hendrix boldly going where no music had gone before, but I knew a good voice when I heard one. It filled the theatre, it swooped and fell and rose again, a thrilling ghost; it nestled in every crevice and it put a light between the shadows. I crept nearer, expecting to see one of the Variety acts, someone I was yet to meet.

The singer was moving across the stage with a mop and bucket. She wore white overalls. It was Terri.

I stayed hidden between the painted flats, not wanting to announce myself because I thought if I did she might stop. Then again, so absorbed was she in her singing that I was sure that even if I'd wandered onto the stage she wouldn't have even noticed me.

I heard the swing doors open from the front-of-house. A voice that could only belong to Colin shouted, 'You finished that yet?'

The song stopped. 'Nearly done, darlin'.

'Get a move on. I wanna be out of here before those fuckers come.'

Her bucket clanked and I heard a few more swishes of the mop before she crossed the stage and took the steps down to the auditorium. Only when I let go a big sigh did I realise I'd been holding my breath. From the shadows I watched her sway up the aisle carrying the heavy bucket. She disappeared through the swing doors. I moved onto the stage and peered out at the rows of dark seats, thinking about the voice I'd just heard.

When my co-workers came in I could hardly wait to mention it. Pinky arrived first. He always had that cigar wedged between his fingers but he was too professional ever to light up in the theatre. When I enthused about what I'd just heard he waved his cigar at the stage. 'I offered to put her on there. But it wasn't allowed.'

'Who stopped it?' I knew the answer before I'd asked the question.

'Who? Vlad the Impaler.'

In the gaps between events that evening I took to drinking the odd pint of Federation Ale, frothy amber stuff, mainly just to try to fit in with all the other male staff who quite casually sank copious quantities. I watched them downing seven or eight pints of the stuff without it seeming to touch the sides or affect their performance. So much of it was consumed by the staff and the campers alike that the slightly vinegary after-tang permeated the entire site. The odour of barley and hops was in the carpets; it was in the plaster and lathe; it was in the timber joints.

As a college boy I was fair game for teasing. Luckily the Federation Ale loosened my tongue a little and I was able to match the raucous banter of the girls who worked in the kitchens. They weren't bad girls, but they could scare the juice out of a man. Strapping figures, most of them, with self-administered bent-nail tattoos, they would grab your bottom as you walked by. It was popular amongst the girls to have the word LOVE written on one bicep and LUST on the other. I seemed to spend a lot of time dodging the goose neck.

After that, when feeding times came around I could identify faces I knew well enough to squeeze next to at the table. At every meal I saw scary Colin and his pretty wife installed at the same table at the distant end of the canteen, eating in complete silence. They cut a lonely sight.

One lunch time after clearing my plate into the slops I passed their spot and I saw him flicker a glance at me. It wasn't an acknowledgement exactly, just a darted look from the corner of his eye. I thought I should speak.

'Thanks for your advice on my first day,' I said.

Terri looked up at me and again the palm of her hand fluttered to her cheek. Colin, though, kept his head down.

He wasn't going to answer me. I felt embarrassed and stupid for having opened my mouth. My cheeks flamed. He lifted his head, but instead of making eye contact with me he looked at his wife. At last he said, 'Nuffing.'

Wanting to get out of the situation with at least a shred of dignity I said, 'Well, I appreciate it.'

At last he turned his gaze on me. There was contempt scribbled in the lines of his face, and I knew I'd made a mistake in trying to engage with the man. His features twisted into a bit of a sneer. But there was something else written into his expression. I knew what it was. It was puzzlement. What I'd just said had somehow perplexed him.

I clattered my empty tray in the clearing area, trying not to look back. But I couldn't help stealing a glance. Colin had his head down and was digging into his food again from the far side of his plate. But his wife, Terri, was looking at me. She wound a single finger corkscrew fashion into her auburn hair.

After lunch we had to run something called the Donkey Derby. This was a major item in the programme, so the full regiment of Greencoats – five out of the six, anyway – plus Tony, alias Abdul-Shazam– were gathered on the sweltering and bone-dry football field for the event. Tony had two modes of operation. Abdul-Shazam, complete with red fez and tassel, was the resident stage entertainer, mostly for the children's programme, but also for a theatre Magic Act supposedly aimed at adults, using some of the same tricks with a different patter. When he wasn't Abdul-Shazam he was just Tony, sans-fez, the camper's friend, the noisy, funny, friendly exhibitionist with a stage tan and an all-weather smile.

Tony took over the PA system for the Donkey Derby, only occasionally surrendering it to the nominally-head-Greencoat-with-the-wig, Sammy from Stockport. Sammy had bucket loads of enthusiasm for broadcasting but little talent and less wit. He would liberally spray spittle onto the hand-held microphone as he chortled and blethered away. Tony winced as the mike was handed back to him; I noted how Tony's ready smile could manifest as a form of violence.

The donkeys arrived with a fairy-tale figure called Johnny, who looked like he lived in the stables with his animals. The crotch of his trousers hung down near his knees and his thin leather belt, having lost its buckle, was tied off in a double knot. He had a bit of straw in his hair and one ear that stood perpendicular to his head whereas the other did not. His team of donkeys smelled less of donkey than he did.

'He spends hours perfecting that look,' Pinky told me, deadpan. 'Just so he can make a case for a better fee next time.' I didn't know if he was joking or not.

I don't know whether donkeys can ever be said to look 'happy' but Johnny's herd seemed totally pissed off with life. Flea-bitten moulting things, they made me nervous. One tried to bite me before I snatched my hand away just in time. I also saw one kick out. I worried that they might try to take a chunk out of one of the children so I kept a close watch.

The jockeys were those children brave enough to scramble on a donkey's back. I was told to grade the children by age so that we could run off five races over the course of the afternoon. Each event had a name like The Seahorse Stakes and the Jellyfish Handicap. While I tied high-coloured silks to the children, Nikki or one of the other girls grabbed the donkey's halter so that Sammy could hoist the child onto the donkey, hopefully without incident. A genuine bookie appeared from nowhere with a blackboard, chalking odds on the board at 3-1 the field. The parents waved shocking amounts of cash at him as they backed their own kid to win the race. I made a quick calculation. Identical odds. For every race if he took sixty pounds he knew he'd only have to pay out thirty; if he took a hundred he'd pay out sixty. For the bookie it was like scooping money up off the beach.

While I was making my calculation I saw Pinky squeeze by the bookie and give him a pat on the behind. It was odd because the crowd wasn't so tight that he needed to squeeze by, but in that moment I saw a brown envelope change hands in Pinky's direction. It was such a rapid sleight-of-hand it could have happened on the *Abdul-Shazam! Magic Show*.

But it was a gala afternoon for the campers, and the sunlight rippled off the dazzling silks while the parents roared as if they were at Ascot. Tony ratcheted up the excitement with a commentary that echoed from the Tannoy around the playing field. As for the race it was impossible to predict a winner because all the beasts did the same thing, which was to bolt five yards and then stop dead, until Johnny, running behind them in his flapping, baggy pants laid his crop over their loins. Then they'd advance another five yards. It reminded me of the mechanical horse race I'd seen in the slot machine arcade.

After five races I was hot, fly-bitten and reeking of donkey but there was still one more race to go. Tony took up the PA microphone and announced The Thoroughbred Fillies Half-Dash Triple Crown, in which mothers – exclusively – were invited to mount the donkeys. For some reason this attracted the most overweight women. It was a struggle for me to get the ladies mounted. The crowd thought I was playing it for comedy. I wasn't. It was hard work to hoist these large ladies onto donkeys that knew what was coming.

The canny beasts side-stepped, backed-up, dipped forward or even bucked to avoid their fate. After a lot of sweating, grunting, endless hilarity and reckless betting from the spectators we managed to get them all Under Starters Orders.

From the off the women screamed, the donkeys brayed and Johnny's whip lashed through the burning afternoon air. Instead of five yards, the poor beasts advanced two or three. Tony kept up an excitable commentary but I doubted whether all the animals would complete the course. They seemed to know it all too well and every time they stopped they tried to munch the parched grass. One of the ladies was in danger of falling, to the wicked merriment of the crowd. I stood aside, watching with a mixture of humour and disbelief, when I felt something tickling the little finger of my left hand.

A ladybird had alighted there.

Bright red with black spots, a seven-spot variety as we called them as children. I don't know why but of all the bugs in creation the ladybird is the only one that doesn't make most people want to shudder or to swat it. Maybe it's because it's known as the gardener's friend. I don't know. I lifted it towards the blue sky to look at it in relief. It was like a bead, a jewel, a drop of blood on my tanned finger. I pursed my lips and was just about to blow it away when someone gently touched the back of my hand to stop me.

It was Terri. Terri the cleaner, the mop-and-bucket singer, the wife of Vlad the Impaler. 'No,' she said. 'You have to say the rhyme. *Ladybird, ladybird fly away home, Your house is on fire and your children are gone.*' And then she blew gently on my finger and the ladybird took flight.

'Flown,' I said. 'We say flown where I come from. Not gone.'

'Well, you're wrong where you come from.'

'No, we're not.'

'Argumentative, aincha? Did you make a wish?'

It was the first time I'd seen a smile on her lips. Her eyes swam at me; she made them squeeze slightly. I hadn't made a wish at first, but I did now. 'I heard you singing.'

She made a little snort. Not even a snort, just a little release of air beneath her nostrils, as if in dismissal.

'You're a great singer.'

She narrowed her eyes at me again, as if to see if I was mocking her. There were very tiny trace wrinkles at the corners of those eyes, whether from laughing or crying too much, I didn't know. I had a sudden impulse and I couldn't stop myself looking round, scanning the crowd of people laughing at the slow progress of this last race.

'He's not here. He's gone into town.'

'Who?' I knew perfectly well who she meant.

'My husband.'

'Oh, I wasn't,' I lied.

'No, you weren't,' she said. She blinked at me and I felt as though she could see right through me, and I felt stupid and young and naive beyond belief. Then she said, 'Next time a ladybird lands on you, you'll know what to say, won't you?'

She turned and went without looking back. And I thought, dumbly, is she talking about ladybirds?

I was pulled out of my reveries by a sharp tug on my blazer.

'Hey,' said Nikki, and I knew she'd seen me talking to Terri. She gave me *the look*.

'What?'

'Just hey,' she said.

3

Of course one had heard speak of Dante

That evening I met the top of the bill, but not before I was accosted on my way over to the Golden Wheel nightclub. It was some time after last orders had been called in the bars. I knew that I should have phoned home to let the folks know things were okay but it was too late and it was as I was passing through the alley leading to the nightclub that a hand reached out of the darkness and roughly grabbed my wrist, whisking me round the corner.

I gasped. The hand released me and I was face to face with Colin the cleaner. He blinked at me, took a pack of cigarettes from the breast pocket of his neat short-sleeved shirt, opened the pack and offered me one. The next bit is ridiculous because even though I didn't smoke I found myself taking one. I mean, I'd smoked a few cigarettes here and there, but it was as if the invitation to take one of his cigarettes – they were the short, unfiltered kind – was irresistible. I put it between my lips and he flicked a smart lighter. I dipped the tip of the cigarette into the flame, knowing that he was still peering hard at me.

'Seen anything?' he said.

'About what?'

Without taking his eyes off mine he lit up a cigarette for himself. He inhaled deeply and then blew out a long thin blue plume of smoke. 'Anythin'.'

I hadn't the faintest idea what he was talking about. 'No.'

He held his cigarette in his left hand and I noticed that his right fist was bunched. He nodded slowly. The he held a single finger up to his face and gave a slight tug on the skin under his eye. 'Keep these open for me, will ya?'

'Sure.'

'How you fixed?'

'What?'

'They paid you yet?'

'No.' He knew that we all worked a week in hand and I wouldn't get paid until the end of the second week. It discouraged quitting without notice.

'Here.' He put a ten pound note in my top pocket.

'What's that for?'

'Help you out, son. Tide you over.'

A tenner was a lot of money. After deductions for food and palatial lodgings I was only being paid £25 per week. I wasn't sure I wanted to keep it. 'I can't take that off you.'

'Leave it out,' he said.

'I'll pay you back when I get my wages,' I said.

He turned very slowly and fixed me with a glare. 'It ain't a loan.'

After that he melted into the darkness. I was left alone with a cigarette I didn't want burning between my fingers and wondering what, exactly, I'd agreed to keep a look out for. I tossed my cigarette to the floor and stamped on it. Then I made my way to the Golden Wheel.

*

The Entertainments Business is hierarchical. As Green-coats we were at the bottom of the well. Then there were the dancers and the Assistant Stage Manager and the DJ. Moving on up came the stage acts and their place in the pecking order was measured strictly by the font size of their name on the billboards. Near the crest were the musicians who accompanied the acts, and Abdul-Shazam. But topping the bill, highest paid and commanding the best dressing room facilities was the *Italian Tenor*.

I'd never even seen an Italian Tenor before I worked at the holiday camp. Mine was an era of rock music, with Punk just around the corner and within spitting distance. Yet in the holiday camp theatre they were still serving up the old-style Variety formula: comedy duos, dancing girls, lady singers in glamorous gowns, magic acts. Beyond that, and somehow connecting low music-hall traditions and operatic high culture, stood the Italian Tenor. Tony told me that every holiday camp theatre had one at the time. Not all of them were from Italy, even though they might have Italian names. Quite often they were from Italy-next-Blackburn.

Our Italian Tenor was the real deal. His name was Luca Valletti. I did the lights for him in The Golden Wheel that evening. Before the show, while I was still shaking off my strange encounter with Colin, he intro-duced himself to me, very politely, and asked if I would do something different.

'Doesn't Perry do the lights?' Perry was the ASM.

'I would like you to do it.'

Luca wanted to finish on a song called 'Autumn Leaves'. He showed me how to mix the gels on the lighting so that we could get green and gold at the outset, move through some appropriate variations and finish on red and gold. It didn't involve much more than gently moving a lever, but Luca wanted it done sensitively and at certain places in the song. Perry was a bit grumpy but cheered up when Luca bought him a drink and explained that it also meant that Perry could quit early. I was impressed with Luca Valletti. I mean with how he managed people.

Luca came out on stage in an immaculate pressed tuxedo with bow-tie. His dark hair was slicked back with hair-oil and he'd accentuated the sharp line of his pencil-moustache. The brilliant white light of the spots flashed along his high cheekbones and quickened the sheen in his eyes. A previously quite boisterous audience dropped into complete silence as the first few chords struck up.

Luca used a microphone but I sensed he didn't need one in that small space. He performed a set of crooner type numbers all of which might have been dismissed by anyone of my generation. Sinatra. Como. Nat 'King' Cole. But to hear this live performance, even I had to concede that some of these old tunes were pretty good.

He wound up his act and went into 'Autumn Leaves'. I did my best with the light gels, as instructed. At the climax of the song he hit a superb, soaring note and as it faded I brought the coloured lights down through a narrowing circle. Luca finished to rapturous applause. When I killed the stage spots and bought the house lights up I noticed that amid the applause one or two women were dabbing their eyes with a handkerchief. I wanted to laugh: not at them, but at myself. It *was* moving. Transforming, even.

There was a small dance floor in the nightclub and the show was followed by a disco, mostly of golden oldies. The fact is that in the 1970s only kids like me listened to 70s music. The music most people listened to in the 1970s – that is everyone over the age of twenty-five– was their preferred 60s and 50s and 40s music.

After a while, Luca came out his dressing room, clutching a make-up case, ready to make a brisk exit. I intercepted him. I wanted to ask him if I'd done okay with the lights.

'Beautiful, my boy!' He had a strong Italian accent. He was a tiny, dapper figure who somehow managed to project himself as much larger on stage. 'Thank you! I appreciate. Very much.'

I said I was glad and all that because I'd been a bit nervous. I was burbling at him. He smiled at me. 'Come. I buy you drink.'

'That's not necessary!'

'I insist.'

We went to the bar and sat on high stools. He ordered a glass of wine for himself – which in 1976 in that place, and had he been an Englishman, was dangerously close to a declaration of homosexuality. I opted for a manly pint of Federation Ale.

'You are studenta? What you study?'

'English Literature.'

'Ah! Shakespeare! But you know in reply I can offer you the divine Alighieri!'

'Dante. I know of Dante.' Well, I'd heard of Dante. I can't say I'd read him. Perhaps I'd read the book cover of a paperback.

'We are all in hell,' he said cheerfully, 'we just don't know what level. What a joy, to have a person of culture in a place such as this.' He offered a hand to shake and I told him my name. He held up his wine so that we could clink glasses.

He asked me what I would do with my studies and with my life. I did have one half-formed and slightly ridiculous ambition, one that I tended to keep very quiet about but for some reason I blurted it out. 'I'd like to be a writer.'

He widened his eyes at me and then tilted back his head. Then he stroked his chin judiciously and leaned forward close enough for me to smell his coconut-scented hair-oil. 'Then I advise you. If you go into this kind of life, you need a strong a-heart. And a strong liver. In some ways it is like show business. You need a strong liver because some days you only eat bread. And find a good woman. This is terribly important. Not one of these silly girls who likes shiny necklaces and bangles and such things. No.' He summarised this advice for me. 'Good heart; good liver; good woman.'

Then he tipped back the remains of his wine, stood up and bowed formally. He wished me a *buona notte* and was gone. I stayed at the bar supping my beer. When I looked round the nightclub I noticed quite a few women in there who seemed to like shiny necklaces and bangles and such things.

But I liked the holidaymakers. They were relaxed, friendly and hell-bent on enjoying their well deserved break from the grubby offices and the scruffy factories and the dirty coal-mines of their industrial year. I saw them at their best for the two weeks when they put down their loads and kicked off their shoes. They laughed easily and loved to share a joke or a story. I saw how the mothers loved and how the fathers indulged their children. Perhaps it was that, and the fatherly talk from Luca Valletti, that made me call home the next day.

The conversation started badly. 'You've remembered us, then,' my stepdad said.

I think I had disappointed Ken. I don't know when or how it started. He was a thoroughly decent man who had provided everything for me and my mother. Ken had spent his life developing his building business. Raised in poverty, he knew the value of a good roof. I think he was always afraid that some misfortune, or a thief, or bad luck would come round and steal some of the tiles from the roof of our own home. Yes, he was a working man made good but he was the kind who wants to pull the ladder up behind him so that no one else from a similar background can make good.

As an only child – he had no biological children of his own – it was somehow assumed that I would follow him into his business. I'd surprised him by wanting to go to college and by standing up to him. He took it badly, as if my rejection of his trade was a personal insult. I don't know why – I'd never once played that despicable game of saying you're not my real dad and so on. Now that I was old enough to understand what he'd done for us, I was grateful to him. But he seemed to take the whole college thing as a rejection of what he'd done for me and my mother, too.

I knew that his plan for me to work with and for him that summer was part of a deeper scheme to embroil me in his business. Presumably he thought I would come to my senses after I'd finished my three years at college. In a sense I had run away from all of this; run away to sea, or at least to the seaside.

The conversation with Ken was short and stilted. He passed me on to my mother, who asked a lot of questions about where was I washing my laundry and where was I doing my shopping. She finally came to the point. 'Why Skegness? Why have you gone to Skegness?'

'I told you. There's a job here. Plus I've got one of the better jobs going.'

'It's an awful place.'

'No it isn't. It's a lot of fun.'

'Of all the places you could choose,' she said. 'Of all the places.'

The days were getting hotter. The thermometer glass was reading the upper eighties day after day. It was all highly unusual for this temperate island of ours so the cool shadows of the empty theatre were a regular seduction. I still wasn't sleeping well and during one of my breaks I knew I could find a seat in the dark corner of the auditorium as a comfortable place to take a nap. I was snoozing in there one evening, drifting in and out of sleep, disturbed now and again as the theatre acts began to arrive to make preparation for the big Variety show we had that night. It was too early for any of the holidaymakers to be inside so the acts breezed in through the front of the house, walked down the aisle and up the stage steps to get behind the wings.

I woke properly to the sound of an industrial vacuum cleaner. It was Terri, pushing the machine around the carpet in front of the musician's pit just below and in front of the stage. I smacked my lips and rubbed my cheeks, thinking I'd better go and throw water on my face. Then to the left of the stage the emergency doors

39

swung open and Colin came striding in. He spoke to Terri. The hoover was still roaring so I couldn't hear what was said; and I was pretty sure neither of them knew I was up in the upper auditorium watching them from the shadows. Terri opened her mouth and said something in reply.

It was like watching a dumb-show. Colin seized his wife by the throat with one hand. He shook her side to side and lifted her a few inches off the ground. It was like seeing a lurcher shake a rabbit. Then he dropped her back on her feet, turned around and marched out of the theatre the way he'd come in.

It all happened in a second. Terri stood with her hands on her hips, looking at the door by which Colin had left. After a few moments she switched off the hoover. She bent to pick up some cleaning cloths and a spray-polish, starting in on the mahogany woodwork that defined the edge of the stage. Whatever had just happened, it didn't seem to faze her much.

I was trying to think how I might slip out without her noticing. I didn't want her to know that I'd just seen that small exhibition of marital bliss. But then she started singing again. At first she sang softly, then after a few bars she let her voice ring out, just as she had the previous morning. Whoever was in her heart when she sang these songs, I couldn't imagine it had much to do with Colin. She was using her singing as antidote to her woes. It was self-medication.

From behind me I heard the swing doors open and then I saw Luca Valletti padding down the carpeted aisle. Luca didn't see me either. He had his make-up bag in one hand and his other arm was flung wide. His face was illuminated with delight.

'My darling girl!' he shouted. 'What is this song-bird I hear?'

Terri stopped in mid-flight. As she turned to him in surprise her palm fluttered to her face in that already familiar gesture.

Luca moved towards her in a skip. 'Beautiful, my darling! Beautiful! Why you not on the stage with me? It's a crime! We should make music! We should make the duet! It's like the Cinderella to see you here when you should be up there! Under the lights! It's a song-bird you are! A beautiful songbird.'

Luca stood with his hand outstretched to her, smiling, his head tilted back and to the side, delighted.

The emergency exit door cracked open. Colin came in. He seemed to be in no hurry and yet something in his step alarmed me. It had calm intention but his face was impassive. As he crossed in front of the stage he was like a postman walking up to someone's front door with a letter.

He attacked the unprepared Luca and with his left hand around the Italian Tenor's windpipe he pushed the singer up against the wall, sweeping him off the ground. He held his right fist bunched and drawn back ready to strike. 'Don't you no never never never speak to my wife like that! No fuckin' never! You don't never you fuckin wop, you what? ? If I ever you fuckin' wop! If I ever!'

I made out the words but it was more like hearing a dog barking rapidly. I got to my feet; not to intervene, because I was too afraid of Colin, but to let him know that there were other people around witnessing this assault. The racket drew others from back stage. Amongst them was Tony, his face half plastered with

41

orange stage make-up. 'Put him down you dozy bugger!' Tony roared.

Colin didn't seem to hear any of it. He was in a zone of his own making. Tiny bubbles of saliva beaded his lips and yet his eyes were cold.

'Colin,' said Terri quietly, but firmly. 'Colin.'

Pinky Pardew appeared on the scene holding a carton of No. 6 cigarettes. 'What the fuck is going on?'

'Colin,' Terri said again.

Finally Colin released his grip on Luca's windpipe. The Italian slid to the floor, gasping, holding his throat.

Pinky was red in the face. 'Enough. You don't come near this theatre again. Nowhere near. Set foot in here again I'll have you off the camp and you can pick up your cards. I'm not having it.'

'He was having a pop at my wife!' Colin stated mildly. He pointed at Pinky. 'What would you do if he had a pop at your wife?' Colin looked around wildly. He pointed at me. 'What would you do if some wop had a run at your wife?'

'Go on, clear off,' Pinky shouted at him. 'Terri, you get on with your work. We've got a fucking show to run around here.'

Colin bared his teeth, put his head down and left.

Meanwhile Tony had helped Luca to his feet. Two of the dancers were fussing around him, dusting him down. 'It's finish,' the Italian was saying. 'It's finish here.'

'Come on, old son,' Tony said, 'let's get you back-stage and straightened up.'

'No I can't. It's no possible. It's finish.'

'Look,' Tony said, 'you know we all worship you, Luca. Never mind that fucking idiot. We all love you. You know that.'

Terri burst into tears. 'I'm sorry, Luca. I'm so sorry!'

Luca suddenly recovered his composure. 'My darling, was it you? Or was it him?' He stepped over to Terri and took her hand, bent his head and pressed his lips to her trembling fingers. Then with a sad smile he released her hand. 'Yes. Si. Si. We have a show, no? We have a show.' He turned and skipped up the steps and onto the stage to disappear behind the wings, followed by Tony and the dancers, all still babbling incredulity at the event.

I was left out front with Pinky. Terri switched on the hoover and moved away from us. 'I saw it all,' I said.

Pinky sniffed. 'Was he?'

'Was he what?'

He nodded at Terri. 'Was Luca having a sniff?'

'Christ, no. Luca was just telling her what a great voice she has. That's all it was. Unless that constitutes "having a sniff".'

Pinky turned away from me and followed the others up the steps onto the stage. He puffed on his unlit cigar. 'Sometimes it does,' he said, 'sometimes it doesn't.'

I was left with Terri as she trawled up and down the aisles with the hoover. I wanted to go but then again, I didn't. I watched her work as if nothing had just happened, and I knew she was aware of me watching her. It was ridiculous. She was beautiful. It didn't seem possible that she had become yoked to a man like that, someone twice her age, someone who was a beast and who could offer nothing but raw violence and meanness and a life of low instinct.

Very slowly she worked her way back towards me with the vacuum cleaner, bringing the thing close to where I was standing. I wondered if I was supposed to lift my feet like I'd seen my dad do for my mum, but when the machine was almost touching my shoe she switched it off. The new quiet pulsed in the empty auditorium. A stray lock of hair had fallen across her face and she pretended to blow it out of her eye but I knew it was a breath of relief. She gave me a deep, searching look. Then she parted her lips and mouthed one single, painful word.

She didn't even have to say it.

4

To fight the savage foe, although

The following morning I got to find out who I was bil-
leted with. It turned out to be the missing Greencoat,
a cheerfully psychotic Mancunian chain-smoker called
Nobby. After another bad night I was actually sleeping
well one morning, only to be awoken when his key hit
the lock from the other side of the door.

If he was surprised to encounter a new room-mate he
didn't show it. He stood over me in a Greencoat outfit
of whites or rather off-whites – and a blazer identical
to mine. 'Are you with us, son? It's a brand new day!'

I blinked up at him from my pit. He was at least ten
years my senior. His hair shook in its tight perm of
dark curls streaked grey at the temples. The tremor was
from an endless nervous energy that would never – I
was about to discover – allow him to be still.

'You the new Greencoat then? Shake a leg and I'll
walk down with you. Though you can have this shit-
hole to yourself cos I'm never here how the fuck they
expect two grown men to sleep side by side in this de-
pressed hen coop for plucked chickens I'll never know
are you up yet? Come on, son, come on.'

'I'll get a shower,' I muttered. I grabbed a towel and
walked out into the corridor.

For some reason Nobby followed me. 'Shower?

Shower? Throw water on your face, you'll be fine. There's a drought on! War rations. I mean war footing! Plus showering every day is bad for you no one ever tell you that scrubs away the natural oils so essential to your vitality, son. Not to mention the pheromones yes yes yes. Did I mention the pheromones?'

There was a communal shower at the end of the building and I walked in and switched on the faucet. 'The what?'

'The what? They told me you was fuckin' educated. Pheromones, son, pheromones. This is what it's all about, in't it? Are you getting plenty? If you are that's cos of your very fine zinging pinging pheromones. If you're not getting plenty that's cos your pheromones are no good. Or rinsed out. Wash it all away and well, damp squib sort of thing.' He stood watching me shower and didn't stop talking except to light up a cigarette. 'Too much fuckin' showering that'll do it. Hey! Hey! Hey! You listen to Nobby. Nobby knows, you know.'

I dried off and padded back to my room. Or *our* room, as with increasing dismay I now felt I should call it.

'Flip-flops! Get yourself some flip-flops. Cos o' the slops they're dirty, lazy bastards in here and you'll get athlete's foot off this shower floor and verrucas and viruses and what else trenchfoot I don't know warts corns blisters in-growing toenails instep fungus hammertoe, hey hey! That floor is like a smorgas board of infection, hey!'

I made the mistake of trying to listen to this barrage but it was impossible. I found my brain starting to tune him out. I'd known him maybe three minutes and already he exhausted me. As I got dressed I said, 'I thought you'd quit.'

'Why? Why's that then? Why?' He went over to the open window, and flung his cigarette butt outside. Then he sat on my bed, took out a fresh ciggie and did that trick of flipping it in the air and catching it in his mouth.

'Well, you'd been missing for a few days.'

'Missing? I haven't been missing. I've been on my other job.'

'Other job?'

'Look at the state of your whites! Bit how's-your-father round the waist I'd say. That the best they could do? That's a joke that. A joke. Go and see Dot and don't take any shit. Better still I've got some as will fit you better.' Then he slapped his thigh and fell sideways on the bed, laughing, a cancerous cackle. 'A joke.' When he'd recovered from the hilarity of laughing at my ill-fitting whites he recovered to light up his cigarette. 'Yes I've got another job up the road.'

'Aren't you full time?'

He did a double-take and then looked over his shoulder as if the management team might be hiding in the tiny wardrobe. 'Course I'm full-time. Full time up the road, too. You ready? You look like shite! Hey! Let's go.'

We walked together to the theatre for the morning briefing. I was keen to ask him some questions, but it was almost impossible to break into his constant stream of chatter.

'Everyone's doing two jobs, son, everyone; and if they're not in the category of everyone they're on the skim, they've all got their skim. Welcome to skim city. Hey! If you find a way to live on these wages you let me know about it.'

47

'Well, we do get food and lodgings,' I suggested.

Mistake.

He leapt in front of me and stopped dead, brought his feet together and leaned forwards at forty-five degrees. 'Food and lodgings! You call that mouse-cage that squirrel-farm a lodging?' We started moving again. 'It's a matchwood tent! A shanty-town! A papier-mâché ghetto! That famous East Coast wind better not blow too hard or it will all come down. Huff and Puff Mr Wolf. What's that? Pigs. Dunno. It's not even a barn. Better not get caught with a woman in your room or they'll have you off the site. And you can't even keep your own alcohol in your own room, have they told you that? As for food, hey!' He suddenly lowered his voice. 'Eyes right! Eyes right!' I thought he was asserting himself, saying '*I is right*' but then he said 'Three o' clock!' and I realised that he wanted me to look to my right-hand side.

A very pretty girl in a tiny bikini was strolling away from us.

'You like school dinner? I f'kin don't. Okay if you want spotted dick and jam roly-poly every Wednesday and pummelled spuds and choked carrots and strangled sprouts and canteen cuisine ... Eyes left! Eyes left!'

To the left, two good-looking full-figured mothers led their toddlers over to the play-sand.

'... and strangled sprouts and canteen catering well let me tell you I had better grub in the fuckin' army and if that's your idea of a good ... Eyes right, eyes right, four o'clock.'

I glanced to the right and a very old lady with dowager's hump came creeping towards us. Nobby howled with laughter. 'Got you there, son, didn't I? Walked into that one you did! Shake hands! Hey! Hey!'

I admitted he'd 'got me' there. Nobby refused to move on until I shook his outstretched hand. Then he started up again with his unbroken patter. I was glad when we reached the theatre. I looked at my watch. It was 9.15 a.m. I hadn't even got to the day's briefing and I was dog-tired.

Nobby's excitable energy wasn't the only reason why I was so shattered. I'd had my worst night so far. I couldn't sleep. I'd had the window wide open but the air was stifling. Every time I thought I might drift off to sleep I had an image of Terri mouthing that single word at me.

In fact it wasn't just while I was sleeping. After the assault on Luca Valletti I'd taken a seat at the side of the theatre watching the show without really seeing any of it. The entire Variety act. Paget and Drum, the comedy duo. Shelly Breeze – I'm not making up these names – doing her diva routine. Abdul-Shazam in his fez inserting swords into a casket containing one of the dancers. Oh yes, Nikki danced at the edge of the stage. She was magnificent under stage lights. All the dancers were and they maintained dazzling smiles that you rarely got to see offstage. But at some point in the show Nikki caught my eye, and she winked at me.

Finally Luca, consummate professional that he was, topped off the show. He had a white silk scarf wrapped tightly around his bruised throat and you wouldn't have known what had taken place in that theatre ninety minutes earlier. He had this farewell song – something about fighting in the Foreign Legion – where he waved a white handkerchief and the ladies in the audience

took pocket handkerchiefs out of their handbags and
waved back at him.

And so I go
To fight the savage foe,
Although I know
I'll be sometimes missed
By the girls I've kissed.

They lapped it up. But I couldn't help thinking about
what was going on in Luca's head as he smiled and
sang and levelled the blade of his hand at his breast.

So I'd spent an entire evening thinking about Terri;
and I'd spent a night tossing and turning in the heat
with her face appearing in the dark. Now I was about
to go into the theatre where I would see her cleaning the stage. I knew I was going to have to fight to
avert my eyes. I thought I was transparent and that
the chirpy mad Mancunian or Nikki or Tony or all of
them would see through me straight away. I was ready-
tailored Music Hall material. I'd only been in the camp
a week and I'd fallen for the old story about rescuing
the woman with the mop-and-bucket.

But when I walked in I didn't get to see Terri at all.
A much older woman with a dry scowl and a giant
hair-pin was up on stage swinging the mop to and fro
giving the boards a good grinding. Tony sat in the front
row of the seats, legs spread far apart, his well packed
midriff spilling over his belt buckle. He looked glum.

'Where's Punch and Judy, then?' I said. I was trying
to sound distant and casual.

'What?'

I jerked a thumb at the new cleaner.

'Chance they'll be fired,' Tony said.

I was crestfallen. 'Really?'

'Yes, really,' he said dryly. 'Turns out it's against camp rules to disconnect the windpipe of your bill-topping Italian Tenor. Who'd have thought it? What's the world coming to?' He yawned; a little theatrically, I thought. Then his eyes fell on my room-mate behind me. 'Nobby, you good-for-nothing Mancunian bastard.'

'Charming, fucking charming,' said Nobby, 'you get one dose of gastroenteritis for a couple of days, one miserly virus and you stay off work to protect your mates from contagion and what abuse do you get? What abuse do you get? I'm glad you asked me that. I'll tell you what abuse you get ...'

But I wasn't listening. I sat down. I was too busy thinking about whether something precious had been torn away from me or whether I'd had a lucky escape. I know that if Terri had asked me to walk over a cliff with her I would have followed, just for the chance of a kiss on the way down.

Nikki, in crisply laundered whites, crashed in the seat next to me. 'Why the long face?' She lifted her leg so that her exquisite right ankle balanced on her tantalising left knee. Her pleated white skirt fell away to expose her tanned thighs.

I realised she was talking to me. 'Can't sleep. Since I've been here.'

'You're not drinking enough, college boy. Or too much.'

'I don't like getting drunk. I'm a mean drunk.'

She looked at me sceptically and was about to speak when Tony jumped out of his seat and clapped his hands loudly.

'Right then, if I can interrupt you love birds,' – he was looking at me and Nikki – 'let me point out we have a big day ahead of us. Before that, please, a big round of applause for Nobby who decided to come to work today.'

Ironic applause followed. I found myself joining in.

'Fucking charming, that!' Nobby said. He started to say a lot more but Tony waved him into silence.

'Girls, whist-drive this morning and round-the-clock. Sammy, you do the Glamorous Grandmother and don't let those old birds grab your wig this week. Nobby, supervise the Crown Bowls if you please.'

'Fuckin 'ell,' Nobby croaked, but to himself.

'Nikki, show David the cheeky on the Junior Tarzan and the Bathing Belle around the pool. This afternoon, everyone in here with me for the prize giving and fare-well. That means *all of you* and that means *you* as well, Nobby. Right, out you go, and smile like it's already home-time.'

By ten o'clock we had the open-air swimming pool arena set up, with the PA crackling and buzzing. It was already sweltering. We broke the rules and took off our heavy blazers and worked instead in our whites. Let them fire us, Nikki said, drawing columns on a sheet of paper attached to her clipboard. Then she looked up, put her pen behind her ear and reached out to hook something off my shirt. It was a ladybird. She blew it off her finger.

'And another,' she said finding a second on my collar. 'They're all over you.'

The ladybirds darting through the sultry morning air were well outnumbered by the Junior Tarzans. The sunshine seemed to bring them out. The Tarzans, that is. About seventy or eighty skinny kids and a dozen fat ones, all aged between seven and eleven, sporting swimwear and lined up around the edge of the pool. It was my job to employ the PA system to rustle up a couple of impartial judges, over which Nikki would preside. I was told to whittle the eighty kids down to a more manageable dozen. I had to 'interview' each kid in turn and keep it interesting. I failed. The only thing I could think of doing was to get each lad to say his name into the microphone and to offer a semblance of a Tarzan-like jungle cry. After the discriminating judges had got the number down to a dozen contenders, we started again, this time with a fiendish question, which was 'Do you help your mum with the housework?' These things passed as entertainment and all the boys got a stick of rock. The winner's name – the boy with the best blood-curdling cry – had his name written down on the clipboard for the prize-giving show.

There was a half hour break before we ran the Bathing Belle competition designed for young women aged between 16 and 21. This time I got to be a judge along with a fresh pair of holidaymakers and Nikki did the interviewing. It all went fine but the heat was building. At the hottest part of the day the girls were forced to swat the flying bugs as they described their hobbies and expressed an interest in World Peace.

We agreed on a pretty winner and Nikki made the announcement. Nikki embarrassed me by declaring that part of the prize was the chance to give me a kiss. I took it all in good part as the winner planted her lips on my cheek. It wasn't exactly a hardship.

As the Bathing Belle competition was wrapped up, half a dozen sexy promotions girls dressed in hot-pants and low-cut blouses moved about the campers with trays of cigarettes. The hot-pants livery matched the design on the cigarette pack. It was a marketing drive for a cigarette called Players No. 6, a market-leader of the time.

One of the No. 6 girls went into action on me, but I explained I was a non-smoker. I got chatting and she said all the girls were 'models on assignment'. I didn't know what that meant. To me they looked like pretty girls peddling coffin nails; though the girls were okay and I kept that opinion to myself. I noticed that Nikki, also a non-smoker, was sniffy with them.

Nikki and I took our clipboards and tin bins – emptied of candied rock – away from the pool and went to the cool of the cafe. I had a question for my fellow Greencoat. 'Nikki, is everyone here on the take?'

I wasn't just thinking about what Nobby had told me. I was also flashing back on Colin's words on my first day. *Give 'em a cigarette but don't never buy 'em a drink.*

'Why do you ask that?'

'Dunno. I thought we were just paid to give everyone a fun time. But it seems like everybody's got an angle.'

As I spoke, one of the No. 6 girls drifted near plying her wares, all smiles, full of easy charm.

'Watch that girl,' Nikki said.

The girl, a willowy brunette, made a sale to a beefy looking man seated at a table with his wife and three children. Everyone was sucking on a straw dipped in a vividly coloured milkshake. Money exchanged hands and the girl took a pack of cigarettes from her tray. She popped the cellophane wrapper, flipped open the pack and flicked the box so that she could proffer one of the cigarettes to the customer. Then she discarded the cellophane wrapper in her tray. The customer, impressed by this sexy, extra little service smiled happily and the girl moved on to the next table.

'What did you see?' Nikki said.

'Nothing.'

Nikki sniffed. 'Not very clever for a college boy, are you?'

'Uh?'

'She makes the sale. She unwraps the pack for him as a nice little service. She flips open the lid and offers him a ciggie and that's when she takes the voucher out of the pack. She tosses the voucher, with the wrapper, back into her tray and lights the ciggie for the dumb customer. Those vouchers trade for goods. It takes an age to save up the vouchers but if you skim one off each sale it's worth a small fortune to you. Watch her again.'

I studied the girl making another sale and this time I saw it: a green voucher slipped out of the pack and dumped in the tray with the wrappings. 'Doesn't anyone ever complain?' I asked.

'Most don't notice. Most who do notice, they let it go. When the one person in every hundred complains she'll apologise and give it back. If the customer complains further she might even pretend to cry and will claim it's the only way they get paid. She'll live with one complaint in a hundred.'

'Well, it's a small thing.'

'It's fucking stealing, is what it is,' Nikki said sharply.

'Okay, okay. You're right.'

But she was exercised now. 'The whole camp is run like this. Who gets the kickback for letting these girls come in? Pinky and Perky, that's who.' Perky I discovered was her pet name for the man in the blue blazer who'd interviewed me while feeding sparrows from his desk. 'Every promo you see on this site. Look at the little ponce who runs the arcade machine. He sponsors the Bathing Belle prize. You'll see why this afternoon. And the bookie who comes on Donkey Derby day to fleece the campers. He pays to get his nose in the trough. Why haven't you got a uniform that fits? Cos they budget for the gear but pocket it rather than give Dot the money she needs to kit us out. Everyone here has an angle.'

'I don't have an angle.'

'Yes, you do.'

'What's my angle, then?'

I didn't get an answer. She slipped on her sunglasses and looked away from me.

'All right then,' I asked her, 'what's your angle?'

'My angle is figuring out everyone else's angle.'

I do believe that Nikki was good at that. I studied her as she stared moodily over at the No. 6 girls moving through the tables.

I felt a stir amongst the people around me. It was Tony – or was it Abdul-Shazam – making his way between the tables, cracking jokes, shaking hands. Before my conversation with Nikki I would have said he was just doing his job, being a fun guy, giving everyone a laugh; but now I could see how he seemed to swell and feed and fatten on the attention until he seemed taller and broader and shinier than everyone else in the room. I thought that it might be possible to do both things effectively at the same time.

He took a chair at our table. 'All sorted?' he asked

me, loudly enough for everyone around us to hear. 'Signed all those boys up for the Foreign Legion? And did you get a date with the winner of the Bathing Belle?'

Nikki saved me from having to think of a smart answer. 'He done brilliant.'

Tony smiled. 'Well, you must be good because Nikki hands out compliments like a Yorkshireman parts with his money. But don't let it go to your head because she's impervious to all offers.' Nikki was about to object but Tony threw his arms wide and burst into song, some old music hall thing about waiting forever for the girl of your dreams. He got a ripple of applause for it.

Nikki looked like she'd heard it all before too many times. She drained her coffee and picked up her clipboard. 'Okay I'll see you lovely boys later this afternoon.'

Tony watched her go. 'Pretty girl isn't she, that Nikki?'

'I'll say.'

'You will say. If she could just relax and whiten up a bit she'd be the perfect woman.' I wasn't sure if he'd said 'whiten' or 'lighten'. Tony ordered a coffee and another for me from a passing waitress. 'Mind you, I can't blame her.'

'Why do you say that?'

'You know something, David? The boys and girls here have taken to you.'

I felt my cheeks flame.

'They like your easy way with things,' he went on. He was over-focused on me, not breaking eye contact for a second and I felt uncomfortable. 'They like your style. You're also smart and they like that.'

'But Nikki is smart, and so are some of the others.'

'*Some*,' he said. He gave me a huge smile. I noticed again that an element of the near-orange suntan was actually residual stage make-up. 'You represent what the smart ones aspire to. College and all that. But there's no side on you. They expect you to be stuck up but you're not and they like that.'

Partly to deflect Tony's embarrassing focus on me, I launched into a notion that I had about ordinary people who didn't get a chance to go to college. I said that I met lots of folk who should get the chance but never did; and that at college I had met a lot of posh types who didn't deserve the chance at all; and that the awful British class system was at the root of a lot of injustice in our society. While I banged on Tony stared at me with shining eyes, as if no one had ever said this before, even though he must have heard it a million times.

He waited until I finished and looked at me seriously. 'You see, David, the people in this country don't know what's coming. There's a recession deepening and things are going to get ugly. But they don't see it. They're like the drunk who doesn't want to leave a party. Well, it's time they sobered up and realised that we've had the party and it's time to pay the cabbie and go home.'

I didn't know which cabbie he meant, exactly, but I nodded anyway. 'What we want,' he continued, 'is more ordinary boys like you going to college. This is the future. Not a gang of toffs quaffing champagne from a lady's slipper while they formulate government policy.' He dropped his voice to a stage whisper. 'They're rearranging the deckchairs on the *Titanic*, you understand that, don't you, son?'

I said I did.

'I knew you were a good 'un as soon as I clapped

eyes on you. You can tell. Only you have to be careful who you're talking to. They don't want to talk politics, most of this lot. They'd rather suck on the titty and leave it all to others. I knew you were different.' He got to his feet and picked up our empty coffee cups, even though there was a waitress to collect them. 'I'll pay for these.' He went over to the counter and made a joke with the girl working the till. I didn't see any money change hands.

When he came back he said, 'You're not doing anything tomorrow, are you?'

The next day was Saturday, changeover day. It was my day off and I had no one with whom to spend it. I shrugged.

'There's some interesting people we want you to meet.'

'We?'

'Midday, outside the main gates. We'll pick you up in the car.'

'To do what?'

'Midday. Tomorrow.' Then he turned and walked away from me, breaking into some old crooning song. There was a very old white-haired lady at a table near the door. He dropped into a crouch, grasped her hand and gazed soulfully into her eyes as he sang. Then he released her and was gone.

The Friday farewell show came and went. It was led expertly by Abdul-Shazam in his red fez. He was good. He had the audience feeding from his hand. He expertly set up his gags (jokes were called gags by showbiz people) with terrific timing. He improvised around the names of the prize-winners and nothing fell flat. I got to help with some of his magic act, around which the prize-giving was structured. It was exciting to see the simple mechanisms at large, the false bottoms, the fake linings of the magic act. Rather than stealing away the enchantment, this insight only made it more fascinating. With light and shadow everything worked. Kids and adults alike were drawn up on stage and induced to stick their hand in a velvet bag or under a steel blade. Their trust was uncanny. They abdicated all responsibility. They let the authority of the stage take over them.

The power wielded under the arc lamps by Tony-Abdul-Shazam was a little bit disturbing. Only I and his other stage assistants were close enough to see the perspiration that went into his act. Everyone who came on stage was given a baton of candy rock they could carry away with them, a multi-coloured magic wand. Yes, when they got back to their seats it would be nothing more than a stick of sugar in a cellophane wrapper, but by then it was someone else's turn to be up on stage, blinking, dazzled by the limelight.

The farewell show was eventually followed by the Friday Revue and I noticed that Luca's attitude had changed. He breezed in before the show and he was polite, he greeted everyone; but he was professional and distant, flinty even. Then he shut himself in his changing room. As soon as the last dancer had high kicked the finale into touch and the show was done he bid a cheery *buona notte* and was out and off the premises sharpish. He showed no more interest in staying behind for a drink. I was disappointed. I was a young man looking to learn about the world and I wanted to hear more of his wisdom. He was an artist: not like Picasso, but still a true artist, living by his talent. His path was different to that of other men, and I was disposed to learn something from him. Colin had put a stop to all of that with a single burst of hair-trigger violence and brutality.

When the curtain went down on the Revue I was scheduled to work the evening cash bingo session, and after that I was free. I had a couple of beers in the giant Slowboat Bar, so called for reasons I never did discover. I laughed and joked with a couple of the scary kitchen girls, but after my conversation with Nikki I had started watched the working staff, too. I saw one of the barmen under challenge from a holidaymaker who claimed to have been short-changed. I wondered how often that happened.

I'd completed my first week. I crashed into my bed and for the first time since I'd arrived I slept soundly.

5

The way forward will require the dismantling of all state apparatus

I'd been wearing whites and a candy-striped blazer for a week solid and it was good to get back into civilian gear, which in my case was a pair of bell-bottom blue jeans and a white T-shirt. I rose early to have a lardy breakfast in the canteen and as I crossed the camp all I could see were suitcases lined up outside the wooden chalets as cleaners tried to get in and campers and their families tried to get out. It was the ritual of the Saturday changeover.

The only thing I could do to find a little breathing space was to go for a walk on the beach. With everyone occupied in the changeover the beach was deserted. It was going to be another hot day. A tunnel gave access from the camp to the beach wall and when I got down to the water I took off my sandals and carried them between my fingers, feeling the warm sand and shingle between my toes.

I still didn't like it. I'd heard all those people talk about how they loved to walk barefoot on the beach. The fact is it gave me the creeps; or even worse, it triggered a mysterious anxiety. I brushed the sand off my feet and put my sandals back on, and then I wiped my hands on my denims. I moved back up the beach so that I could walk on the reassuring pebbles.

I started walking north, towards Ingoldmells. The sand settles out in banks at angles to the shore and when you get past the housing and developments there are impressive dunes. I'd read that the Vikings found natural harbours behind these now-dry dunes and I thought I might take a look. Way up the beach I saw two figures sitting, huddled together on a railway sleeper that had been deposited on the beach by a high tide. The sun at my left hand was a bright yellow blister over the water and the bright sunlight sparkled electric blue on one of the figures.

It was the man in the blue suit I'd seen on the day of the sandcastle competition. He was hugging a child – presumably the boy I'd seen. Maybe the blue suit was made of some synthetic material because its threads caught the sun's rays and darted light. He had a rope coiled over his shoulder.

But then the sun darkened and I felt dizzy. My breath came short. I head a groan from way off – way out to sea and I felt an unaccountable panic, triggered by something very old shifting deep inside me. I looked up. The man and the boy had turned to look at me, per-haps because I was acting oddly. But their faces were in shadow. It made no sense. They were turned full on to the sun, but their faces were grey and flat and smooth like beach pebbles, almost in silhouette. Even though their faces were indistinct, they peered back at me with suspicion, as if I somehow meant to harm them. I felt a wave of revulsion. My teeth chattered.

The sun appeared to come out again, and I had to blink, because I wasn't looking at a man and a boy at all. All I could see was the railway sleeper they'd sat on.

I'd somehow hallucinated them in the morning light. I recovered and paced up the beach to the sea-blasted railway sleeper. It was festooned with the usual debris of the beach: a bit of rope, a plastic bottle, some dried bladderwrack, an old coat hugging the sleeper. But of the man and the boy there was no sign.

I cast around, still looking for them. The empty beach was now a hostile, echoing place. A sudden stench came off the water and turned my guts. I told myself what I'd seen was all a trick of the light. But I didn't believe that. Not for one second.

I recovered and moved on. I glanced back a few times to see if I could see anything until finally I had to challenge myself not to keep looking back over my shoulder. Now I didn't feel at all like going to explore the lonely dunes. Instead I walked on for about two miles. There was a very faint breeze coming off the water, and the bad odour went away. I'd been holding my breath against it. Instead, salt air and the mild electrical charge of the gentle waves was something I could inhale again. I walked on, starting to feel better, with the sun rising steadily over the water.

At midday I stood outside the main gates of the camp, waiting for Tony. I knew he drove a smart Wolseley saloon. Instead a two-tone Hillman Minx pulled up, with a cheerful pip on the horn that was clearly directed at me. I noticed two figures in the back but I couldn't see the driver. The passenger door opened.

I was astonished to see Colin behind the wheel. He was wearing a dark suit and a blue tie. I hesitated.

He leaned across the seat. He tilted his head sideways and closed one eye. 'Get in, son.'

I climbed into the passenger seat. Colin set off without a word and when I turned to check out the passengers in the back I recognised a lad from the kitchen. I didn't know his name. He had buck-teeth shaping his mouth into a permanent sneer. The other passenger I didn't know at all. He had his head back on the seat upholstery and, with his eyes closed and his mouth open, appeared to be dozing.

Pretty soon we were heading away from the coast into the flat, open countryside of Lincolnshire. I didn't want to stare at Colin, but he looked very different in a suit and tie. I wouldn't say he looked neat: he was one of those men for whom even a close shave can never quite get rid of a blue shadow. He caught me looking.

'Nice car,' I said, wanting to break the uncomfortable silence.

'That's cos it's British,' the lad from the kitchen said.

'Where are we going anyway?' I said.

'Fifteen minutes, twenty at tops,' Colin said. 'Most traffic west will be goin' another route.' It wasn't an answer to my question but I gathered that it was the only answer I was going to get.

Colin had scrubbed up and I could smell something like carbolic soap on him. That and a metalwork smell. He switched on the car radio. A local news reporter was banging on about the unusual drought conditions. A hosepipe ban had been introduced and several grass fires and woodland fires had scorched areas of land in Southern England. Colin cursed the government, as if they had engineered the drought conditions to blight the country.

'It's the mad scientists,' said the boy in the back with bad teeth, 'puttin' ice seeds in the clouds.'

'Oh fuck off with that,' Colin said, and he snapped off the radio.

After he'd put another few miles on the clock, without taking his eyes off the road Colin said, 'Where from?'

It took me a couple of seconds to realise he was asking me a question. I hardly finished answering him before he asked me another question.

'What's yer Dad do?'

I told him about Ken's building business.

He sniffed noisily. 'Movver work?'

'No.'

He had an odd style of driving, tucking his chin into his chest and looking up from under his brow. It reminded me of a boxer's defensive stance. We drove through the Lincolnshire countryside with all the windows of the Minx wound down. The land was dusty and parched and we occasionally passed roadside signs: Danger You Are Entering A Drought Area Conserve Water. But somehow it didn't concern me and I had faith that every natural order would soon be restored.

Eventually we drew up at a pub with a thatched roof. It was called The Fighting Cocks and it had a lovely beer garden with a tall slide and a play area for children. Though there was no breath of wind to move the flag, a smart Union Jack hung from a freshly painted white pole. A number of cars were drawn up in the car park but Colin stopped at the entrance.

'Out,' said Colin. 'See you inside.' I made to open the door but Colin put his leathery hand on my arm. 'Not you.'

The other two lads got out as directed and hurried into the pub. I noticed that they were both wearing highly-polished Doc Marten lace-up boots. Even though it was ridiculous footwear in this heat it made me feel exposed in my open-toed sandals. My stomach fluttered. Colin eased into the car park at the back of the pub where a steward beckoned him into a reserved space. Two tall and rather impressive men in dark suits were leaning next to a highly polished Bentley. They were exchanging a few words and both were smoking cigars.

We got out of the car and Colin walked over to the smoking men. I assumed I should follow. Colin shook hands with each of them in turn. If they noticed me loitering in the background they didn't show it.

One of the men, completely bald and with a very thick neck, said, 'Mills has cried off.'

'Oh the cunt,' Colin said.

'About two hours ago, what do you think of that?' said the second man. Unlike his colleague he had a thick head of black hair, swept back and fixed with Brylcreem.

'That's what happens,' the thick-necked man said, 'when you give people like that the opportunity.'

Colin rolled his neck as if to relieve some muscle stress. 'Tony here?'

'He's in the pub,' the second man said. 'But he says he don't want to do it.'

'He'll do it,' Colin said. 'He'll warm 'em up til Carter gets here. No worries.'

At last the bald man acknowledged my dithering presence. 'Who's this then?'

'This is David,' Colin said, 'Student. Just here to take a look at us.'

The man held out his hand and gave me a warm handshake. 'Good to have you here, David. I'm

Norman Prosser and you are very welcome amongst us. Student, are you? Well, good for you, lad. We need more students. You see, we need to get amongst the students and explain properly what we are about.' He took a step back and looked me up and down. 'If Colin spotted you, you must be all right. You look smart, handsome and you look the part.'

What *part* I was supposed to look in my T-shirt and sandals I had no idea. But then the second man with the oiled hair stepped forward and gave me a very firm handshake – too hard – and told me his name. 'John Talbot.' Though he didn't say any more, he looked hard into my eyes as if to prove some kind of a point.

We went into the pub and, as I blinked into the darkness of the bar after the brilliant light outside, I felt Norman Prosser's hand in the small of my back gently steering me. 'Now let's buy you a drink, young man. What will it be? A fine single malt or a pint of ale?' He spoke like he'd already adopted me. 'And you just remember the name Norman Prosser and you come to me for anything, you understand? Any problem, however big or small, come to me. Because once you're in our circle we look after each other.'

Colin, crowding me on the other side, winked at me. I had no idea what the wink meant. It did nothing to put me at ease.

'Can I be honest with you, David, can I? Do you want a cigar by the way?'

'Thanks, I don't smoke.'

I was given a pint of bitter and a glass of malt whisky, even though I hadn't asked for the latter.

'The truth is we don't get as many students as we'd like. This is because we get a very bad press. Those newspaper people, they hate the working classes and they want to keep them down. So they misrepresent us over and over. But we do want to get amongst the students, so I'd like to get your views. But not now because I'm going *through*.' Prosser nodded to his left and gathered up his own beer and whisky. His cigar he left smoking in the ashtray on the bar.

I glanced around. The pub wasn't busy. A few elderly couples were enjoying a lunchtime drink and chicken-in-wicker-basket type meals; a pair of young lovers holding hands and flirting, oblivious to the world. I couldn't see anything distinctive about the place.

'Bring those,' Colin said, 'we're in the pavilion at the back.'

I picked up my drinks and he led me through an echoing corridor that ran behind the bar. We passed into a large concert-type room illuminated by harsh electric strip lighting and there it was immediately apparent as to where I'd been brought. Though I think I'd already guessed; I just hadn't wanted to be right. Because Tony had been the source of the original invitation, part of me still clung to some preposterous idea that I'd been brought to an exclusive entertainment-business elite; perhaps a meeting of the Magic Circle; or even an afternoon strip-club.

Well, there were no strippers on show. The entire room was decked in the flags of the British union: the same flag that looked so cheerful and harmless and reassuring hanging from a painted pole outside the pub. Every inch of wall space was draped with the red, white and blue. At one end of the room was a platform with tables and a microphone at the ready. These tables were draped instead with the white background and red cross of the flag of St George. The wall immediately behind the platform was also decorated with the flag of St George.

About sixty or seventy plastic chairs were drawn up in neat rows before the platform and most of these were already occupied, mainly by middle-aged males, many of whom wore a collar and tie on this hottest of days, but there was a fair scattering of women there too. In some of the seats but also patrolling the room were a number of young skinheads in bomber jackets and high-laced Doc Marten boots. They had a paramilitary swagger. It was obvious that they regarded themselves as foot-soldiers, or as some kind of unofficial security force.

Some years earlier, when I was thirteen, I walked home from a youth club happy at having got my first kiss from a girl. I had to pass by a chip shop and a group of skinheads in Docs and braces were laughing and joking outside. For no apparent reason they attacked me – maybe I made the mistake of making eye contact with one. There were five of them. Kicked to the ground, I cradled my head in my arms as I felt the boots going in all over my body. I was rescued by an elderly lady who told them they should be ashamed. I got to my feet and limped home. I managed to hide my bruises from my parents, but from that day I always treated any skinhead in the same way you would regard a rabid dog.

One of these skinheads immediately approached me, peddling some publication pitched between a magazine and a newspaper. It was called *Spearhead*. I became aware of a lot of eyes on me. My clothes were all wrong. The long hair, the open-toed sandals. Whatever the 'other side' might be I was pretty sure I resembled it. Some self-preservation instinct kicked in and I found myself digging in my pocket for a few coins. The skinhead became friendly and let me know that someone was going around with a great pamphlet about how we should support Welsh nationalists' campaign of burning holiday homes. I said I'd look out for it and he gave me a wink. Colin had disappeared and something was about to start so I quickly took a seat.

Of course I was furious with myself for being so naive. If someone suggests you follow them your initial question should be: *where to*? You don't just go along with the first person who charms you into following them. Or do you? I think that's what I'd done pretty much all my life. I still think that it's what most people do, whether we are talking about social activities, or about politics, or about falling in love.

After a short delay in proceedings, the two men whose hands I had just shaken in the car park took their places on the platform. I noticed one chair remained empty. Then a familiar figure leapt onto the stage.

It was Tony from the holiday camp. Just like Colin, he'd found a suit and tie for the event. He blew into a microphone to check it was working and then launched into a relaxed welcoming speech, saying how good it was to see so many old friends and so many new faces, too. He came down from the stage and strolled about the place, smiling, winking and shaking hands with one or two people on the front row without breaking his patter. Then he effortlessly segued into a few Paki jokes.

They were new jokes and he was very funny. He easily drew laughs from the audience and I found it impossible not to laugh with them. A very edgy joke about the Jews followed and that went down very well, too. At some point a third man arrived and without fuss took his place on the platform. I assumed this to be the man they'd referred to as Carter.

Tony threw in another Paki gag about an Indian family eating dog-food and while the audience were howling he handed the microphone back to Norman Prosser. Prosser got to his feet and thanked Tony not only for his 'wonderful humour' but also for his lifelong commitment and dedication to the serious business for which we were all assembled. And, he pointed out, while we can all laugh, and that it's good to laugh, the things that were happening to the country were no laughing matter. The Reds and the Jews and the Immigrants were hand in glove – and on this phrase he paused and looked searchingly round the audience – *hand in glove*, presiding over the demise of a once great nation and the government were like the Emperor Nero, fiddling while Rome burns. Well that's all coming to an end, he said, the party was growing and change was coming. There was evidence of all sorts of new people coming forward, workers, school teachers, people from industry and students. In this latter category I knew with absolute certainty that I was his evidence. I even felt a few eyes flicker in my direction. Prosser went on to say that we were fortunate today in being able to welcome Harold Carter to the meeting who will outline for us the Way Forward.

Prosser handed Carter the microphone and Carter got to his feet, taking some early applause from the floor. He was a tall, slightly stooped man with thinning sandy-coloured hair. In a cut-glass accent he told us that the people of the country were awakening. Evidence of this was to be seen in the numbers of votes the party had received in the last election and the number of deposits that were not lost in that election. Furthermore, he told us, memberships of the party had increased by several thousand in the last two years alone. Awakening, he said ominously. The people are awakening and beginning to arise.

This last bit of rhetoric not only got enormous applause but it got a standing ovation. It also pulled me to my feet. Not because I thought that what he was saying was either brilliant or even convincing but my sense of self-preservation was working overtime. Perhaps I'm a coward. It's possible. But I'm not stupid. This wasn't a rational position to be in. To have resisted the mob in this context would have been like standing in front a herd of stampeding cattle. As I joined in the hand-clapping, as lightly as I could, I noticed the way that Carter, lapping up the applause, darted his tongue rapidly between his lips, or shoved his tongue into his cheek to bubble out the side of his face. It was a tic I observed in him every time he paused in his oratory to take the applause from the floor.

The Way Forward was very clear. Immigrants who were stealing our jobs would be repatriated. They would be deported. Incentives would be found to encourage them to leave the country and if that was not acceptable then secure methods would be found to make the deportation happen. When that was done legislation would be passed to disengage the Jewish monopoly of the financial institutions. After that the Reds would be systematically exposed and their stranglehold on all public national and local apparatus of the state would be broken.

I give you only a summary of the Way Forward, but this speech went on for an hour, punctuated by regular outbreaks of wild applause. The audience got to its feet on numerous occasions, and I of course with it, even though nothing I heard made any kind of sense to me. Maybe I was too fixated on the man's darting tongue.

The speeches concluded and the platform group rose to disperse. As the audience stood up the skinhead foot-soldiers went around with plastic buckets encouraging donations. Norman Prosser and some others at the front made a show of putting large denomination notes into the buckets but I noticed most people dropped in a bit of loose change and when the bucket came my way I clattered in a few pennies.

I felt a hand on my shoulder. 'Couple o' minutes an' we're out of here.' It was Colin. He shoved a fiver into my hand. 'Get another drink and a whisky for me.'

I was grateful for the role. I dodged another bucket and an incoming *Spearhead* vendor and made my way to the bar. There was nothing I could do but wait out my time before getting a lift back to the camp. At the bar I bought myself another pint of bitter, a whisky for Colin and a whisky for myself. I didn't want the latter but I felt like I needed it. I leaned against the bar sipping my drinks and watching buoyant party-members leave in small groups, some of them resting ceremonial flags on poles across their shoulder.

Colin re-appeared. He had a way of ghosting to your side. 'What you make of that then?'

'Interesting,' I said.

His face was like a sea-washed stone. 'Interesting, eh?' Then for the first time ever I saw him laugh. It was a cynical laugh. 'Listen, I'm not a cunt. I know it ain't where you're at. I told Tony but he thought you deserved a chance.'

I'm not sure what *chance* it was that was being offered to me, but I nodded my appreciation.

'Listen,' he said again. 'You're honest. I like that. You come to me for anything. You got that?'

'Yes.'

'No,' he said. 'You 'aven't got it.'

'Yes, I have.'

'No, you don't get it. You come to me for anything. Any reason.'

I was embarrassed by the idea that Colin was telling me he'd taken a liking to me. I didn't know what to say so I offered to buy him a beer, but we were interrupted by Tony. 'Enjoy any of that, David?'

Colin rescued me from having to think of an answer. He said to Tony, 'Any word?'

'Suspended without pay, old son, and banned from the camp for two weeks.'

Colin swore. 'Cowsons.'

Tony put a forefinger under his own right eye and pulled down the fold of skin there. 'You're lucky that I put a word in for you,' he said. 'Be grateful. Could have been a lot worse.'He switched his gaze to me. His lower lip was moist. 'A lot worse.'

I recalled what Norman Prosser had said about them looking after their own. It seemed that Colin's party membership had come in useful: Tony would have some sway with Pinky and the rest of the camp management team. In the next moment I heard someone call Colin by his name but he didn't look up. Instead, while Tony was buying more drinks at the bar Colin drew me aside and tapped me with extreme delicacy on my breastbone. 'While I'm away I want you to keep an eye open.'

I shuffled. 'Keep an eye open for what?'

'If she talks to anyone, I want to know.' He fixed me with an intense look. It was like having someone insert their thumbs into your eye sockets.

Most of the party members were drifting away, with their flags and regalia, while we knocked back our drinks. Tony seemed upbeat, cheerful. He wanted us to stay but Colin was ready to leave. But not before Norman Prosser came bustling through.

'Where's my young student?' he said loudly. The whisky had given him a red complexion and there was a glow of perspiration on his jowls. When he put a hand either side of my face and gently patted my right cheek I could smell his cologne. He was all smiles. 'I saw you listening. I saw you listening. And that's all I ask, that you students give us a fair hearing and then spread the word. That's not unfair, is it? You want another drink?'

'He doesn't,' Colin said. 'We're away.'

'Now you've got Colin if you need anything from us,' Prosser said.

'Colin's not going to be around for a bit,' Tony said.

Prosser tipped his head back to look at Tony. From that simple remark he seemed to gather all he needed to know. 'Well, in that case he's got you.'

'Give the lad a breavin' space,' Colin said.

Prosser brushed some imaginary lint from my shoulder. 'Never mind these two. Colin's a good spotter. We're like family and you come to me for anything at all. Are you all right for a few quid?'

'I'm fine thank you, Mr Prosser.' I said.

'Norman to you. And you come to us for anything at all.'

Out in the car park the two back-seat passengers were waiting by the car. They stood in their high-laced Doc Martens with their arms folded, fists bunched behind their biceps. I hadn't seen them in the meeting though I knew that's where they'd been. They sized me up like I was the Prodigal Son. Or the fatted calf, ready for the knife.

We climbed in and set off to return to the coast.

'Ignore Norman,' Colin said. 'He can't hold his drink.'

'What's Norman said then?' asked one of the lads in the back.

Colin ignored the question so I thought I should, too. There was no further discussion about the meeting and I certainly wasn't going to bring up the topic. Meanwhile Colin drove in silence, utterly focused on the heat-shimmering road ahead.

At one point in the journey Colin stopped the car and took out a cloth to wipe away the huge number of bugs that had splattered the windscreen. I studied his face as he worked. It was flat and emotionless; but it was full of history. Deep diagonals raged across his forehead and twisted over his brow. I wondered if there were people who could read faces, in the same way that a palmist looks at your hands.

He caught me looking and I glanced away sharpish.

Shortly after he started again, the buck-tooth passenger in the back said, completely out of the blue, 'Is he a poof, then?'

'Ask him yourself,' Colin said.

'Are you a poof, then?'

I realised he was talking about me. I turned and looked him in the eye but said nothing.

After a while the same boy piped up again. 'He thinks we're all cunts,' he said.

I turned around a second time. 'No,' I said. 'I don't think Colin is a cunt. And I don't think your mate is a cunt either.'

'Ha!' shouted Colin, and he hooted his horn. 'That's fucked you!' Then he hit his horn again. 'You're out your league wi' this boy! Haha!'

After that we drove back to the camp in complete silence.

6

The extraordinary seduction
of marine phosphorescence

I spent the rest of the afternoon sleeping. I wasn't accustomed to drinking in the day-time – whisky or beer – and, what with the heat, when I got back I just crashed on my pallet bed. By the time I awoke I'd missed tea at the canteen. I remember sitting up on my bed in a semi-stupor, gazing down at the floor where my sandals lay alongside the copy of *Spearhead* magazine while a stupid newspaper shoutline *Was Jesus A Fascist?* looped around my head. It was half an hour before the paralysis left me and I was able to drag myself off to the shower.

It had been my plan to wander into the town of Skegness that evening, to get away from the camp, but I still felt sluggish and I decided it was too late. I needed to eat. I trailed over to the Fish & Chip bar but even that failed to shake me from my stupor.

Several drinking venues were available on the site. There was a licensed ballroom where older couples did the foxtrot and the cha-cha-cha but following my afternoon with the National Front I didn't feel up for either. There was another watering hole known as the Tap Room featuring a stout and rather warty lady called Bertha who slapped the piano stride-style for a traditional singalong. 'The Old Bull and Bush' and all that. Then there was the strip-lit giant aircraft hangar of the Slowboat. If you didn't like any of these, the last recourse was a tiny bar situated in a corner of the theatre foyer, a hideaway favoured by the professional acts if they wanted a drink after a performance, and that's where I decided to go. But of course there was no Variety show on a Saturday evening, so the Review Bar as it was titled, was closed. I settled instead for the Slowboat.

The residency three-piece band bashed away on stage at the far end of the hangar: drums, organ and bass artlessly covering standards and classics. Dozens of circular table-and-chair sets filled the space between the band and the bar, populated with new holidaymakers relaxed and drinking at a hearty pace that would last all week and quicken on Friday. I made for the bar and was surprised to see Luca Valletti sitting near the band and in his civvies. He was smoking a cigarette and he had a glass of wine in front of him. I wanted to go over but he seemed deep in conversation with a woman I knew to be the girlfriend of one of the band members. Anyway, I was immediately distracted when I was rounded on by a coven of kitchen girls.

'Hey it's him from the college of knowledge! Show us your IQ!'

I was learning how to racquet back the banter but I still couldn't stop myself from blushing. I said my IQ was too big for any of them. It got a big cheer which made a lot of people turn round to look at us. The girls took every thing as a *double-entendre*, even if there wasn't one. They wanted everything to be a *double-entendre*. You could say *I once knew a man who kept an aardvark in his garden shed* and they would treat it as a sexual remark. They were always excitable, and always thirsty for lager.

'Come and drink with us, college boy!'

There was no way out.

'He fancies you, Rachel,' said Pauline, a girl with luscious lips and thick eye-liner. 'You could teach him how to fuck.'

This sort of thing could go on for hours. They bought me a drink. It was all teasing, all talk. At least I suspect it was. I had no idea what would happen if you tried to take one of them up on all this. Not that I was interested, and neither would I have had the courage. I bought a round of drinks back, for Pauline and Rachel and for two other girls. It was while I was waiting for my change at the bar that I felt someone's eyes on me.

Terri stood alone at the far end of the bar. When people say 'my heart missed a beat' I don't believe that phrase exactly describes the experience. I felt a sudden suffocation, a noose tightening around my throat, an instant of time freezing when all sound was sucked out of that giant hangar of a bar. I had the uncanny and stupid notion that she had been able to do that to me just by looking, like a moment of witchcraft. And then just as quickly everything was normal again.

I turned away with the drinks I'd bought for the girls. Did my hand tremble? When I looked again at her she was still gazing back at me. She almost huddled into the corner of the bar, as if she was trying to make herself small. Her arms were folded and she was shrunk into herself. She wore a simple black dress, somewhat low cut and reaching halfway down to her knees. The reason I was so struck by her dress was that this was

81

the first time I'd seen either her bare arms or her bare legs. The lustrous dark hair that she always wore tied back now fell forward in a loose wave across one side of her face.

I went over to her, just as if pulled by a magic thread. As I approached she dropped her eye contact and looked away, squeezing herself with her folded arms. 'I thought you'd been banned,' I said.

'No.'

'Or that you were suspended?'

'Not me.' She averted her face, as if she'd found new interest in the band. Anyone looking at our body language would assume that she was bored but trapped by my conversation. She wore large gold ear-rings and a gold bangle that reminded me of something Luca had said about women.

'I saw Colin today. At a meeting.'

That surprised her. She flickered a glance at me and then looked away again.

'Not that I'm one of them,' I said.

'So why were you there?'

'It was a mistake.'

'You went to a p'litical meeting by mistake? Not very bright, are you?'

'Did I claim to be bright?'

At last she looked at me. Her eyes had a feline flame, but with a dissolving quality, an intelligence behind them as if she processed and documented every detail that came before her. She wore eyeliner and a little lipstick, again something I'd never seen on her before. Some instinct told me I should back away. Instead I said, 'Can I buy you a drink?'

She looked away again. 'No, you can't.'

'Why not?'

'Because everyone will see you buy me a drink.'

'Do you want me to go away?'

'Of course not. Why do you think I'm here?'

The remark left me open-mouthed. 'So ... I can't buy you a drink. I can't talk with you because you won't look at me. What am I to do?'

'You figure out a solution. You're the one who is supposed to be clever.'

Not *that* clever, is what I wanted to say. I asked her where Colin was and she said that following the meeting he had gone back to London. He would be staying down in the capital while his suspension was in force. When I asked why she hadn't gone with him she said that they simply couldn't afford for her not to be working. I flashed on what Colin had said in the pub that afternoon and it occurred to me that this, at least, might give me permission to be seen talking to her. I would also be keeping any predators away.

But even that was no use if she couldn't look me in the eye. I felt emboldened and I said, 'It will be dark in an hour. We could go for a walk on the beach.'

'Up to the dunes? Bit obvious, aincha?'

'That's not what I meant.'

It really wasn't. For one thing the idea of the dunes at night didn't appeal; secondly you would be in serious danger of tripping over any number of fornicating couples in the dark.

She unfolded her arms. On the bar and in her glass of gin-and-tonic was a pink plastic straw. She took a sip through the straw and set the glass back on the bar. Still without looking at me she said, 'Do you know where the wreck is?'

'Yes.' Way up the beach in the other direction a very old shipwreck lay offshore. At low tide the masts and the rotting prow of the boat were exposed, festooned with lime-green seaweed.

'Meet me opposite that. There's a break in the wall.'

She didn't wait for an answer. She just left me and her unfinished gin-and-tonic without a backward glance. I was still watching her go when I felt a shadow at my side. I turned to see a row of perfectly white teeth smiling at me. It was Luca Valletti. He put his mouth very close to my ear. 'Stromboli,' he whispered, 'you play with a-fire.' Then with a tiny, formal bow he walked away, leaving by the same door as Terri.

I'd said one hour. I glanced at my watch. Then I rejoined the rowdy kitchen girls. If they had thought anything of my talking to Terri they said nothing. They were gathering themselves together to drift off to the Tap Room, ready for a raucous sing-song with Bertha at the ivories, so I joined them, knowing that I could easily melt away from the Tap Room without anyone noticing.

It was a beautiful evening, still very warm but with the lightest of breezes streaming from the seaward. I left the camp by the north gate, passing the little white caravan with the palmist's board outside. Though I'd never actually caught sight of the said Madame Rosa I couldn't seem to resist trying to steal a glance inside every time I passed by. The caravan, though, was locked up for the night.

The wreck was a fair stroll up the beach. Terri had chosen the direction that the fewest people went and a place that was poorly lit. When I got there she was

84

loitering near the gap in the wall, her arms still folded.

'We'll walk along the beach.'

'Yes,' I said.

'Hang on, I want to take my shoes off.'

We walked down to the water's edge with Terri carrying her shoes. The water was midnight blue and a foamy phosphorescence emanated from the surf. It was like being in the Golden Wheel nightclub when they switch to ultra-violet light. She flicked her head in the direction she wanted to walk, away from the streetlamps. After a few yards she turned towards me and I saw the flash of her teeth and the whites of her eyes, but the rest of her was in semi-darkness. She seemed to me like a species of beautiful demon in the ethereal light.

But she looked away again and we walked on in silence. She took a deep breath of the air and then she made a strange gesture at the sea, raising her palm towards the waves, as if she could conjure the water. Then she stroked the back of her white neck and shook her hair free.

After a while I said, 'Shall we sit on the sand?'

'Yes,' she said. 'You're not kissing me.'

'I wasn't about to,' I said. Though the thought had crossed my mind. Of course it had.

She lowered herself to sit cross-legged onto the sand and I sat beside her, but not too close. We stared out at the foaming, electric-blue discharge of the phosphorescent waves. 'It's beautiful!' she said. 'Beautiful!'

'I know,' I said. 'It's something to do with microscopic creatures reacting with oxygen to reflect—'

'I'm not talking about the sea, you idiot!' she shouted. 'Oh?'

'The freedom! A minute's freedom! All this! Just

being here with you!' She looked at me and smiled and I realised it was the very first time that she had allowed herself to smile. 'You don't know what I'm talking about, do you?'

'Not really.'

'You don't know how I live!'

'How do you live?'

She looked out to sea again. She compressed her lips and narrowed her eyes. Then she flicked at her dress. 'See this dress? I keep this in secret. He doesn't know I have this dress. He decides what I wear and when I wear it. I'm not allowed to go out. I'm not allowed to go shopping. I'm not allowed any friends. I'm definitely not allowed to stroll along the beach at night.' She picked up a pebble from the sand and tossed it into the lapping water. 'You see those Muslim women who wear those bloody awful all-over things?'

'It's called a chador.'

'Is it? Well. He treats me like they treat their wives. He covers me up. He hides me.'

Forgive me, I thought, but at this moment I would want to hide you, too. She was a spark of light and he wanted to keep her under a glass jar. He knew that if he let her go the light would go out of his life. 'Why don't you just leave him?'

'Ha! Don't you think I have? Three times. He came after me and he beat me black and blue. Plus I've got nowhere else to go.'

'That doesn't make sense. You can go anywhere.'

'It's all right for you to say. You have all of life in front of you. I'm stuck, cleaning floors, stuck with a man I don't love. Jesus, I'm being a boring bitch.'

'No, you're not.'

'Change the subject.'

I took a breath and described my life at University. I told her that my life wasn't very exciting either, consisting of lectures in the daytime and drinking in the evening even though I wasn't a great drinker.

'What sort of lectures?'

I didn't know what to tell her. I started with some guff about William Faulkner, but then I tailed off. What could I say? *Sorry, you're not allowed to go to University to know about Shakespeare and William Faulkner because you were born the wrong side of the tracks?* I supposed if she exhausted herself at night-school for three years and starved herself for a further three she could do it. But it wasn't anywhere in her own expectation of herself.

'That all sounds rubbish,' she said. I was relieved that she didn't want to hear any more about my University life.

The conversation returned to Colin and she told me how she'd met him.

'He rescued me,' she said.

She was fourteen and living in Chingford when Colin had 'rescued' her. He was twelve years older than she was. She'd been in and out of foster care and ended up with a violent uncle who was getting ready to put her on the game. Her life back then was a kind of hell that she said I didn't want to know about. Colin was handsome enough, he was strong and he had his own flat. He took care of her. He took her away from the life she was living. She shacked up with him and carried on going to school for another year, cooking his breakfast, making his dinner, tidying his flat. She fell pregnant but it didn't work out.

Colin was sometimes flush with money. He knew some bad people and she had a good idea where he was getting it. But it seemed exciting. Then Colin had to do a stretch in prison. It was lonely. She got some cleaning work in a pub to make ends meet. In the pub she got a little too friendly with one of the bar staff, a young man more her own age. Colin came out of prison and first he dealt with the young man and then he dealt with her. She ran away from him. He came after her, beat her again and brought her home.

'You don't want anything to do with me,' she said. 'I'm trouble wherever I go.'

'No, you're not,' I said.

She got to her feet. 'I'm going to swim,' she said.

'What?'

'I don't know when I'll next get the chance.' In one moment she lifted her black dress over her head and stripped it off. Then she unhooked her bra and let her breasts fall free. 'Get an eyeful, why don't you?'

'You expect me to look away?'

'No. You can look.'

She left her white cotton knickers on and walked into the water. The blue-white threads of phosphorescence foamed around her calves, and then around her knees and then lapped at her thighs, as if the water had become excited, charged. Again I had the eerie notion that she was a dark spirit. She didn't look back at me to see if I was going to join her. The truth is I was a little bit afraid. She went out deeper and began to swim.

I waited on the sand until she came out again. She was shivering. She smoothed water from her shoulders and her breasts and from her hips and thighs with the palms of her hands. Then she slipped her bra on again

88

and pulled her dress over her. 'We'll walk back now.'

I didn't want to. But I got to my feet and we started walking very slowly back towards the lights of the promenade. 'How was it?' I said, dumbly. 'How was the water?'

'Oh.'

Then she skipped in front of me and reached up and, taking my face in both her hands, she craned her neck up to kiss me. I know I sound like a little girl, but I felt dizzy and faint. I tasted saltwater on her lips. Saltwater and the soft phosphorescence.

I had kissed girls before. I wasn't a virgin. But she wasn't a girl and this was all new to me. There was a less pliant quality to her kisses, a brittleness that said the thing had to be more hard-won. She broke off and let her hands fall at her sides, staring hard at me. Then she turned and made towards the promenade. Before we reached the first lights she said that she would go on ahead and that I should follow after a decent interval.

'But I should walk you back!'

'I'll be fine.'

She skipped off the beach and up onto the promenade, quickening her pace, tossing her hair as she went. I watched from the shadows. When she'd disappeared from view I sat back down on the concrete platform of the sea wall. I held my hands in front of my face. They were trembling. I could still taste the saltwater from her lips. And the honey. And the fire.

7

Whereupon they gather to drink bitter tears

Sunday was our start of the week. When I got to the theatre for Pinky's up-and-at-'em briefing most of the team were already assembled – Tony, Perry the ASM, George who ran the disco in the nightclub, and all the Greencoats except for Nobby. I was hoping that Terri would be up there on the stage in her cleaning whites, swabbing the floor with a mop. But she wasn't. It was probably a good thing. I would have found it impossible to take my eyes off her.

Nikki perched on one of the front row seats so I went over and settled myself next to her. I said good morning but she didn't answer me; instead she instantly got up and went to talk to George. I thought little of it at the time and anyway after a moment Nobby bustled in, huffing and puffing and blaming everyone but himself for his lateness. He crashed down in the seat Nikki had vacated and continued to talk nonsense about missing milk and no cereals and traffic and ducks waddling in the road until Pinky, unlit cigar wedged between his fingers, waved him into silence so that the various duties could be assigned.

The Sunday programme was fairly light. Pinky nominated me to do the Treasure Hunt. I was hoping Nikki would volunteer to do it with me but she elected instead to run the Whist Drive with Nobby in the Slowboat. I was paired with another dancer called Gail, a pretty and dreamy girl who, when not dancing, spent most of her time examining the split ends on her long hair or studying her fingernail varnish. Before leaving the theatre I glanced up on stage, but Nikki had already disappeared behind the curtain.

The Treasure Hunt was for kids between five and nine years. Gail and I led the kids around in a mob as they tracked down clues and locations all previously configured. The clues led to a set of plastic spades and then identified a spot on the beach where the treasure (a tin casket full of sticks of rock) might be dug up. I thought it was a bit lame so I suggested we tell the kids that Captain Blood the pirate was trying to beat them to the treasure, and that so they should look lively. Of course there was no Captain Blood so I slipped off to the props room behind the stage. Behind the sword casket used for the magic-act I found a headscarf and a belt with a huge buckle, plus a black eyepatch and a hook. I crept up behind the thirty or forty kids and roared.

They turned and looked at me in complete silence.

I was regretting my input, and then they charged. I really had to run fast to get away. Luckily I knew the lay of the camp and I gave them the slip. I have no idea what they would have done had they caught me. I took my pirate kit off, stashed it away and went to rejoin the Treasure Hunt. Out of breath, I told the kids I'd just seen Captain Blood on the beach and off they charged again, screaming for his hide.

'This is brilliant,' Gail said, 'we can forget about the clues.'

We rounded up the kids from the beach and I said I was going to look for Captain Blood but that I was a bit scared, so if they heard me blow my whistle they should come to my aid. On my way to put my gear on again I was intercepted by Pinky and Tony.

'What's going on?' Pinky wanted to know.

I explained the game.

'This is like the old days,' Pinky said brightly. 'Go up on the theatre roof and when they see you, duck out of sight.'

There were stairs onto the roof of the theatre and I went up there to slip on my pirate gear. When I blew my whistle they came running. They saw me on the roof. They pointed and shrieked. Pinky and Gail led them in a chant of 'We want Captain Blood!' I ducked out of sight. There followed a chorus of boos and another round of chanting and then there was another chorus of excited screams. I looked over the parapet and the kids were no longer looking in my direction. There at the poolside was another Captain Blood in an almost identical get-up, this one waving a sword at them. I could see it was Tony. He legged it and the kids went charging after him.

I could see right across the resort: the playing fields, the offices and staff dorms, the blocks of chalets, the pool with its gay flags drooping in the windless heat of the day. I could also see the sandy beach beyond and the still blue sea rushing towards the vanishing point. The kids chased Tony down and at the crucial moment I would pop up so they would chase me. It was wonderful: Captain Blood had magic powers. But I made a foolish mistake and almost killed myself.

When the kids approached again looking for Captain Blood I decided I would cross the roof and roar at them from the other side, but in order to do so I had to spring over a low wall running down the middle of the roof. I cocked my leg over the wall and was about to let go when I glanced down. Where I expected to see a flat roof inches under my foot the ground thirty feet below flashed at me like the edge of a shiny blade. Down there stood the man in the blue suit and the boy. The man had his palm extended towards me.

In that moment it looked as though the man was reaching forward as if to grab me, to pull me, or at least to encourage me over the edge. The flat roof of what I took to be the same building was divided by a narrow alley. I hadn't realised. I was horribly arrested with one leg dangling over the wall and my eye fixed on the man with the outstretched palm. A fraction of extra momentum would have taken me clean over.

Brought to my senses, I staggered backwards and lay down on the roof, holding my heart where it punched at my ribcage. If I had let go I would have fallen either to my death or to certain serious injury. I lay on my back for a long time, thinking about what had just happened. When I got up to look over the edge again, both man and boy had gone.

Finally, I crept down from the building. The only thing that seemed to bring the game to an end was the midday heat and the cloud of bugs – ladybirds – that were starting to become a nuisance. We gave in. I allowed myself to be 'caught' by the grown-ups and marched to the swimming pool at the point of the sword. There I was made to walk the plank, or rather the diving board, into the swimming pool. It got a big cheer. The casket-treasure of rock was dug up and the children were fed with red sugar.

Tony and Pinky took me for lunch. They told me I was no longer on probation. I hadn't known that I was on probation. You're *one of us*, Pinky said. I wasn't certain whether that meant I was good at wearing an eye patch or draping myself in the flag of St George.

'Speaking of the old days, who's polishing the Brass?' Tony said, and Pinky looked glum. Nobody wanted to polish the brass, it seemed. Every Sunday afternoon the camp was visited by a brass or silver band representing a colliery or a village somewhere in the North of the country. The musicians travelled a long way by coach to play. All that was required of the Greencoat was to place deckchairs around the bandstand and then fold them up again after everyone had gone. It was hardly onerous and I said I'd do it.

Tony and Pinky looked at each other. 'Why can't they all be like you?' Pinky said. A ladybird settled on his brow and he seemed not to notice. 'Where's that fucking Nobby?'

I was very glad of the chance to sit still. I hadn't felt right since I'd almost plunged to my death. The jolt had put the world out of joint. Meanwhile the brass band was a sadly outmoded feature of the entertainment programme; notionally it was kept on 'for the oldies' and in truth that's who turned up to listen. The white-haired old folk. They bought with them thin white-bread processed-meat sandwiches and thermos flasks filled with tea.

I helped the brass band set up, too. They were the Brigthorpe Colliery Band in smart sky-blue cotton blazers. They had already appeared earlier in the season. As I was tightening a music stand the bandmaster said, 'Are you new? What happened to Nigel?'

Nigel, I gathered, was my predecessor in the job. 'No idea,' I said. 'He cleared off.'

'Shame. Good lad, Nigel was.'

After everyone was settled I slumped into my own deckchair with a printed repertoire programme and the band struck up. The pure sounds of the brass band went to work on me at once. My breathing returned to normal. I started to drift into a world where I was half asleep, floating and soaring and falling with the music. These unfashionable musicians carried with them a beautiful sadness even when they played something jaunty and up-tempo. We had the William Tell Overture. They played the Floral Dance. They were into Largo from the New World Symphony when I felt someone settle lightly into the deckchair next to me, and I felt sand closing over my head. I lurched awake, opened my eyes and found Terri sitting next to me. She said nothing.

'I don't want you to think,' she whispered, 'that I've come here just because you are here. Because I come here every week.'

Maybe I looked sceptical.

'It's the only place he will allow me to come on my own where he knows I'm not going to get chatted up.' She indicated the snowy-haired audience with a nod of her head. 'But I like it. And I knew you would be here.'

I waved away one of the ladybirds that were becoming a plague. 'How?'

She shook her head. 'It's all all right. All of it. It's meant to be. You'll see. It's meant to be. But it's all all right.'

The band stopped for a breather and to swig water. The sunlight winked on their tubas and trombones and cornets. Sweat ran down the faces of the musicians and pooled in the crevices of their armpits. Then on a command from their leader they picked up their instruments and started up again. I went to speak but she held up a hand to stop me. I looked at my programme: Adagio for Strings. Terri sat forward in her deckchair, hands clasped under her chin like someone praying. Every now and then, as the movement began to swell, I stole a glance at her. Then I saw that she was indeed weeping. Not just a pretty tear rolling down her lovely cheek, but bitter, bitter, tears expressed in silence. I felt my own chest constrict. I wanted to do something but I couldn't. The music had completely taken her over and it was almost as if she no longer knew I was there.

A ladybird alighted on her face, on the angle of her cheekbone. I do believe it was drinking from her tears. She brushed it away.

The afternoon was evaporating in a shimmering haze. I felt very strange. For a moment I hallucinated that the men and women and boys and girls of the band were all made of glass, and their instruments, too. They were transparent and fragile, and I feared for the hammer that could so easily break them. The sun refracted off the brass instruments, but slowly, and air was filled with music, fat glass globes of sound rising from the band and drifting across the camp like bubbles blown from a child's water-pipe. I know I wasn't asleep, and anyway it only lasted for a second or two. But I felt like I'd had a glimpse at a world just behind the physics of this one. I'd been delivered into a state of unaccountable bliss, happy just to be sitting next to her all afternoon.

'Do you ever think,' I said 'that you might have someone watching over you?'

'Never,' she said, a little sharply. 'Do you?'

'I think I might have,' I said.

'Like an angel?'

'No, not at all like an angel.'

She looked at me sideways. Then she settled back into her deckchair and closed her eyes.

The concert came to an end. The elderly folk got up from their seats and shuffled away. We were the last to get out of our chairs.

'Come on. Someone will see,' she said, standing up.

'What will they see? Two people sitting in deck-chairs?'

'Yes. And that will mean a lot more than two people sitting in deckchairs.'

I made out I didn't understand that, but I suppose I did. 'Are you around this evening?' I said.

'No,' she said sharply. 'Madness.'

Then she walked away from the bandstand, across the grass, in the direction of the sea wall.

But she was around that evening. And how.

I'd spent the early evening as a checker on the cash bingo in the Slowboat. Nobby called the bingo from an elevated chair, with a glass cabinet powering numbered ping-pong balls through a Perspex tube. When one of the punters – it had taken me about a week to graduate from calling people punters instead of camp-ers – shouted for a line or a house it was my job to collect the winning ticket, take the ticket over to Nobby and run through the numbers. If all was correct – and it usually was – play could continue and the winners collected their cash at the end of the session. It was mind-numbing, oddly comforting and hugely popular with both the campers and the punters.

When the bingo was over, most of the players drifted back to their chalets to get washed and changed for the evening, whereupon they would float back again to the very same venue. It was all a bit like the sea ebbing and flowing. During that time the Slowboat residential band – three amiable Brummies in silk shirts and sparkling waistcoats – would set up ready for the night's steady stream of cover versions. One of the band – Eric the drummer – was telling me a joke, something about an adulterer who was in church when he remembered where he'd left his bicycle. I sensed but didn't hear him getting past the punch-line.

'You're not listening,' he said. Then he scoped where I was looking. 'Don't blame you, matie.' Eric moved away and rippled his fingertips along the edge of his cymbal as if to underscore some point or other.

Terri stood against the bar. Wearing that same dark, figure-hugging dress, this time she wore opaque black tights and a pair of shiny black high heels. Her eye-lashes had been highlighted with mascara and she wore a thin trace of lip-gloss. I saw her in front of me and it was like I was speeding along a motorway with a car crash happening way up ahead, but instead of slowing down I was accelerating into it.

'Are you back at work?' I said.

'Yes. But they've taken me out of the theatre. I'm cleaning the refurbished chalets in D block.'

'You look amazing,' I said.

She smiled at me but then said, 'Hush!'

'What am I supposed to do?'

She flicked her hair and glanced at me sideways. Then she looked away again.

'What's going on?' I said.

She let out a little moan. 'I don't know.' Then she picked up her handbag from the bar and leaving her drink unfinished she said, 'I'm going into town.' Without a backward glance at me she walked out of the Slowboat bar.

I stood frowning at the space she'd vacated. She was going into town? Dressed like that she was going into town? I had to fight myself to stop from running out after her and bringing her back. I turned away from the bar. Eric the drummer, perched on his stool behind his kit, was watching me. He blew on his hand and flapped his wrist, as if to cool burned fingers.

8

A sequined costume and a sword casket

Monday I woke after a bad night. Every time I slipped into sleep I was tortured by images of Terri giving herself to men in town. It was ridiculous. I didn't own her. But I was torturing myself with pictures played out on the back of my retina. Perhaps it was something of this that made Colin the way he was.

Yet Terri wasn't a flirt. She didn't toy with people's feelings, nor did she smile or flash her eyes or lick her lips or swing her hips. Just the opposite. Neither did she ever play the double-entendre game that gave the kitchen girls so much fun. With the exception of one impulsive, stolen, dry kiss, she'd held me at arm's length. At almost every moment she'd avoided giving me any kind of signal. Either she was the most manipulative woman since Mata Hari or she was genuinely trying to stay true to her monster of a husband. Even so, as I tossed and turned, I couldn't get rid of feverish pictures of her lavishing her favours on the men in the town.

I didn't see Terri all of that week. Since she'd been taken off the theatre duty she was deployed in various places. I didn't see her in the daytime and she didn't show up again in any of the evening bars. I felt as though I was always looking over my shoulder for her.

On the Wednesday morning I went into the briefing and I caught Nikki glaring at me. I tried to catch her eye but she looked away. She'd been frosty with me for some days now and I had no idea what I'd done to upset her. I was determined to ask when I got the chance.

It was the morning of the magic show. Tony asked me to ready the props and I started by wheeling the sword casket from the props cupboard, which was actually an alcove adjacent to the theatre. After a few moments Nikki appeared. She was Tony's assistant in the show and as such she was required to wear a sequined costume and to climb into the sword casket. I made some lame remark to her about dodging the swords and she completely blanked me. Turning her back on me, she stripped off and wriggled into her fishnets and her sparkling costume. Then she started brushing her long, lustrous black hair.

I'd had enough. 'Right,' I said. 'Will you tell me what I've done?'

She narrowed her dark eyes at me and brushed her hair with angry vigour. I wondered if she somehow knew about what was happening between me and Terri, and disapproved.

At last she spoke. 'Let's just have a think, shall we? A think.'

It didn't seem to me possible that she could be jealous. It didn't seem possible that she could even know. I shook my head. I had no idea.

'Didn't take you long to team up, did it?'

'What?'

'Fun, was it?'

'What fun, Nikki?'

'Joined the gang, have we?'

'The gang?'

'You went to one of their meetings.'

'Meetings?'

'What do you think that says to me, David? You know what they want to do to people like me and my family? They want us sent off in cattle trucks, that's what they want.'

I felt embarrassed and stupid at the same time. I hadn't realised that in Nikki's lovely dark looks she carried the genes of a different race. Nor had I thought what others might think about my attendance at that meeting. I was horrified. 'No! Wait! Nikki! I didn't even know you were ...' I couldn't find a word or phrase that wouldn't compound the problem.

She supplied one for me. 'Half-caste? Mixed race? Oh fuck off, David.'

'I swear! I didn't know what I was getting into! Tony said come and meet some people and I thought it might be like a conjuring circle ... or I don't know what. Next thing I found myself up to my chest in flags and skinheads and ... I had no idea.'

'You came home with all their horrible literature though, didn't you?'

'Literature?' I suddenly recalled the copy of *Spearhead* in my room. 'Who told you that?'

'Nobby saw their papers in your room.'

Nobby had reported to Nikki! My room-mate had grassed me up.

'One. One paper. I was about to throw it out. That's the truth!'

'So why have you even got one? Why, David, why?'

Her dark eyes were moist with anger and hurt and

my protestations were getting me nowhere. 'I swear to you, Nikki, I have nothing to do with those people.'

She shook her head. 'David. You're like ... like a little puppy. You'll follow anyone anywhere. You've got to be careful about where people will lead you.'

'I'm sorry! I really am.'

She gazed at me in silence before someone came blundering into the semi-darkness of the backstage. It was Tony, still wearing his fez. 'Lover's tiff, is it?' he said cheerfully. Then he began singing loudly, something about the course of true love never running smooth. Nikki sighed and headed off towards the ballroom.

Tony took off his fez and became serious. 'You have to be precise about how all this stuff unpacks and gets put away afterwards, look here. Take hold of that box.'

Later I asked Nikki how I could make things up to her.

'You can buy me an ice-cream.'

I agreed, as if to do so would solve the pressing problem of racism that was hawking the country.

'On the pier. Saturday.'

9

Your future foretold with yellow underlighting

When Saturday came I had breakfast in the canteen in my civvies. Every time someone came in I looked up, thinking it might be Terri but fearing it might be Colin. Neither appeared. I was eventually joined by one of the security guards who asked me if I was interested in Formula One car racing. I said I wasn't and he proceeded to tell me about the history, business and current state of competition in the sport, just as if I'd said yes. When he finally paused for breath, I asked him if he'd seen Colin.

'You don't want to have anything to do with him,' he said.

'No. Have you seen him around?'

He shook his head. 'What's he to you?'

I gathered up my tray and said, 'Look at the time. I've got to put my foot down.'

Nikki sat on the sea wall just outside the camp. We were going to walk together into Skegness and spend some time there. She looked very pretty. She wore a simple pink dress that bared her shoulders and she had tied her dark hair back into a ponytail. She dipped her sunglasses as I approached, and squinted at me. 'That ice-cream,' she said. 'It has to be a big one.'

'I can do that.'

She linked arms with me, as if we were a couple, and we walked along the promenade in the direction of town. Where the promenade ran out we crossed the dunes of the North Shore Golf Course and we walked a little way along the beach before going up onto the road called Roman Bank into the town. Nikki took off her flip-flops and carried the straps between her fingers as we crossed the dunes. Before we'd gone but a short distance she trod on something sharp and let out a little yelp. I made her sit down while I had a look at her foot. There was a bead of blood under her toe, a bead the size of a ladybird, already clotted with sand. I could see a thorn in her toe and I pulled it out. I put a bit of spit on my finger and cleaned her toe.

She dipped her sunglasses again and looked at me strangely.

'What?' I asked.

'Nothing.'

I suggested she'd be better off wearing her flip-flops because there was quite a lot of thorny debris amongst the dunes. She did what I told her.

'You're funny,' she said.

I couldn't think of anything I'd said that was funny.

When we got into town I bought her the promised ice-cream. I wanted to sit somewhere up on the Grand Parade and look out to sea. But she studied her thin gold wristwatch and said, no, we had to go and find somewhere to sit on Castleton Boulevard. I said I didn't think Castleton Boulevard offered much of a view.

'Who's in charge of this trip?' she said.

'You are.'

So we went to Castleton Boulevard. There we found

a bench and we ate our ice-creams. She glanced at her wristwatch again. 'Are we waiting for someone?' I said.

'Be patient, will you?'

I finished my ice-cream. The sun was already hot in the sky. You could feel it pulse. I felt a trickle of sweat run under my collar as we sat in silence. Then a lion came down the street.

The lion was on a leash. It was a young lion but it was already the size of an Alsatian dog. Bigger even. It pulled at the leash, and only just managing to restrain it was a small man in a lightweight suit. His companion, a middle-aged woman in heavy-make-up and an extravagant, broad-brimmed hat, clutched a small handbag tight to her side and walked with a slightly theatrical swing.

Nikki jumped up, almost as if to greet them. 'Beautiful!' Nikki said.

The dapper little man stopped and the lion stopped pulling. It blinked patiently. 'Good morning, my darling,' the man said to Nikki. His companion smiled. She looked about her as if expecting more people.

'Is that a lion? I said, quite stupidly.

'None other,' said the man.

'We met before,' Nikki said.

'We did indeed,' said the man. 'Though I'm very poor at names.'

'I'm Nikki. This is David.'

The man turned to me. 'Lion of the Serengeti. Born in captivity. Live ten to fourteen years in the wild though up to twenty in captivity. They prey mostly on large ungulates and can run the length of a football pitch in six seconds. This is Hector and Hector is eating twelve pounds of chunk meat fed five days per week.' I had the feeling that this man regularly said the same thing through a microphone. He blinked at me.

He seemed about to say more but Nikki spoke up. 'You let me stroke him last time.'

'As I said to you before, it's at your own risk.' He held a finger up to me and said, very pointedly, 'Please witness that I said so.'

I nodded.

Nikki stepped forward and gently stroked the lion's incipient mane on the top of its head. It reacted like any cat, narrowing its eyes in pleasure. Nikki was mesmerised. She ran her elegant fingers through its fur and stroked along its flank. Then she turned to me. 'You going to have a go?'

The man made an extravagant gesture of checking his wristwatch. 'Go ahead, young man. But I do repeat the warning.' His companion cocked her head at me and smiled.

I stepped forward and gently brushed the lion's mane. It opened its eyes wide and looked at me hard. I know it's ridiculous but I felt like the beast had calibrated my soul. Then it closed its eyes again. I thought maybe his fur would be like that of a cat's, but it wasn't. It was much more brittle and coarse but it had extraordinary movement in it, and my playing with it seemed to trigger a smell of musk and dung.

'He likes it,' said the woman.

'I do,' I said.

She giggled. 'I meant Hector likes it.'

The man checked his watch again. 'We really must be on our way. Good morning to both of you!'

We watched them amble down Castle Boulevard, the

man with his lion and the woman swinging her but-
tocks and fixing her hat in place as she went.

'How did you know he'd be here?' I asked Nikki.

'He has a route he walks every Saturday morning
at the same time. Everyone around here knows him.
He's the man with the lion. It's free advertising for
his circus. The police wanted to stop him in case it's
dangerous; but they decided there's no by-law against
walking your lion.'

'You know what I think?'

'What do you think?' she said.

'I think you are a lioness.'

She made a lovely cackle. 'I'll take that.'

I think I smiled but the smile must have vanished
on my lips because I suddenly thought about Terri. I
wondered where she was. I wondered *how* she was.
Nikki had succeeded in doing exactly what I'd wanted
her to do, which was to take my mind away from Terri
and Colin. But now that it had happened I felt guilty.
I don't know why. Nothing had happened between us,
but I was dogged by the feeling that I'd already made
Terri some kind of promise.

It was insane. She was married to a violent attack-
dog and here I was feeling responsible for her. Whereas
I was spending my time in the company of a stunning
and beautiful dancer with no complications. One gave
me lions, the other, snakes.

Nikki linked her arm in mine. 'Come on. I've got
other things to show you. What's an ungulate.'

'Dunno.'

'Mr clever-clogs college boy doesn't know what an
ungulate is.'

'No he doesn't. Happy with that?'

'Very happy with that. Shows you don't know everything.'

'Did I say I did?'

'Not in so many words.'

We had a wonderful day together. Nikki was fun company and made me laugh. She wanted to show me what she called the secrets of the town. After encountering the lion we went to the old esplanade with its formal gardens. After that she took me to an Art Deco theatre. It had been closed and turned into a hideous penny-arcade with a nasty plastic hoarding covering half the front of the building; but you could go inside and see some of the hidden glory of the old theatre. The same thing had happened to a cinema. She told me it was going to be washed away; all of it, and she didn't feel sad.

'It's just had its day. The holiday camp is living on borrowed time, too. People don't want all this any more.'

By 'all this' I knew she meant Abdul-Shazam, Luca Valletti and dancing girls rehearsing jaded routines in clapped-out Variety clubs. She meant the holidaying habits of the industrialised working classes. She meant a way of life that had reached the end of its commercial utility. These were the last days of working culture ended not through earthquake or tidal wave or volcanic eruption, but through the obstinate ticking of the cash register.

We went to a pub and had chicken-and-chips-in-a-basket. I asked Nikki about her future in dancing. I wanted to hear about her next career step, her plans, her dreams. She took off her dark glasses, folded them and put them on the table next to her chicken-in-a-basket. Then she took a sip of lager.

'I don't know. This sort of work is dying out, too. I'm going to have to do something else.'

'But there must be better work.'

'And the better you have to be. If you're really good you could work in the big London shows.'

'But you are really good.'

The skin around her eyes crinkled when she smiled. I wondered how old she was. I figured she was about twenty-five but I didn't want to ask. 'You know nowt about it.'

'I know what I see on stage.'

'So who are the good dancers? Go on! Out of me, Gail, Rebecca and Debbie. Who is good and who isn't?'

'Gail is pretty shit.'

'Gail is classically trained.'

'Really?'

'Really. Though in a way you're right. She's got no sexiness.'

Not compared to you, is what I thought.

'There is work,' she said, 'if you want to take your top off and show your tits to Arab oil sheiks. There are also cruise ships. I don't really want to do that either. But I'm never going to be a top dancer and I got used to that idea a while ago.' There was sadness in that. She was a bird with a broken wing.

Some middle-aged men at a table nearby were eaves-dropping. They were utterly fascinated by her. Why wouldn't they be? She was stunning to look at and here she was talking about dancing topless in front of Arab millionaires. I could tell they thought she was wasted on me. I felt their envy and their lust. They were like lions in a sawdust pit who had surrendered to the whip. I didn't give a damn. They could gnaw on their own livers as far as I was concerned. I could afford to feel superior, so when she offered to buy me another drink I held up my glass to the staring men before draining it. They all looked away. I wanted them to hate me.

After lunch we decided to go onto the pier and as we came out of the pub, a man nodded at me briefly and passed us by. I knew him from somewhere but I couldn't place him.

Once on the pier we strolled past a small arcade of fizzing, pinging and gurgling slot machines. There was a glass case with an upper-body manikin of a lady fortune-teller. Zorena. It was an impressive name for a fortune-teller. Better than Rosa. Sadly, Zorena looked like Punch, but with a dark veil over her head. The paint on her hands was peeling, and in front of them were spread a few playing cards: aces and queens.

I felt oddly fascinated by it. I was sure I'd seen one of these before. Nikki saw me staring at the thing.

'Give me a coin,' she said and I fumbled in my pocket. Some tinkly music struck up and the dummy was underlit with weak yellow light. Zorena rocked and whirred and her flaking mechanical hands made a pass across the cards. There was actually a tape recording of some wise words but it was so distorted and muffled we couldn't make out what was said. When it stopped, a card spat out of a slot.

Nikki grabbed it and showed it to me. *Know Thy elf* The print mechanism had lost its S. We both laughed, but the laughter was won from very different places. Nikki wanted another coin and the machine spat out a second card. *Choo e your future wi ely.*

'There you are,' Nikki said.

As if by contract we walked the boards all the way

to the end of the pier, where in grander times passengers would be loaded on or off pleasure steamers. We leaned easily against the rails looking far out to sea. Nikki turned the conversation to my own future. She asked me what I would do with my life. I wanted to say to her that my immediate ambition was to avoid having my arms and legs broken. Instead I told her some cock about going into journalism or copywriting or teaching, none of which career I'd seriously entertained for more than a few moments.

'Journalism? Do you get to go around the world breaking big stories?'

'I guess.' That was the fantasy anyway.

'You could take me with you.'

I laughed. Not because of what she'd said but because of what a great time I was having just being with her. She looked at me strangely. Perhaps she was offended, but I was distracted because in that moment I suddenly realised who the man was outside the pub. I remembered where I'd seen him before. It was at the National Front meeting. He was the second man Colin had introduced me to, the oily-haired man called Talbot, John Talbot.

Nikki sighed.

'What?' I asked.

'You. There's always something else going on inside your head. You're never fully there. Or here.'

'Is that true?'

'Oh yes it is. You've got a noisy inner life.'

'Have I?'

'If a woman waved at you with a barn door, what would you do?'

I didn't know what she meant and I said so. Then she

turned away and started to wander back up the pier. I was about to follow her when I was distracted by the sound of a motor boat cutting across the water.

It was a dazzling white power launch, about twenty-five foot, cruising the shallows at low throttle and turning in a wide arc as it approached the pier. Behind it trailed a frothy wake, rolling from its rudder like silvery earth from a ploughshare. I couldn't make out who was at the wheel but a man stood on the deck looking towards me. I was struck by his strange posture. He stood at a right angle to the line of the boat, looking over the gunwale at the pier. His feet were planted together and one hand seemed to grip his lapel. His chin was raised and he stared right at me.

As the boat approached the pier my heart scraped. It was the man in the blue suit I'd hallucinated when I'd almost fallen from the roof of the theatre; the man I'd seen on the beach with the little boy. He wasn't holding his lapel at all: he had a rope coiled over his shoulder. Though the light made a shadow play of his grey features there was no mistaking that familiar jaw. Worse than that was the awful confirmation in the shadow of his face. Even though the sun shone full on him and should have lit him like a stage spotlight, his face was grey, blue-grey, smoky even. As if his face was made of smoke.

He held a rope coiled over his shoulder and he was coming for me. Another shiver of revulsion went through me. I felt cold, lonely and very small. My tongue stuck to the roof of my mouth. I had never before known what it meant to quake. I felt my heart ice over.

The man gazed right at me with what can only be

described as a menacing grin. I gripped the rails of the pier, leaning out to get a better look at him, willing the light to reveal that I was mistaken. But just as easily as the boat had cruised in, it followed the clean line of its arc and the man, still gazing me and holding his rope, was taken away again. I watched the boat complete its turn and go deep out to sea. A man in a dark blue suit, in a boat, in the sun, in the bay of Skegness.

There was a coin-operated binoculars mounted on a stand. I swung it round to follow the boat and though I fumbled in my pockets I didn't have the right coin. By the time the boat had diminished to a dot far out to sea Nikki had returned to find me. 'Are you okay?' she said.

'I've been here before,' I said.

'What? Like déjà vu?'

'Yes. No. I mean literally. I stood here. Exactly in this spot. I held his hand.'

'Who?'

I couldn't bring myself to say it. 'I was here when I was a little boy. I stood here. Right here. I'd forgotten. But now I remember it.'

The pupils of her dark brown eyes dilated as she searched my features. There was a frown line on her forehead, like an omega. If I was pale or if my hands were still trembling she didn't see it.

'I'm okay,' I said. 'Someone just walked over my grave.'

Oddly that banal phrase made her feel reassured. Whatever it was that had just happened, those six words made it all right, made everything proportionate. Just to show her I was okay I linked arms with her and nudged her towards the other side of the arcade. The cash machines and winking lights of the games arcade made everything normal again.

An elderly couple asked if we would take their picture, which we did. Then as we made our way back down the length of the pier Nikki drew up by another one of those absurd glass cases. Inside this one was not a fortune-teller but a manikin of a jolly-jack-tar sailor, its face painted with an evil smile, like an early-period ventriloquist's dummy.

'Do you remember these from when you were a kid?' she said. 'These are great! Another coin please.'

This time I found the right coin and she dropped it into the machine. The mechanism rumbled. The manikin's shoulders began to shake and its arms moved. Then a recording of muffled laughter bubbled up from within the bowels of the machine. We stood and watched the manikin howl and laugh, as if we were both five-year-olds. But the laughter seemed to have a nasty edge that sawed against the sea air. I don't know how long the thing went on for.

'I suppose we'd better get back to that fucking place,' Nikki said, when the sun started to drop in the sky. The sun was a big golden-red balloon, like something you take home from the funfair. She grabbed my wrist. 'Can we get some sandwiches and a drink and just go to the dunes for an hour before we go back?' She was like a child begging for an extra hour of play.

I said, 'Sure.'

We strolled along the beach and she suggested we find a place in the deep dunes. I started to feel uneasy about the dunes so I suggested we sit on the pebbles but she insisted we go deeper into the spiky marram grass and the hills of sand. It was still hot. She said she wanted to get some sunbathing in. I gave in.

As soon as we settled down she wriggled out of her skirt and took her top off. 'You don't mind do you? I want to get some air to my body.'

I assured her that I didn't mind. She lay on her back with her hands behind her head. I sat down near enough to her but with a couple of feet of distance between us. I felt too agitated to lie back. I opened a can of cola and it frothed over. The spray went onto her midriff. She wiped her flat belly with a tanned and elegant finger and sucked her finger to clean it.

With the heat diminishing by the second, the day had distilled itself into a wonderful calm, even if inside I was fighting my own inexplicable anxieties. Were I not still troubled by the apparition of the man in the boat I would have said it was a moment of paradise. We could hear the sea, gone far out now, rhythmically sucking at the sand. I had to force myself not to scan the dune hills. I had this idea that I would see a boy and his father there. Finally, I forced myself to lay back with my tormented thoughts and I thought Nikki had gone to sleep.

I felt a finger trace my neck. I opened my eyes.

'Ladybird,' she said. 'Look, they're everywhere.'

She had one on her arm, too, so I flicked it off. I lay back again but Nikki flopped lazily on her side and reached out a hand towards me. At first she rested her hand on my thigh and then she moved her hand to cup my genitals inside my jeans. I felt a jolt inside my jeans. I gasped.

Yes she was beautiful. Yes she was sexy. She was extraordinary. But I had to stop it. I wasn't ready to stop thinking about Terri. It was ridiculous: it hadn't gone anywhere with Terri, but I was still obsessed.

I knew what I should do. I should speak to Terri and remind her that she was married and tell her straight up that I didn't want the complication. It was the right and decent thing to do. I could honestly say to Terri that nothing had happened with anyone else and that I'd made a moral decision about her situation, and after that the way would be clear with Nikki.

That was what I *should* do.

I lifted Nikki's hands from my balls.

'What's wrong with it?' Nikki said.

'Look, Nikki, there's someone else.'

'Who?'

I shook my head.

'Is it a man?'

'God, no!' I said.

Then Nikki screamed, right in my face. She pulled her T-shirt on, scrambled to her feet and stormed over the dunes and ran towards the beach. I waited for a while and then decided to go after her.

She stood on the sand in her T-shirt and knickers with her back to me. Her arms were folded and she appeared to be gazing out to sea. The tide was out. With the sun dropping behind us her lonely figure cast a long shadow across the sand. I didn't say any thing, just stood abreast of her, gazing out to sea.

'I could have any man back at that camp,' she said. 'Any man. I know it. That's not being vain. I just know it. I would just have to point at one of them. So why is it I pick the one man I can't have? Why is it? I always do it. Always. Something in me sees that I can't have this or that one, and that becomes the one I want. If I can have them I don't want them; if I can't have them I want them. Who are you seeing?'

'I can't tell you … just yet. I want to get it sorted out.'

'Oh? Well, I think I know anyway.'

'Really? Who?'

'Never mind.'

'Go on.'

'No.'

'Please tell me,' I said.

'You don't want to say; I don't want to say; let nobody say.'

I looked hard at her. I couldn't tell whether she was just playing games or if she had seen something that had suggested it was Terri.

She sighed. 'Oh, come on. Let's walk back to't camp.'

She linked her arm in mine and we walked along the sand back to our workplace.

'Anyway,' she said when we got back to the gate. 'I had a great day.'

'Me too,' I said.

We kissed briefly. Somehow in that moment I popped my tongue inside her mouth. She drew back and shook her head minutely, as if she didn't understand me.

She wasn't the only one.

10

Things that could get one evicted from the Magic Circle

Before turning in to the theatre the next morning I made my way over to the canteen for breakfast. It was hard going. The ladybirds that had been bothering us for a couple of days had begun swarming in the hot air. They pinged at my face as I walked across the yard. One flew in my mouth and I had to spit it out. I could see campers batting them away with the flat of their hands. What had been a nuisance was becoming a plague. It was a relief to get to the canteen and shut the door on them.

The ladybirds were the talk of the breakfast tables. No one had seen a swarm like this before. Someone said there was a plague of hover-flies one year. Another declared that it was happening because the greenflies were plentiful that season and the ladybirds fed on greenflies. A third reported that it was caused by the drought and the ladybirds were coming to the coast looking for water. I had no wisdom about ladybirds to contribute to this vigorous debate.

After finishing my breakfast I cleared away my plates, stashed my tray and headed over to the theatre. The ladybird blizzard had got even worse. If anyone was out and about, they were running. On my way to the theatre I passed by the reception and one of the office secretaries opened a window and said to me that I had a call.

My first thought was that it was from home. I had an idea that my stepdad would call at some point and tell me that mum was sick or would find some other way to pressure me into coming home. I picked up the receiver and pressed the earpiece to my ear.

'All right, son?'

'Oh! Hello, Colin.' Of course, Colin would know my exact moves. He would know exactly what time I would pass by the offices on the way to the morning briefing. This was all surveillance.

'Anything I should know, son?'

'No, I don't think so.' One of the secretaries was eavesdropping, so I moved away as far as I could and turned my back.'

'What does that mean? You *don't think so.*'

'It means nothing to report.'

'Right. You all right for everything?'

With Colin it was like speaking in code. 'What do you mean?'

'Are you short for a few quid? I'll get it to you if you're short.'

'No, no, I'm fine.'

'Good lad.'

'Where are you right now?'

'I'm around. I ain't allowed on the camp.'

'Colin.'

'What?'

'If I see her out, am I to buy her a coffee or whatever?'

There was a long pause. 'You can buy her a coffee. But not a drink.'

'Okay. I've got to go to work now, Colin.'

'Right.'

I put the receiver back on its cradle. The secretary looked at me and compressed her lips.

When I got to the theatre, Pinky and Tony were hastily revising the programme.

'What's it like out there?' Pinky asked.

'You couldn't cut it with a knife,' I told them.

We were scheduled to organise a Swimming Gala around the pool. 'Can't do it in this,' Tony said with finality. 'Right let's get 'em all in the ballroom. We'll have another fuckin' magic show.'

'Right.' Pinky said. 'Another fuckin' magic show.'

'We need,' Tony said, 'someone to jog up to the pool to see if there's anyone hanging about. Bring 'em all down to the ballroom.'

'I'm not going out there!' Nobby shouted. 'Have you seen out there? It's like a biblical fuckin' epidemic out there is what it is. A fuckin' biblical fuckin' plague I mean. Cecil B. DeMille, without the toads. Four horsemen of the fuckin' ladybirds. That's right. Apopolypse. No, what is it? Apocalypse. I open my mouth to speak and ten ladybirds fly in.'

'What a shame you have to shut your mouth,' said Sammy the elder Greencoat, adjusting his wig.

'Hey!' went Nobby. 'Hey! That's not nice!'

While all this was going on, Tony leaned over to me. 'Will you go, David? Someone has to.'

'Yeah, I'll do it.'

Pinky opened his office and reappeared with a battery-powered megaphone. 'Use this, if you like. You'll need to hang around up there for half an hour collecting the stragglers and latecomers. Good lad.'

Off I went with my megaphone, into the ladybird storm.

I didn't jog. I made my way pretty smartly up to the deserted swimming pool area and switched on the thing. The airborne insects were pinging into the metal funnel as I mouthed a few words about everyone going down to the ballroom to have a great time. The trouble was there was no one there to hear me. Hardly anyone was actually outside in the ladybird storm. I let the megaphone fall at my side. 'There's a magic show waiting for you,' I said to no one, or maybe just to the flying bugs.

The ladybirds seemed attracted to my blazer. Maybe the green stripes had them confused into thinking they were settling on a lush leaf. Thankfully they didn't seem attracted to my white trousers in the same way, but I wiped about two or three dozen ladybirds off my blazer sleeve alone. Tony had told me to stick around for half an hour but what with the insects targeting me I didn't feel like standing still so I went about the chalet blocks, trying to be inventive with what I gabbled into my megaphone. Something unfunny about emergency anti-ladybird legislation. Occasionally a door would open and a bemused family would peer at me trying to fathom what I was saying.

Ladybirds were crawling inside my collar and in my ear and I'd had enough. I walked past block D mouthing about an all-star magic show with *Abdul-Shazam!* and all the gang when one of the chalet doors opened. It was Terri. She'd been cleaning one of the refurbished chalets. I went over to her.

'Look at you,' she gasped. 'Come inside.'

She pulled me in and slammed the door on the cloud of insects.

'Look at you!' she said again, this time pointing at me.

I looked down. The ladybirds had swarmed over my blazer. There was barely a patch of cloth to be seen under them. They were live but motionless, anchored to the coloured threads. My blazer was a live garment, like something from a dream.

I was shocked.

'Let's get it off you,' she said. Very gently she reached a finger under each lapel and eased the blazer off my shoulders, like she was determined to lift the thing off me without killing a single ladybird. I felt the thrill of her fingers stroke my collarbone. She stepped in closer to me and delicately slipped the blazer down the length of my sleeves. I could smell the shampoo in her hair. I could smell something like sunshine on her skin. She was close enough for me to feel her breath on my neck. When she'd lowered the blazer sleeves free of my arms she stepped to one side, holding the blazer in one hand, and then she gently hung it over the back of a chair before stepping back. I don't think she lost a single ladybird in the process.

For a long time, we were motionless, staring at the ladybird-sheathed coat. Then she turned and stepped over to me, and pressed her mouth on mine. We were still kissing as she popped the buttons on my shirt and tore it from my back. The shirt cuffs wouldn't go over my wrists as she tugged the shirt behind me. There was a new, uncovered mattress on the bed and we fell on it. I was still manacled by my shirt as she worked my trousers down. I remember gasping, and looking up, and seeing the live ladybird blazer on the back of the chair, and then closing my eyes.

The magic show was hitting its stride by the time I got to the ballroom. Tony had some kids on the stage, fumbling for coloured handkerchiefs in a soft blue velvet bag. When they pulled out white handkerchiefs instead of coloured ones he pretended to be annoyed. Nikki was up there with him in her fetching costume of sequins and fishnet tights. I avoided eye-contact with her.

'Thought we'd lost you,' Pinky said dryly, eyebrows aloft.

'I swallowed a bug and it stuck in my throat,' I said. 'I had to go and get a drink from somewhere.'

'Ha,' said Pinky. He flicked imaginary ash from his unlit cigar. 'Haha.'

Tony – or should I say *Abdul-Shazam!* – wrapped up that part of his conjuring act and I saw Nobby and Sammy wheeling the large sword casket on stage, carefully settling it between two chairs. Tony went serious for a moment and changed his microphone style. He asked for quiet because, he said, the next trick was genuinely dangerous and the swords he would be using were sharp. He invited someone to come up and check the swords. He held a piece of ribbon at arm's length as one of the campers cut through the ribbon with a whisper. He warned us that they had tried to get insurance against any mishaps but no insurance company in the land would offer a premium. And with that, Nikki climbed into the casket.

Tony perspired visibly. I thought he looked anxious. I glanced at Pinky but he was poker-faced. Nobby and Sammy looked pretty serious too. A hush descended over the audience, broken only by the clink of glasses or the sound of the till opening at the bar. I knew the trick would be perfectly safe, even though I didn't know how it worked. I just had an awful feeling in my stomach that something was going to go wrong.

At that moment I felt an astonishing surge of protectiveness towards Nikki. I had to grip the sides of my chair to stop myself getting up and interfering with the show The casket was closed and locked with Nikki in it. There were five swords in all, and after a little bit of strutting on stage, as if he was pumping himself up, Tony forced the first sword through the cabinet with rather shocking violence. There was a gasp from the audience as the second and third swords were thumped in swiftly and without ceremony. The last two swords were inserted from the top

. Of course, no one was really surprised when the swords were taken out again, the casket unlocked and Nikki stepped out prettily in her sequins and fishnets. It seemed to me not that Tony had performed a fabulous illusion; but that that the audience had given their permission for the illusion to work on them. There was wild applause and more gags from Tony, who pretended to be rather relieved that the trick had worked.

Tony announced that the morning's entertainment would be concluded with a yard-of-ale competition. Nobby and Sammy were dispatched to the bar to collect the yard glasses while I was asked to clear away the magic props. I started by wheeling the sword casket from the ballroom back to the props cupboard behind the adjacent theatre. When I got there I found Nikki backstage behind the scenery flats, wriggling out of her sequined outfit.

'That seemed to go well,' I said. I still hadn't

recovered from my explosive and unexpected sexual encounter with Terri just a couple of hours earlier and I was trying to sound casual.

She beamed at me. Then she frowned and patted the side of her face with her forefinger.

'What?' I asked.

She found a tissue and stepped across to me. She was wearing bra, pants, fishnet tights and stiletto heels, and her tawny skin had on it a bloom of perspiration. She wet the tissue with her mouth and rubbed something from the side of my mouth, near my lip.

'What is it?'

'Lipstick.'

'Really?'

'Yes, really. It's gone. You're clean.'

I didn't feel clean. 'Must have been one of the campers. You know how they grab you.'

She didn't blink. She ran her tongue across her top lip and said, 'Wow! You smell like a whore's handbag. Did she throw perfume all over you?'

Tony breezed in, wiping sweat from his brow with a white handkerchief. 'Funny!' he said loudly. 'Funny how I keep catching you two backstage. Put her down, David, and let me explain how all this packs away.'

I could barely pay attention as Tony explained how to stow all the props and demonstrated how to collapse the sword casket. He went to great lengths to show me how the casket worked: there was a frame inside the box in which Nikki had rotated her body into a very precise position with her ankles tucked back. The swords ran in fixed trammels between the backs of both knees; under her armpits; behind her neck and so on. It was completely safe since the frame moulded her body in an inflexible position, and the invading swords were tracked along smooth rails. The sharp demonstrator sword, identical to all the others except for a single identifying bead in the pommel, wasn't used.

I pretended to be well focused on all of this. All through it I was acutely aware of Nikki watching me watching Tony.

'I'm showing you things,' Tony said seriously, 'that would get me kicked out of the Magic Circle.'

11

A *fine* casket built for sturdy illusion not service

I missed lunch. Terri was still working on the refurbished chalets and I returned to her, as I'd said I would. On my way I walked past the palmist's white caravan. Madame Rosa had the door shut firmly against the bug swarm. She was looking out of the window, directly at me. I averted my eyes. The ladybird storm had subsided a little but it was still unpleasant to be outside. Dead ladybirds crunched underfoot; they lay in piles where they had hit a wall or a window and had fallen back.

She'd left the door ajar for me. When I stepped inside, the door clicked behind me and she was already unbuttoning her thin nylon overall. She was completely naked underneath and it slipped to the floor with a hiss. 'What kept you?'

She didn't give me a moment to answer because she leapt on to my hips, folding her arms behind my neck and clinging to me with her legs, kissing me. The scent of her mixed with the perfume Nikki had got wind of had me dizzy. Any doubts I had about Terri were dispelled the moment she wrapped herself around me. With her still clinging to my neck I walked her across the room and collapsed onto the bed.

'Wait,' she said. 'Not like that.'

She got up and moved across to the table. She shifted a chair aside and bent across the table, spreading her legs and pushing her bottom into the air.

'Spank me.'

I laughed. Wrong.

'Spank me,' she said again.

'What?'

'Do it.'

I moved towards her. It wasn't something that would ever naturally occur to me. The request seemed more comical than erotic. I lifted my hand and let it fall across her buttock, but without conviction.

'Harder for Chrissake.'

But I was already losing my erection. I felt ridiculous.

Perhaps she sensed it wasn't going to happen. 'Oh just fuck me, you prat.'

I had to clear my head. I managed to slip away from that chalet with some free time before my next duty. I stepped out of the camp with the idea of recovering on the beach for half an hour, but the ladybirds were still swarming, pinging at my face and settling on my clothes. As I turned away from the camp gates I sensed a car cruising alongside me. I knew it was the same car in which I'd been chauffeured to the National Front meeting. It was Colin's green-and-cream Hillman Minx.

My guts squeezed as my instincts kicked in and I pretended to be deep in thought. I kept walking. The two-tone Hillman purred alongside, keeping pace. Then the horn sounded.

I had no choice but to turn. The car came to a halt. I faked a startled look, then processed a smile on recognising Colin at the wheel. His face was expressionless, staring back at me.

I froze as he leaned across the seat to open the passenger door. Everything about his demeanour said to me that he knew. I thought if I got in that car I was finished.

'Get in then, you fucking drip,' he called softly.

In a flash it occurred to me that if he didn't know, then my hesitation would make him suspicious. I had no choice. I climbed in. The car smelled of leather upholstery and something like gun metal. He reeked of smoky, fresh sweat as if he'd just been exercising.

Colin put his wipers on to sweep the ladybirds away. 'Fuckin' things. Everywhere.' He released the clutch and we drove off. 'What's a matter wiv you then?'

I looked back over my shoulder as if we were being followed. 'I think they were watching from the gate.'

'Watching for what?'

'Well, they know you're banned, don't they?'

'Oh,' he said, threading the big steering wheel through his rough hands as he turned the corner. 'They don't give a monkey's. Neither do I.' He didn't go very far, pulling up at a nearby modern brick-and-glass pub called The Dunes. Before we got out of the car he pushed a fiver into my hands. 'Get 'em in; I need a slash.'

While he went to the toilet I went up the bar and ordered two pints of bitter. I was glad he wasn't there because when I went to carry the pints to a table my hands shook so badly I slopped some of the beer on the carpet. I sat down and took a deep breath. I took a sip of beer and as I lifted the glass to my mouth my fingers reeked of Terri's sex.

Colin came out of the toilet, sat down opposite me and lit up a cigarette. Players No. 6. He took a deep drag, exhaled and sat back. His change from the fiver lay on the table. 'Well?'

'Good as gold.'

'Yeah?' He looked out of the window and then took a deep gulp from his pint. His Adam's apple bobbed aggressively as he drank.

'As far as I can tell.'

He snapped his head back away from the window, too quickly. 'As far as you can tell. What's that mean?'

'Well, I can't watch her twenty-fours a day, can I? I'm trying my best to be where she is or somewhere near her as far as I can. I tried to buy her a coffee a couple of times but she wouldn't have it.'

He nodded. 'Seen her talk to anyone?'

'Only staff about cleaning. She's been taken off the theatre and put on other jobs. Last time I saw her she was down at those reconditioned chalets.'

He blinked at me.

'She seems to have her head down,' I said. 'Working hard.'

He blinked again. I lifted the glass to my mouth and once again I could smell Terri on my fingers. It seemed so strong. It seemed impossible that he couldn't smell his wife on me. My guts squeezed again. I felt like I might throw up. 'How long have you been back?' I asked him.

'Just got here today. Sat outside for an hour or two, waiting for you to stick your nose out the door. Tried to call you but that bitch in the office said you wasn't around.'

That meant that while he was trying to call me, Terri

and I were fucking in D block. 'I was probably in the canteen,' I said.

'No, it was just after lunch.'

'Dunno,' I said.

'You look fuckin' knackered, son.'

'I can't sleep properly here. Dunno why.'

'You sure you ain't been on the nest?'

I looked him in the eye.

'You 'ave been, aincha?'He smiled and lowered his head. It was an evil smile. He drew back his lips but compressed them so that he showed no teeth. 'Aincha?'

'I should be so lucky.'

He downed the rest of his beer. 'Go up the bar and get us another, will ya?'

I didn't see why he couldn't take his turn at the bar but I wasn't going to argue. I got up but he called me back and told me to take it from the change that lay on the table. I got him another pint and a half for myself.

'What's that then?' He looked at the half pint glass as if he'd never seen one before; as if it were some new and silly marketing idea for ladies.

'I don't like to be pissed while I'm working around kids,' I said.

He considered this. 'That's fair enough.'

We both took another glug of beer.

'She's up to something.'

'Oh?' I said.

'You get so you know.'

I shook my head as if to indicate that I knew nothing about that kind of thing.

'She wasn't much more than a kid when I found her,' he said. 'Don't look at me like that.'

'Like what?'

'I know what you're thinking: why does he keep her on such a tight leash. Well, I'll tell you. She was on the game when I found her.'

'You what?'

He held his hand up to quiet me. 'Fourteen, and on the game. Not good. I had to dice up a ponce to get to her, and then another. I looked at that gal and I said if I do one decent thing in my life I'm gonna pull that little gal out of that life. You with me?'

I nodded. This wasn't quite the same story that Terri had told me.

He went on. 'It ain't easy though. They get a taste for it. That life I mean. Know what I'm talking about?' He looked out of the window. 'It keeps calling 'em back. Like a drug. Like one of these junkies. It's like, in 'em. They gotta 'ave it. Cock-happy. It's there for life, ain't it?

'So I has to keep pulling 'er back. Why don't I let her go? I could. I could let her go her own way. But I made this promise. To myself. To her. It's hard work, I tell you. Women are crafty. Very crafty. They'd have you stitched up in seconds. You think you see 'em coming but you don't. Look around you. Ain't a woman in this pub you couldn't have if you set your mind to it. Married, boyfriend, it don't matter.

'And that's what I know. As for her, I keep her on the straight and narrow. Served time for her, I have. Protected her. Put up with hardships. Stop her slipping back into it, you understand me?'

I said I did.

'Ha! Look at your face! You don't know nothin' about it, do you?' He stubbed out his cigarette in the ashtray with a series of rapid, hard jabs and took his wallet out of his pocket. He found two ten pound notes, folded them and flicked them across the table to me.

'What's that?'

'Don't ask.'

Once again, this was almost what I was paid weekly in addition to meals and lodgings. 'What am I supposed to do with it?'

'Do with it? Do what you want with it, you dozy fuck. I'm flush. Ain't anyone ever give you no money before now?'

'Well. No.'

He shook his head. 'You're a right one, incha? Fuckin' college boy. Listen: I have a kid somewhere. They wouldn't let me see him. Be about the same age as you. I like to think he wouldn't be cleaning or in no factory or fuckin' coal mine. Maybe he'd be at college, smart-arse like you. Maybe someone somewhere will sling him twenty notes.'

'It's too much. I can't take it, Colin.'

'Take it.' He looked at me when he said take it and I knew he meant that I had no choice. I picked up the money and I put it in my pocket. 'Anyway, it's nice to know I've got someone on the inside looking after my interests.'

'I've got to go, Colin. I'll be late for the yard-of-ale competition.'

'Want a lift back?'

'It's two minutes.'

'Okay. I'll be in touch.' He lit another cigarette and sat back.

I still can't believe that just an hour after having sex with his wife I walked out of that pub with twenty of his pounds in my pocket.

Later, in the cooler evening, the ladybirds began to sub-
side. After I'd finished work I made my way up to the
same dark place on the beach. After my encounter with
Colin I didn't want to go but I'd arranged to meet Terri
there again before Colin had intercepted me. I assumed
she knew Colin was back on the scene, and I was quite
prepared for her not to turn up. But when I got there
she was waiting with a blanket and a couple of beers.
She did of course know that he was around, but she
was very surprised that I'd seen him that day.

'What's he want with you?'

'I'm supposed to keep an eye on you.'

She found that amusing. 'Jeez!'

'Maybe we should leave it. Are you sure he's not following you?'

'Not tonight. I know exactly where he is tonight.
Cards club. Once a month to piss his money away.
That's why he's back. He ain't here to see me.'

I looked back up the beach. 'I don't know about this.'

'It's all right. I'm sure. Look at you. You got the jit-
ters now, haven't you?'

I felt trapped. After what had happened between us
I was afraid she might think I was drawing back from
her. We walked on a little way and then she spread
the blanket on the sand and popped open a beer. The
luminous ripples of the waves did nothing to calm my
nerves.

'Relax, will you?'

The sea was blue-black, calm with a light, foamy
tide. What had seemed like a beach in paradise a few
nights ago now seemed to have a smoky edge. The
phosphorescence in the waves was still at large, but

now it had a wormy quality. But it wasn't the beach that had changed.

Terri would talk about other workers on the camp in quite brutal terms. Somehow she got onto the subject of Nikki. She called her a half-wog.

'Stop,' I said, 'stop. You know what? Nikki is amazing.'

'You think,' she said dryly.

'Yes, I do. She's become a good friend. The only friend I do have here, not counting you.' That last phrase came out like an afterthought.

'How good a friend is she then?'

I knew exactly what she was hinting at but I said, 'How do you mean?'

'Never mind. What about Colin? Sounds like he's your big buddy now.'

I ignored that. Whatever relationship I had with Terri, I wasn't going to allow her to slag off Nikki. Already the evening wasn't playing out in the expected way so I tried to change the subject.

I took my wallet out of my pocket and showed her the photograph of my biological father. I've no idea why. It wasn't something I went around discussing freely with anyone. In fact it was a kind of secret. Perhaps I'd made the basic error of thinking that emotional intimacy automatically follows sexual intimacy. I told her I had this idea that my biological father was always close. That he was somehow here for me.

It now sounds impossibly naive. It was a half-baked idea. I hadn't worked it out, but if I'd hoped to develop the notion any further by talking with Terri, I was mistaken. I told her the little bit I knew. She examined the photo briefly and then slung it back at me. 'You think you've had it rough?' she said.

'I'm not saying that at all.'

'You've been brought up in cotton wool.'

'That's not what I meant. I was just telling you that—'

She wasn't going to let me finish. 'I could tell you things about my own life that would make your hair fall out. At least you know who your dad is – or you think you do. I've no idea and you don't see me crying about it.'

'I'm not crying about it.' Her hard-hearted posturing only made me smile.

'I don't see why you're smirking.'

Her irritation only made me smile more. Heaven knows, I thought she was faking being cross with me, but I misread her mood. 'That's it,' she said with a nasty wheedle in her voice, 'you can fuck off. You're not getting it tonight.'

'What?'

'You heard. I said you're not getting it.'

It, of course, being sex. I was taken aback. Firstly, I had never imagined sex as a bargaining token or a credit chip to be offered and withdrawn in this way. Secondly, I couldn't imagine anyone who wasn't in the mood being open to sex. Here I was facing the withdrawal of privileges I hadn't even asked for. The evening had turned sour and I wasn't entirely sure why. I felt the second argument had something to do with the first. Quite apart from the fact that I was worried about Colin prowling the beach, the episode stirred deeper doubts in mind about what I was doing. If I'd ever seen myself as Terri's rescuer I'd been a fool. It now occurred to me that in her mind she might have thought she was the one doing the rescuing.

She swallowed the last mouthful of beer and slung

the bottle into the sea. I wanted to say something about children cutting their feet on broken glass but I let it go. She was already up and folding the blanket. Without a word she set off ahead of me, moving toward the lights of the promenade.

I didn't see Terri the next day, but the following morning we almost collided in front of the theatre. She behaved as if our spat hadn't happened. She'd been re-assigned to clean in the theatre again and that meant she'd been obliged to return her keys for the refurbished chalets. Our love nest was taken away from us and we had nowhere private to meet.

'What will we do?' she asked.

I said I didn't know. The truth is it was almost a relief. Then she suggested we use my room.

'That's not a good idea,' I said.

She narrowed her eyes at me. I was afraid that she suspected I was withdrawing. I couldn't tell whether what I saw in her eyes was contempt or hurt. She could seem vulnerable one moment and then cast-iron the next. I weakened and we arranged to meet in my room at lunch time.

We'd been in my room for maybe ten minutes when we were brought to our senses by the sound of a key hitting the lock from the other side of the door. Fortunately I'd secured the door with my own key and left it hanging in the lock.

There was a loud thumping. 'Got someone in there, you maladjusted boy?' It was Nobby, making one of his rare visits back to his room. 'Wickedness. Fire and brimstone shall come to thee, young man. Plus I'm going to 'ave to report you to the Secret Masters who

138

run this august lodge since you are in clear violation of rule number seventy-seven which expressly prohibits the wayward practice of afternoon nuptials etcetera etcetera etcetera can't you open this fuckin' door?'

'Jesus!' Terri whispered.

I shouted through the door. 'Nobby, can you come back later?'

'Later is tomorrow is no good is surplus to tomorrow's requirements. Did I leave my dicky in there?'

'You what?'

'Dicky! Dicky! Dicky bow! Formal neckpiece throat-butterfly fuckin' bow-tie is it in there my friend I need it for tonight? It'll only take me two seconds to ascertain presence of said couture oh for fuck's sake!'

'Where? Where is it? I'll look.'

'I dunno, in the drawer, stuck in my drawers in the wardrobe under the bed fallen behind the fuckin' walrus secreted in a shoe stuffed under the mattress, come on chief, I don't know, let me fuckin' well look an' I'll find it!'

'You can't come in. I'll have a good look for you and bring it to you later.'

I resisted all his protests until finally he went away. We heard him go out of the building, blethering incomprehensibly. I lifted back the curtain to see him trotting across the yard away from us, still prattling to himself.

'Is he on drugs?' Terri asked me.

'No, he's from Manchester.'

She was already getting dressed. 'I don't want to stay here.'

I made a half-hearted effort to get her to stay. Before leaving she suggested we meet backstage in the theatre.

'You're joking!'

She took a deep breath. 'Now that I'm working there again we both have a reason to be there. It makes sense. We should only meet in places we are supposed to be.' She cupped my face, kissed me, and gave me a precise time when I would find her backstage early that evening, while everyone else was eating.

The ladybird storms were subsiding but the ground was littered with their carcasses. Workers were mobilised to sweep the bugs into neat pyramid-piles so that they could be disposed of. One man was shovelling the things into a paper sack. I had never seen so many insects. It reminded me of biblical stories about swarms of locusts.

But the spectacle of all those bug carcasses told me that the madness was over. I'd made a mistake and I knew it. I hated myself for having raised Terri's expectations about me; but I hated myself more for having to pretend that I wanted to carry on. I decided that when I saw her in the theatre that evening I would tell her that it all had to stop.

At tea-time I ate early and quickly and I went hurrying over to the theatre. I had to fight off the notion that I was transparent, that everyone knew where I was going and whom I was seeing. It seemed like I passed everyone who knew me. Nikki, Sammy, Gail. Even Luca Valletti, who wasn't usually to be found outside his performance hours, was there outside the offices having a smoke with Pinky. They all looked up and gave me a knowing smile. Or so I feared.

I went into the theatre through the front entrance, through the hushed and shadowy auditorium, skipped up the steps onto the stage and behind the thick red curtains. There was no one around. I found a stool to sit on between the upright wing-flats and waited in the dark.

A darkened backstage is a place full of ghosts. You expect silence, but things creak. You feel the tension of hanging wires, and pendulum weights and flimsy flats. After a while a crack of light appeared briefly as the rear door was opened and closed again.

She came in. 'This is crazy,' she said.

'Yes.'

But she flung herself at me and we kissed. All the time we were kissing I felt like a meteorite falling to the earth. I wanted to pull back but the taste of her mouth inflamed me all over again. Her kisses sparked memories of that phosphorescence on the dark beach as she invited me to go further. She put her hand inside my shirt and raked my back with her fingernails. I was weak. I had a sense of myself as a moral coward as I kissed her back.

Just then I felt a draught, and one of the flats wobbled slightly. Someone was backstage with us.

'Slutcha.'

The gravel voice was unmistakable, coming from out of the darkness, somewhere between the unsteady flats.

'No,' Terri breathed. 'No.'

'And you, you *cowson*.'

I still couldn't see where the voice was coming from but I could almost scent the toxic breath on which it travelled. Colin knew we were there but it was plain that he could only see us in shadow. Perhaps he thought that I was Luca Valletti. My instincts were conflicted. I wanted to run but with Terri in my arms I felt emboldened. 'Slip out the back way,' I said to her. 'I'll face him.'

I felt her peel away from me as I turned. I took a step towards the voice. Colin moved from behind a black-painted flat, making it quiver. His face was in darkness. I could see his teeth bared in the shadows. He powered forward at me but in his momentum he tripped over one of the iron weights holding down the stage-braces and he went sprawling, down onto his knees. One of the flats at the edge of the stage fell forward on to him.

Terri grabbed me. She put her face right up to mine. 'Get out,' she hissed. 'Get out or you're dead.'

I saw him throw off the fallen flat and my fight instincts liquidised and turned to flight. I squeezed between the back flat and let myself out of the back door, slamming it behind me. I ran quickly up the alley behind the theatre, sure of the route from when I'd played Captain Blood with the children. I took the steps three at a time and went out onto the theatre roof.

Once on the roof it occurred to me that I'd trapped myself. I'd left myself no way out. There was a low wall on the east side of the roof and a space between a humming ventilator and it. I squeezed in between them and lay down. The ladybirds were still swarming. Though their numbers had diminished they seemed to target me as I lay behind the ducting.

I was breathing hard. I lay there listening, trying to filter the sounds. I hadn't heard anyone come from behind me or up the steps to the roof. There was nothing to be heard from inside the theatre. Above the hum from the ventilator I could hear snatches of conversations of holidaymakers. There was the occasional laugh or cry of mirth; and I could hear the low-level buzz of some familiar voices from below me. It was Luca and Pinky, having a smoke below. Though I identified their voices easily enough I couldn't make out what they were saying.

Colin might have seen Luca chatting with Pinky; in which case he would have realised that Luca was not his man. If he hadn't seen them I feared that he would attack the Italian Tenor on leaving the theatre. I had no doubt of the violence of which Colin was capable. Terri had told me of previous convictions for grievous bodily harm and a whole number of assaults for which he'd never been brought to book. I lay in my cowardly hiding place praying that at least he'd spotted Luca outside the theatre before going inside.

I stayed there for a long time, not daring to move. It occurred to me that he was waiting; that he had an almost supernatural instinct for knowing that I was still in the vicinity; that he could smell my fear. Eventually I started to hear more and more people draw up outside the theatre doors below. I was already late for my next duty. My heart had stopped hammering and I came to a decision that I should go.

It was then that I heard tiny steps making their way up onto the roof. They were very slow steps, as if made by someone who was trying not to be heard. I had to strain my ears to listen to them over the hum of the ventilator. But my hearing was so focused that the steps were unmistakable. I had to still myself all over again.

The steps reached the rooftop. And though they were still small steps, they were easier to distinguish now because of the gravel on the roof that crunched very lightly underfoot. I held my breath. The steps seemed to approach me and then moved away again, towards the edge from where I'd almost fallen. I tried calibrating the steps. Was it a tiny step, suggesting that Terri had come up onto the roof to look for me? Or did the step belong to Colin, rolling his foot like a hunter in the woods?

I lay there in agony as the steps moved across the dusty, gravelled surface of the roof. I considered raising my head to see if I could look around or across or through the humming ventilator. But I was afraid any movement might alert the hunter. Then a ladybird flew directly into my mouth, into my throat. I reflex gagged and I managed to roll the bug out of my mouth on a tiny wave of saliva.

The footsteps had stopped. I felt certain that I had alerted the hunter to my presence. Surely enough, the footsteps started to approach me. I quickly decided that if discovered I would spring to attack. It seemed better than lying down to be beaten. I coiled myself in readiness.

The footsteps stopped again closer to the ventilator. I felt a scratching on the side of the humming metal. Then a slight tapping, like fingers drumming. Slowly a head appeared from around the side of the ventilator.

I sprang to my feet. But it wasn't Colin at all. Neither was it Terri. It was a child, a small boy. I had startled him and he put his hands to his face to protect himself though he made no noise. For a moment I thought it was one of the camper's children who had wandered up onto the roof.

When he took his hands from his face I saw that his eyes were clear glass. I saw through the glass. When I say clear glass I mean I could see through them to the cloudless blue sky behind him.

Inconceivable. But that's what I saw.

Of the boy's father this time there was no sign. Though his face was distorted with fear, the boy was no longer cast in grey shadow. I recognised him easily. I knew perfectly well who he was. And as soon as I recognised who he was he rose slowly into the air, like a helium-filled balloon. He went higher and higher into the warm summer air, rising steadily into the blue. At last, he waved at me; a tiny gesture, like the time he had waved at me on the beach during the sandcastle competition from which he was excluded. The pinkness of his sunburned face was the last thing I remember as he rose even higher in the early evening sky, until at last he was the tiniest dot in the blue, and then he was gone.

I don't know how long I stayed there. Ultimately I had to go and face whatever was down there waiting for me. I decided that if Colin attacked me I would do my best to defend myself and hope that there would be other people around to help me. I got up from my hiding place, dusted myself down and cautiously made my way down the steps from the roof.

12

Blacker than night were the eyes of Felina

I stepped lightly as I made my way down from the roof but my head was broiling. I was short of breath. My anxiety had given everything an intensity of colour and sound and my senses seemed super-sharp. I made certain that no one was at the bottom or hanging around by the back door before I followed the wall of the back of the building. Of course I was expecting Colin to call me back at any moment. I kept walking and turned up the side of the building, eventually breaking free from the shadows into the sizeable crowd moving into the theatre. My heart hammered, though there was comfort to be had in the crowd.

The ladybirds were even now dotting the early evening air but their numbers had dropped massively. The task force was still sweeping the carcasses into piles, and some of the workers had incinerators with fuel-tanks strapped to their backs. The insect piles crackled and sent up twists of black smoke as they burned.

A friendly camper walking to the theatre with his wife and three children stopped on the way. He looked concerned. 'You all right?' he said to me.

'Touch of migraine,' I said.

'Coffee,' he said. 'My mother used to swear by coffee. She got migraine. She always said—'

'I'll try it,' I said, skipping away and forcing a laugh at the same time. I hurried into the theatre. I was late for my evening duty. My hands were quivering. I took a deep breath and I knew I was going to have to quiet myself.

That evening we had the talent show. The campers were the stars: they made up the evening programme with singing and dancing routines and the winner walked away with a decent cash prize. Tony and all of the Revue performers had an evening off while the talent show was run by my fellow Greencoats. Sammy with the wig acted as the show's compere. I was supposed to be there ahead of the others, taking names and forming a schedule.

The talent show always seemed to feature a tiny five-year-old performing some cute but charmingly inept dance routine that they would forget halfway through. The idea of one of them out on stage while Colin beat the crap out of me in the auditorium had me sick with anxiety. But the talent show was scheduled to start within five minutes.

I made my way to the front of house where Nikki presided behind a desk, doing my job of listing a schedule from the queue of would-be performers. Mike, the organist with the Beatle-haircut I'd met on my first day, was sitting next to her making his own running order.

Nikki was cross. 'Where have you been?' She jabbed a pen in the direction of the folk in the queue. 'Find out what music they want Mike to play for them.'

I did exactly as I was told. I shuffled down the line asking what compositions they wanted. Most of them didn't know. One man was doing a song from the musical *Fiddler On The Roof* but he couldn't remember what the song was called. When it was hummed for me I recognised 'If I Were a Rich Man'. Another man said he wanted to do an American country song called 'Rosa's Cantina' but when he sang a few bars for me I knew he meant 'El Paso'.

I didn't even look up for Colin. I was running on auto-pilot. I could see myself from an astral point twelve feet above my head, and I could hear my own muffled voice from a short distance saying, 'That'll be fine, just tell Mike you want "El Paso" and Nikki over there will give you a number, okay, good, thank you, who's next then?' An elderly and very large lady said she was going to perform 'The Laughing Policeman'. Seven-year-old twins wanted to do 'The Good Ship Lollipop'.

I somehow got to the end of the line but then I came unglued.

'You look really pale,' Nikki said.

I hurried to the toilets and I managed to reach the porcelain in time. I rinsed my mouth from the taps and threw up again. Sweat rolled from my face in great beads and yet my face in the mirror was white like the moon. I splashed water on my cheeks and on my neck and rinsed my mouth a second time. I looked in the mirror and gave myself a stiff talking-to, cut short when someone else came in.

It was another friendly camper, not one I knew. A burly man with a red face and ringlets of blond hair. 'So this is where all the big knobs hang out then is it, heh heh heh.' It was a mirthless laugh. A spoken laugh. *Heh-heh-heh*. That was what my life as a Greencoat had become. One weak joke after another. One forced smile beyond that. I grinned back at him, but I knew it was the smile of a skull. I felt too weak to speak.

By the time I returned to the front of house, everyone had gone into the theatre. I heard the muffled report of Sammy, in his bad toupée, patting the stage microphone, not to see if it was working but to advertise his authority over the event.

'Grab one of the campers,' Nikki said, 'cos we need a third judge.'

I patrolled the front row looking for a likely suspect to agree to do it and finally I found a heavily made-up lady who was delighted to be steered into the limelight. The houselights came down, the stage lights went up and at last the show got underway. Sammy made a lot of himself. He told a couple of weak jokes that just made me want to shit. With his spittle darting in the limelight he introduced the first turn, which was 'If I Were a Rich Man'.

At this point I was visited by a curious calm. I wish I could say that it was the performance of the singer on stage, but it wasn't. In fact the singer was hopeless. The pop-eyed, rotund figure on stage swaying slightly in a minor concession to the theatrical demands of the song did, for just a moment, make everything seem all right. He was up there faking it. He must have known he was a poor singer. The audience certainly knew he was a poor singer but they were all generously prepared to forgive. The only thing they didn't know was the drama that had taken place backstage and up on the roof a short while ago. I knew those details only too well, but I could almost fool myself into believing it had all been a piece of theatre. Inept and ill-managed, yes: but still theatre. It was all right. It was all going to be all right. Colin and Terri would have a furious row; but strong girl that she was, she wouldn't identify me.

It was all going to be all right.

I don't know where my thoughts had been but when I looked up onstage the next turn was already in progress. It was the seven-year-old twins shouting out 'The Good Ship Lollipop' and Mike on the organ was whipping up a nice noisy storm in support. Mike went early for the big finish on the organ and the audience showed wild appreciation for the children. Sammy took the microphone and advised the audience that they should keep an eye on those two young ladies because they were destined to go far.

My mind wandered again because the next time I blinked up at the stage an elderly gentleman was playing 'Ave Maria' on the musical saw; eerie and unaccompanied. I knew I was losing small sequences of time. My mind was like a bingo ticket, with only certain numbers belonging to the full set. I'd come back to consciousness to find another act in progress. After a few bars of ethereal saw-music Mike started to come in with his organ.

After the musical saw came the gentleman who wanted to sing 'El Paso'. He'd chosen to appear on stage wearing a massive straw Mexican sombrero. The song was a ridiculous, warbling gunfighter ballad, but at least the singer had a reasonable voice. Something about a challenge for the love of a maiden and a handsome young stranger lying dead on the floor.

Life, in a sombrero, was mocking me square in the face. The elderly woman I'd pulled from the audience to be a judge put her hand on my knee. 'Looks like we have a winner,' she said.

After the talent show was over, I had to work the bingo in the Slowboat. Nobby did the calling and all I had to do was check the winning tickets. I scanned the rows of tables of people with their heads down, ostensibly scrutinising the players but really I was hunting for any sign of Colin or Terri. There were two doorways into the Slowboat and I planted my back against the wall so that I could scope both entrances.

Up there on the microphone Nobby was an enthusiastic proponent of bingo-lingo. *'Five and nine the Brighton Line.'* I had no idea what some of these things even meant, though I started to ascribe my own meanings. Nobby's microphone had a bad echo to it and everything he said sounded sinister, like he was in on a joke. *'Was-she-worth-it, 56.'* My paranoia made me 'see' Colin come into the Slowboat a couple of times; but it was just someone with the same stocky frame.

I didn't know what he would do to me. I didn't know whether his style was to make a public, fist-and-toecaps full-frontal assault; or whether he was more likely to wait for me in the dark, with a blade at the ready. Either way I was no street-fighter and I hadn't much idea of how I might defend myself if and when the attack came. My mouth was dry, I was in an advanced state of fear, but I was super-alert.

I got through the bingo session and I was supposed to do the lights again at the Golden Wheel. I cried off sick. George agreed to cover the lights. I couldn't face walking back from the Wheel through the dark to the staff quarters. Instead I stayed with the crowds and, checking over my shoulder every yard, made my way back to my room. Even before I got there I had an idea that maybe Colin had already let himself in. I unlocked the door and checked through the crack at the hinge that Colin wasn't standing behind it with his back to the wall. I stooped down to make sure he wasn't under the bed. I gave the flimsy wardrobe a push to test its weight before opening it. Then I closed my room door, turned the key in the lock, checked the window was bolted and drew the curtains.

It was going to be a long night.

13

The Ladybird Patrol:
tooled, equipped and ready to burn

I lay awake, listening. Footsteps in the corridor, doors opening and closing. Each individual returning from the bars was going to be Colin. I heard someone outside my window and I thought Colin might be planning to break his way through the glass; but it was one of the waiters trying to get a kiss and a cuddle in the dark from a girl who kept protesting that she would but she was afraid her father would find out.

When I finally did drift off to sleep I had dreams. I was on the pier standing before the mechanised fortune-teller. The glass case had been smashed and the mani-kin leaned forward out of the broken face. Her tongue lolled from her painted mouth. It was an absurdly long, fat, moist and lascivious tongue and she seemed to produce from her throat one of the prediction cards. In the dream I took the card but I couldn't read what was on it because the printed letters changed before my eyes, now Greek, now Chinese. It was a matter of great torment to me that I couldn't read what was written on the card.

I felt so anxious about not being able to read the card that I woke up. In the dark someone was sitting on the end of my bed. But I couldn't sit up. My chest was compressed. It was like I had a claw wrapped round my lungs. I could hear myself trying to breath. I was so frightened I tried to shout out but I couldn't get my breath. It was the man in the blue suit. He was sitting on the end of my bed regarding me steadily.

But his eyes were pure glass. Clear glass, no pupil. They reflected the light and shadow of the room; and even though his eyes were clear glass I could see he was looking down at me. But because his eyes were clear glass I couldn't see if he wanted to hurt me. I tried to sit up but couldn't because of the weight on my lungs. I thought he must have a hand pressing on my chest.

With a superhuman effort I forced myself upright, and as I did I woke up. I'd had a dream within a dream. I'd woken up only to wake a second time. I got up to put the light on. The man on the edge of my bed had gone. I prowled my tiny room, lifting things and setting them down again: my clock, a newspaper, a shoe. I was scared of waking up again.

Finally I went back to bed. I left the light on. I lay awake for a long time, blinking at the ceiling. I must have fallen asleep again because I overslept. I was already a few minutes late when I threw on my Greencoat outfit and hurried over to the theatre. There was a smell of burning accelerant in the air. The ladybird patrol was up and about, fuel tanks strapped to their backs, sweeping dead ladybirds into piles and incinerating them. You would hear the spit and brief dull roar of the incinerator and a little black puff of smoke would ball in the air.

Pinky's morning briefing was already well under-way when I got to the theatre. Nikki gave me a look of maternal disapproval. Nobby, slumped in a chair, winked at me as if I'd done something good. I looked for signs of Terri performing her cleaning duties but there was no sign of her. I sat through the briefing, rubbing my eyes and trying not to yawn.

'Are you with us then, son?' It was Pinky.

I realised he had just asked me a question. 'Sorry,' I said. 'I had a night from hell.'

'Not letting that Nobby have a bad influence on you, are you? Not going to turn out like him?'

'That's fucking nice, that is,' Nobby spluttered. 'Charming. Fucking nice, that.'

Pinky ignored him. 'Sandcastles with Nikki then?'

Nikki had one eyebrow raised, waiting for an answer. 'Sure.'

'Go easy on the sticks of rock,' Pinky said as we got up to leave. 'It has to last all season.' I looked up at the stage again, expecting Terri to emerge from behind the flats and wiping her mop this way and that as on so many other occasions during our briefing. Normally, the hoover and other equipment would be around as she worked. Not this morning.

'Are you all right?' Nikki asked me when we got outside.

'Yes. Why do you I ask?'

'Nothing. I thought you looked a bit …'

'A bit what?'

'I worry about you, for some reason. God knows why. But I wondered if Nobby had been up to his tricks. Getting you involved.'

'You're speaking in riddles, Nikki.'

Nikki brought her hand to her mouth and made a quick back-and-forth smoking gesture. 'He's a doper,' she said. Then, as an afterthought, she said, 'And a dope.'

Gosh, I wanted to say to her, I wish it was as innocent as smoking pot. Instead I said, 'No. Nothing like
that. I don't even like the stuff. I tried it once at college
but it made me throw up.'

'Me neither,' she said as we passed through the beach
wall tunnel and emerged onto the sand. 'I prefer fresh
air and sex for entertainment.' She looked at me pointedly. 'Right, let's get cracking. You do the over-sevens
and I'll do the tiddly-pots.'

My only salvation was to fling myself into the work.
It was a way of shoving aside all thoughts of either
Terri or Colin, even though they were like demons
barking at either ear. I got down on my knees with the
children and exhorted them to dig. I helped them to
make models of horses and of boats, trains and planes.
One little girl even complained that I'd snatched away
her blue plastic spade in my fervour. I was manic.

I'd already decided that Colin would just have to
come and do his worst. I would fight him. I would go
down fighting. As I worked the sand and flipped shiny
plastic buckets amongst them, the innocence of the
children almost made me want to cry. I very nearly did.

Nikki stooped beside me and whispered in my ear,
'You're putting me to shame.'

I looked at her. The sun was up hot and I was sweating. I must have been wild-eyed.

'It's okay,' she said sweetly. She lifted my hair out of
my eyes and parked it behind my ear. Then she went
back and lay down.

I thought some of the parents were looking at me
oddly so I left the kids to their sand designs and went
to sit next to Nikki. She was stretched back on the sand
with her hands behind her head and her eyes closed. I

tried to copy her, but as soon as I put my head back and closed my eyes I saw Colin standing over me. I sat up. There was no Colin. 'I'm really sorry about that thing,' I said.

'Without opening her eyes she said, 'What thing?'

'That meeting. They're not my kind of people.'

'Oh forget it.'

'I didn't know what I was getting into. I just went along for the ride. Literally. I mean I was invited to get into a car without knowing where it was taking me. Next thing I know I'm up to my jaw in flags and regalia and spearheads and all this about the commies and the unions and the Jews and the blacks and—'

'Look, we've been through all this. I've forgotten it. Why don't you?'

'I would never have gone if I'd realised.'

'Realised what?'

'Who they were. How it would offend you. All that.'

Now she opened her eyes and sat up.

'I mean to say, what if those people ever got into power?'

'They won't,' she said.

'How do you know?'

'They're a hate club. Most people are decent, you know.'

'You say that. But it has happened. In history.'

'What do you think we should do?'

'Well. Organise.'

'Organise? Right! This afternoon. We'll go after them with an iron bar and a cricket bat. You and me.' She closed her eyes again.

I vented a deep sigh. I know I sat there for a while pinching a loose bit of skin above the bridge of my nose. At least it was better than forcing small children into making over-complicated sandcastles.

Eventually Nikki got to her feet. 'Come on. Put on a happy face. I'll pick the winners while you give everyone a stick of rock. Sod it, give them two sticks apiece.'

14

The reward of a cigar while Saturday comes

More than ever I needed to find Terri, to re-establish *terra firma*, to stop my world from spinning out of control. But I couldn't locate her anywhere. A sweet-natured grey-haired woman called Elsie supervised all the cleaning staff. I tracked her down and asked where I could find Terri.

Elsie wore a pair of plastic-framed spectacles patched together with clear Sellotape. Metal hairgrips pinned back her hair and she was weighed down by an enormous silver ring of keys dangling from a leather belt looped round her thin waist. She seemed too frail to be carrying such a bunch of keys. 'What do you want her for, duck?'

'She left some stuff in the theatre. I want to take it to her.'

'Give it here. I'll see she gets it.'

'No problem. I'll return it to her myself.'

'Please yourself, duck. Only she hasn't been in today.'

'Oh?'

'Happen she'll be back tomorrow, eh?'

'Happen,' I said. I don't know why. I never say *happen.*

I thought briefly of home. I don't know if these are

the sort of things young men discuss with their fathers or their stepfathers or not at all, but I was in serious need of someone to talk to. Though the idea of me telling all this to Ken seemed ridiculous. I'd always kept him at arm's length as if, through no fault of his own, he wasn't to be trusted with intimacies. As I passed by the palmist's little white caravan I couldn't help glancing through the door. Tony was in there, laughing and sipping tea from a china tea-cup, his feet crossed at the ankles. I couldn't actually see Madame Rosa, but I could hear her talking in animated fashion

No, I didn't think that she could see my future, or that she could see into my past. But a kind of desperation made me look towards the caravan. Not that I was ever going to give her the chance: I'd found out that Madame Rosa charged four pounds fifty for a reading. That seemed to me to be an astonishing amount of money: the equivalent of about fifteen pints of beer. I didn't need a palmist to tell me that I was serious danger of getting my head kicked in, and that it was all of my own doing.

Nikki had a direct way of speaking. 'You don't look happy and you don't look well,' she said.

'I'm not sleeping well.'

Nikki sighed. 'This place. It can really get to you. That's why your predecessor left. He just couldn't stand it. Long hours of the happy face. It's dangerous. Doing a happy face when you really want to scream. Is anything else bothering you?' She looked at me with dark eyes full of intuition.

I was close to telling her everything. I wasn't in love with Terri but I felt responsible for her. I couldn't see how I could spill the beans on any of this without seeming like I'd made it all happen. 'I'm just not sleeping. That rabbit hutch doesn't help.'

Of Colin or Terri there was neither sight nor sound. A new cleaner had been drafted in to take care of the theatre. I got her to switch off her noisy hoover so that I could ask her about Terri. She didn't know anything. She said that all she knew was that she'd been taken off Block B where she was happy and put on the theatre where she didn't know a soul.

In blistering heat we judged the competitions around the swimming pool. The heat and the lack of sleep exhausted me. Nikki wanted me to go to the canteen with her for lunch but my need to sleep was overwhelming. Images from the previous evening's escape were washing over me and the dreaming part of my brain was flooding my waking mind. I went back to my room and was relieved to find no sign of Nobby. I locked the door, flung myself on my cot and instantly fell into a deep sleep.

Though it seemed like only seconds, it was maybe a couple of hours later when I was roused by a hammering on the door and a woman's voice calling my name. It was Nikki.

I got to my feet and opened the door.

'You're supposed to be preparing for the farewell show,' she said. She peered round me into my room, as if to see if I'd got anyone with me.

I felt drugged. I was like a zombie. 'Need a shower,' I slurred.

'You haven't got time. They're all there. Only you missing.'

I ignored her and in a stupor I shuffled to the shower room, stepped out of my clothes and ran the shower cold over my head. I stood under the icy water for a moment and began to revive. When I opened my eyes Nikki was there, shamelessly watching me. Her arms were folded. She was holding one of my towels. She flapped it at me. 'You'll need this.'

We hurried over to the theatre where the preparation for the farewell performance and prize-giving ahead of the Friday Review was already underway. Tony and the others were already onstage, setting up. As I came in he asked me to go backstage to wheel out the sword casket and his fez in readiness for his *Abdul-Shazam* routine.

It was the first time I'd been alone backstage since it had all kicked off. Before then I'd made sure there were others around, people I could talk to, just so that I didn't have to confront the loaded silence of the place. Backstage in the theatre is awash with ghosts. It is a memory bank for every cue missed by an actor; every gag that died; each muffed line and dance routine gone awry; each dropped catch, muddle, mix-up and mistake: the tragic moment that turns to farce. For all of this there is a dark audience perched and waiting.

The sword casket was covered with props and stage junk. I was thinking about Nikki, who would be called upon to get into the box as I took all the junk off the box and unlatched the lid. When I opened the lid and looked inside I let the lid slam down and I toppled backwards.

There was a woman in the casket.

I sat back on the bare boards, paralysed, staring at the glittering box. The truth is I was waiting for the lid to open.

It didn't.

I knew it must be a trick of the light. But even in the dimly lit recess of the props chamber the image of a woman stuck in that coffin of a magic box had been vivid. Slowly, and on my hands and knees, I crawled over to the casket and lifted the lid again.

It was Terri. She was jammed in the casket, her feet drawn up beneath her and wedged into the dividers. She wore just her bra and pants. I could only see one side of her face, and that was in darkness. Her skin looked grey. Her nose and mouth were squashed up against the padded sides of the box. Her eyes were closed. A trickle of liquid had dribbled from her mouth and across her chin, leaving a snail-trail. A rope was tangled around her legs.

Her eye opened. In the light and shadow of the back stage her eye glimmered briefly in a way that made me think of the phosphorescence of the waves. She was trying look back at me, but her head was trapped, firmly lodged, and she couldn't move it. She stuck her tongue out of the side of her mouth and licked her parched lips. 'Get me out,' she said in a faint rasp. 'There's a good lad.'

I grabbed at the plastic dividers, trying to give her some room to move. One of the dividers broke in my hands but it wasn't enough to give Terri any relief. She was still horribly compressed. So grey were her features in the shadows I honestly thought she was near to death. Her breathing was shallow. Still trying to break her free I grabbed another of the dividers and it cracked noisily in my fingers, cutting the side of my hand.

The sound of the plastic splitting in my hands seemed to have shattered a spell. I was left with a shard of broken plastic in my hand, staring down at an empty box. There was no Terri inside it, compressed or otherwise.

The casket was empty.

I clawed at the velvet padding at the base of the box, just to see if I was the victim of some illusion. There was nothing. Just the hollow casket with its now cracked and broken dividers.

I let the lid fall and stared at the casket for some time. The hallucination had been so strong that I couldn't figure out what had happened. I'd seen Terri in the casket. I'd smelled her yeasty sweat. I'd heard her raspy voice.

I went back out front. Tony was laughing about something with Nikki and Gail, the dancer with whom I'd run the Treasure Hunt. 'Where's the kit?' he said to me when I got to the ballroom.

I had no time to compose myself. 'It's been damaged,' I said. 'You'd better come and look.'

Tony knitted his eyebrows. He spun on his heels and marched ahead of me to where I'd just come from. I'd already decided that I would be there when he opened the casket. I followed Tony backstage and into the props chamber.

'What a fucking state, this place,' he said, pulling the casket out of its corner. He flipped open the lid and then he stepped back, just as I had done. His eyes bulged. 'Jesus Christ!' he said. 'What the fuck?'

I advanced up to his elbow and peered into the casket.

'Who's done that?' Tony shouted. 'It's smashed to fuck!'

He turned to me with an accusing look. I shook my head.

'It's that fucking Nobby,' he said. 'He brings women down here.'

'What?' I said. I was still reeling from what I'd seen – what I thought I'd seen – in the box.

'Fucking gets 'em playing around in the box, shows 'em how it's done to impress 'em. I'll swing for the little bastard.'

'How do you know it's him?' I said reasonably.

'How do I know? How do I know anything?' He kicked the casket, as if he wanted to break it some more. 'We can't use that now. That's fucked that for this afternoon.'

He was furious. I pressed past him and peered into the casket. I stooped down and ran my hands over the broken trammels, not for any other reason than to check for warmth, or blood or any other evidence that the box had contained a body less than three minutes ago.

'Leave it,' Tony said. 'You can't fix it. We'll do the plate-spinning, for fuck's sake. Sort it, will you?'

He stormed away. I was left standing over the empty sword casket. There in that place of shabby conjuring tricks, it occurred to me for the first time that someone might be messing with me. It was impossible that there could be someone in the casket one moment and then not the next; but then it was also impossible to get a woman to climb into a casket and to stick swords into her only to have her pop out of the casket unharmed moments later.

My heart hammered and my brain was like a nest of spitting snakes. I was in a kind of fever and my head was boiling with notions. I needed to see Terri, to speak to her, to see if she was all right, to find out what was happening.

I practised deep breathing and my heart-rate started to come back to normal. I collected the gear for the plate-spinning routine. The set of plates spinning on poles have deep dimples under them so that they can easily be set spinning; meanwhile you invite an idiot from the audience to try his hand and you give him a fragile, similar-looking plate with no dimple that, of course, crashes to the floor and splinters, all to the cruel merriment of the audience. It began to seem like all the conjuring was a cheap deception rather than the noble art I'd first taken it to be.

I hauled the plate-spinning gear over to the ballroom. Nikki and Gail were still there. Tony had gone.

'He's not best pleased,' Nikki said.

'Wouldn't like to be in Nobby's shoes,' Gail said.

'No,' I said.

Nikki took some of the plates from me. 'Come on, let's set up.'

The farewell show passed without event. I say without event: plates crashed to the floor but that's what they were supposed to do. Winners were announced and prizes were given. After the show, a little girl, who had a habit of following me around, tapped me on the hand and gave me a cigar in a tube. No doubt her parents thought this a nice gesture, and I did, too, even though I don't smoke. In fact, when I looked into the sparkly innocence of the child's eyes it almost made my own eyes water.

In the Golden Wheel nightclub I operated the lights for Luca. The show was the same and the song was the same. Amid the lyrical references to summer kisses and sunburned hands I improvised a few touches with rotating gels for 'Autumn Leaves'. After his performance, Luca didn't hang round to talk. He made a little salute in my direction before leaving.

With Luca's song playing in a nightmarish loop in my head I made a point of finding some company with whom to walk back to my quarters in the dark. I was a bag of nerves, scanning the shadows. Once again I locked the door behind me and closed the curtains. I lay down on my pallet bed and eventually fell into a bewildering sleep.

I was back on the pier again, standing before the smashed glass case of the mechanical fortune-teller. I put a coin in the box and instead of Zora the manikin, there was the boy, screaming. His head was shaved to the skullbone. He covered his head with hands as he screamed and his forearms were tattooed. The tattoos were all red and black ladybirds. The boy's mouth was wide open and his ear-splitting cry faded slowly, as did the boy, leaving scraps of himself hovering in the air. Eventually I reached out a hand to where the after-images floated. The scraps stirred as if I'd put my hand in water to disturb them, and finally faded altogether.

In the dream a card was spat from the machine. It read, *Wait for the card.*

15

Will no-one fix the malfunctioning strip light

Some movement awoke me in the early hours. I opened my eyes and in the darkness I could see Nobby sitting on his bed. There wasn't enough light to see his face but he sat with his hands on his knees, staring at me.

'You all right, Nobby?' I said.

'Tain't Nobby. It's me.'

The gravel voice was unmistakable and it did two things. It iced my blood and it sent me scuttling up from my bed and against the window, to the nearest point of escape.

'Calm your nerves, son. It's Colin.'

I knew perfectly well who it was.

As I forced my back up against the window the curtain rucked to admit a thin ray of moonlight to fall on Colin's angular face. In that light his eyes shone like the carapaces of shiny black beetles. If I tried to speak, my mouth was too dry. I was paralysed with fright. I couldn't move again if I wanted to.

'What the fuck are you doin'? It's Colin,' he said again. He laughed. 'Look at you!'

'How did you get in?' I managed to say.

'Are you joking? Have you seen these locks? Get dressed. I need some help.'

He stood up and moved towards the door as if to give me room. Slowly my heart rate came back to normal. My legs trembled. I felt I had no choice but to do exactly what he said. I pulled on my jeans and my denim shirt and my trainers. Colin flicked his head in the direction of the door and went out. I followed. I looked down at the lock to my door and it was hanging off its fittings.

'Fix that later,' he said.

A malfunctioning strip light fizzed at the end of the corridor. No one else was around. The whole unit snoozed. I wanted to bang on someone's door and shout for help, but I couldn't. Colin stopped under the light and turned to me. 'I'm not allowed on the camp so this was the only way to get to you.'

'Right,' I said. It was all so normalised. I felt like I was being marched to the electric chair by someone whose job it was to throw the switch at the end of the walk.

We passed through the shadows between the chalets and he led me to a low wire fence behind a privet hedge. It was a way into the camp I'd never even seen before. He cocked a leg over the fence without looking back to see if I followed. A path between the camp and a caravan park led out onto the road and there Colin's Hillman Imp was parked.

Without a word he unlocked the driver door and got in. It didn't seem to have occurred to him that I might bolt. Everything was telling me to run, but another voice in my head was asking me to stay calm. I thought that if Colin was going to attack me he would have done so in my room. After a couple of seconds Colin leaned across the seats to pop the button lock on the passenger door. This was my last moment to make a run for it.

I opened the passenger door and I got in. Colin started up the engine and pulled away from the kerb. The car didn't smell good. Something was 'off'.

'Where are we going?'

'You'll see.'

It was after one a.m. and the roads were deserted. We drove in complete silence. After we got out of town Colin said, 'Open the glove compartment.'

I popped open the glove compartment. In it was a folded map. 'You can navigate,' he said. 'There's a torch.'

I got the torch out of the glove compartment and I unfolded the map. A clumsy X had been marked on the map with black biro. It was a place just across the Lincolnshire border into Nottinghamshire, near a town or village called Barlston. 'What is it?' I asked.

'We stay on the A158 for a while. Keep your eyes peeled.'

Progress was slow. The road was single carriageway pretty much all of the route to Lincoln. More than once oncoming drivers blared their horns at Colin, angry that he hadn't dimmed his headlights for them. Even in the dark some of the route looked familiar to me, and just before we reached Horncastle we approached a pub that I knew. It had a thatched roof and there wasn't a breath of wind to stir the union jack on its smartly painted pole. It was The Fighting Cocks.

I said nothing. I thought: this is it; he's brought me here so that he and his National Front cronies can have some fun with me.

But the car swished by without Colin even acknowledging the place.

It was a long journey in silence and the car still
smelled bad. It was a smell that seemed familiar yet
I couldn't identify it. Eventually, Colin alerted me to
look for a turn-off. We found Barlston easy enough. It
was a Nottinghamshire mining village.

'We're looking for a place called Black Bank,' Colin
said.

We'd been driving for maybe an hour and after crawling through the village we found Black Bank. About
half a mile from the village a field on the embankment
of a hill had an area fenced off with steel mesh wire.
A sign hung lop-sided from a single screw: DANGER
DEEP SHAFT NO ADMITTANCE. Colin parked up and
switched off the car lights.

'What is this place?'

'Old coal mine. They're capping it over. If anyone
comes,' he said, 'we just pretend we're queers.'

'What?'

'There's two bags in the back behind you. And there's
another three bags in the boot.'

'What's in the bags?'

'We're slinging 'em down that shaft.'

'Why?'

He looked at me like I was simple, a half-smile on his
face. 'Jus' fuckin' do it, all right?' He opened his door
and got out.

My mouth was dry. I got out of the car and looked
out across the field. Someone had already peeled back
the steel wire mesh to get to the shaft. I don't know
what had been dumped down the shaft but there was
a pile of hardcore rubble outside the protected area,

and a lot of building materials – sand and gravel – plus industrial drums inside the fence. There was a five-bar farmer's gate leading onto the land. Colin went up to the gate and gave it a shake. It was padlocked.

'We have to carry it. I'll help you wiv it over the gate. If anyone comes while you're up there I'll drive away, turn around and come back. You just keep low.'

Colin went back to the car and opened the back door. He started wrestling with a black bin liner that was in the foot-well. It looked heavy. 'Come on.'

I went over to help him. The bin-liner was tied at the top so I couldn't see what was in it, but I could smell it. It was the source of the odour that had been bothering me. I noticed he was still wearing his driving gloves. When we got the first heavy bin liner out I knew what was inside. 'Look, what's in it?' I said again, pointedly.

'Condemned meat,' he said matter-of-factly. 'We're dumping it.'

'Why?'

'Questions fuckin' questions. Get it over the gate.'

The bags were heavy. We dumped two from the back of the car over the gate, and then we carried the other three from the boot, and dropped those over the gate.

'You're gonna have to take them up there and drop 'em over the edge. I'll sit 'ere.'

'Why can't you help me?'

'Told you. I'll drive away if anyone comes. Get on with it.'

Carrying the bags on my own was difficult. I started shaking again and the strength drained out of me. But I half-dragged the first bag along the parched and baked clay, stirring up dust. I managed to manoeuvre it through the broken fence and right up to the edge of the shaft.

There were over a dozen metal drums near the shaft, all stamped with biohazard symbols. The shaft was no more than a shadow in the ground. It had been shored up with wooden planking on three sides and it had a rough derrick structure straddled across it. I dropped the bag on the dry earth and looked back at Colin in the car. He was some distance away and he had the courtesy light on and appeared to be studying the map. I was sure he couldn't see me in the dark. While I could see his shape behind the wheel I knew that at least he wasn't planning to shove me down the shaft. Not until I'd disposed of the bags, at least.

I tore open the bag and sure enough I found raw meat. I had no way of knowing what kind of meat it was. It smelled worse now that I'd opened the bag. I thought about the other four bags. I was trying to calculate how much meat there was in each bag. More than would comprise one human being, I was certain. More like two people, at least.

I put the toe of my trainer against the bag and tried to push it in but I couldn't put enough force behind my foot. I was also afraid of getting too close to the edge, maybe losing my footing and going down with it. I needed Colin to help me but there was no way I was going to invite him up there with me. I found a plank of wood and I managed to lever the bag of meat closer to the edge. At last it went tumbling over the edge and into the gaping black hole. I didn't hear it hit the bottom.

I stared after it. My shoulders were shaking. I looked down at the car. Colin had got out to see what was holding me up so I made my way back down to collect a second bag.

'Whassup?' he said.

'Heavy.'

'Pussy.'

I took the second bag up to the shaft. This time I dropped it on the end of the plank of wood, so that all I had to do was to lever the plank. The second bag dropped without a sound. I took a deep breath and went back for the third bag. Colin saw me coming and got back into the car. I dumped the third bag and by the time I got the fourth up to the shaft I saw headlights coming towards me along the unlit country lane. Colin moved off in the Hillman Minx. I left the bag next to the shaft, slipped through the mesh fence and ran to the edge of the field, keeping in amongst the shadows. The car approached and cruised by. After it had gone I went back to the shaft.

Colin hadn't yet returned. Something sharp was pressuring the black plastic of the fourth bin liner. I had a moment or two before Colin came back so I tried to see what it was. In the darkness I was pretty certain it was the longish fingernails of a human hand. I tried to tear open the plastic, but it was very thick, durable stuff. Colin still hadn't come back.

I found a rusty nail in a piece of scrap wood and with shaking hands I worked it out so that I could use the nail to tear at the black vinyl. I was hyperventilating trying to get it open. When it did pop the sharp thing I'd taken to be human fingers popped through the plastic.

It was a pig's trotter.

I was drenched in sweat. My breath started to come

back. I staggered out through the mesh, went down to the gate and fetched the final bag. I dragged it along the dust, took it up to the shaft and placed it on the end of my plank-lever. As I levered the bag down the shaft Colin cruised back into position by the gate and killed his lights. I tossed the plank down the shaft after the bags and made my way back to the car.

'All done and dusted?' Colin said when I got in beside him.

'Done.'

He started up the engine and flicked his headlights on again. 'Look at the state of you! Worked up a bit of a sweat, son.'

'Yeah.'

He smiled. 'Fuckin' schtoodents.'

On the way back he told me 'they' – and he didn't say who 'they' were – had been caught selling condemned meat. It was slaughterhouse waste they were repackaging. When I asked him why he couldn't dump it anywhere, like in the sea, he said that it was legal evidence. It had been confiscated by the authorities, stamped and frozen to be exhibited in a court of law. 'They' had had to steal it back. Colin said he wanted to dump it where no one could find it. If there was no evidence there was no case.

I sat in the car feeling cold and with my sweat chilling on my skin, wondering whether to believe him. I tried to speak a few times and then finally got up the courage to say, 'By the way, I haven't seen Terri for a while.'

His jaw set. He fixed his eyes on the road ahead.

'You still want me to keep an eye on her, right?'

'You know what?' he said. 'I was wrong about that fucking Italian geezer.'

'Oh?'

'It wasn't him.'

'Oh?'

'Don't you worry about Terri no more.'

'Why is that?'

'I told you: don't you worry about Terri no more.'

That was his last word on the matter.

When we got back to the camp he shoved something in my breast pocket. 'What's that?'

'I'm looking arter you 'ain't I?'

It was about 3.30 a.m. when I got out of the car. He drove off. I pulled three ten-pound notes out of my breast pocket.

16

Zen and the art of ignoring archery

Next morning I was assigned to archery on the football field. Whereas I was hoping to work with Nikki again I was given Nobby instead. I understood that Nobby had the previous week cocked up the whist drive, resulting in a silver-haired uprising, so Nikki had been drafted in to pacify the octogenarian rebels and run it instead. Nobby, along with me, was presumably trusted not to cause too much upset with a bow and arrow.

We walked together from the theatre and he was in high spirits already, even though he'd been given a formal warning that if he didn't buck up his ideas he'd be out of a job. He claimed no one would tell him why.

'But I know why,' he said as we approached the white-painted shed where the straw clouts and archery equipment were locked away. 'I know fuckin' well why; someone busted Sheik-Ben-Gaza's sword cabinet, that's fuckin' why and then cleverly got the finger pointed at me.'

I unlocked the shed and I started the job of carrying out the target stands and the clouts. They were heavy and Nobby showed no signs of helping, though he did keep pace with me to keep up his cheerful prattle. As I was setting the first clout in the middle of the field he told me, 'They won't say that's what it is; but it *is* what it is; and I *know* what it is. Do you know what it is? Do you know anything about it?'

I shook my head and pretended to look puzzled by the unfolding of the A-stands for the straw clouts. I'd got my own, other mysteries to figure out. My sleep-deprived brain was clacking like beads back and forth on an abacus but without ever adding up to anything. I was running events over and over in my mind. Like the fact that Colin had worn a pair of gloves while we were dumping the meat. Which of course meant that were there any fingerprints on those plastic bags, they would be all mine.

I was a bit short with him. 'I've got my own problems, Nobby.'

Nobby wrinkled his brow at that, and followed me back to the shed in a unique silence. When we got to the shed he pushed me inside, and closed the door behind him.

'Sit down,' he said. 'Go on, sit down.' I sat on one of the straw clouts and so did he. He whisked a tobacco tin from his jacket pocket and from it he withdrew three cigarettes papers. 'Now listen to your Uncle Nobby, because he understands and he has what you need and what we all need and what everyone needs; and in fact he's not here just to be a figure of fun oh no he's here to help and that's Nobby's mantra if you can be of help be of help, right, this is the answer which comes from the ting-ting!' During the course of this prattle he licked the gummed edge of the papers; rapidly skinned up a joint; took from his other pocket a bag of grass; crumbled it into the tobacco; rolled it; lit up; and blew a big cloud of smoke into my face. It took him maybe

178

seven seconds. Then he took another drag and passed the joint to me.

I looked at it. 'I don't,' I said.

'Ah, resistance! The mind is moving. But you must still the mind before the mind can move. This is the answer that comes to us from the ting-ting!'

When he said ting-ting he floated a finger towards heaven. 'What?' I said.

'Just fuckin' smoke it and your problem will be as smoke. Trust old Uncle Nobby, who is here to help.'

Well, I needed something. I accepted the joint, took a drag and inhaled. As a non-smoker I was determined not to let it make me cough. I held the smoke back in my lungs and immediately felt light-headed, probably from the effects of the tobacco rather than from the grass.

He nodded encouragement for me to take another drag. 'Which is a medicament of oriental persuasion, yes, a beneficial herb, derived from the many-splendoured alternatives to a reality-check; now be a good chap and let Nobby have the joint back because what you're doing is called bogarting the joint in hipster terminology otherwise known in Manchester as please pass the fuckin' Duchy.'

I took this to mean he wanted me to give the thing back to him, which I did and he received it magnanimously, as if I'd been the one to provide it in the first place. We shared the joint until it was finished, then tumbled out of the shed, probably along with a great belch of smoke. Meanwhile, the children waited patiently, with their mums and dads, for us to finish setting up.

When the set-up was complete I ordered Nobby to

stand at the side of the targets to make sure no one wandered behind. Still talking, he did as instructed, mainly because it required no effort. Then I flung myself into advising and helping the campers, offering the bit of technique that had been shown to me. I even tossed in a joke about not aiming an arrow at Nobby unless they were certain they could hit him. I got distracted for a moment when I was rather taken by the depth of hue of the brilliant red, white and blue targets; but largely the grass had done its job of relaxing me. Meanwhile, a little girl decided she wanted to stand next to me and hold my hand throughout the event.

After a while I called a halt to collect arrows and Nobby used this opportunity to wander over and tell me how he planned to give Sheik-Ben-Gaza – which of course was his name for Abdul-Shazam *aka* Tony – a piece of his mind if anything else was said. 'You know why they don't like me, don't you? You know that? Eh? Eh?'

'Cos you don't do any work?'

'No, you lout. It's because I'm the only one who has called them on their evil politics, that's why. It's like history didn't happen with this mob, they've got collective amnesia; they all wanna get dressed up in buckles and boots and eagles and leather and the whole Nazi regalia and if you have anything to say about it you're stuffed. What if we were to tell all these holidaymakers their entertainment programme was being run by the Nazi party? Eh? Eh? What would they make of that? How about that? Ladies and gentlemen, the Junior Bathing Belle is brought to you today courtesy of the Panzer Division of the Skegness Reich? Eh?' Then he laughed. Quite seamlessly and with no pause for breath in the middle of this tirade he said to me, 'Are you tapping that Nikki?'

I nodded at the little girl who'd held my hand throughout most of the proceedings, indicating that Nobby might be a little more careful in what he had to say. It was a pointless gesture.

'You are, aren't you?'

'No, I'm not.'

'Yes you are. That's who was in your room, wasn't it?'

'No.'

'Oh yes it was. Uncle Nobby knows. That time when you wouldn't let me in. That's who it was. You can tell me. I know the meaning of discretion.'

'Do you?'

'Oh yes. Oh yes.'

'No, it wasn't Nikki.'

'Oh yes it was.'

'I'm not arguing with you, Nobby.'

'If it wasn't Nikki it was that Terri, wasn't it?'

That went through me like a sword.

'It was, wa'n't it? She's a right blue blazer that one. Bing bang bong. Careful there my son, careful there. Remember Nigel? He who came before you? He had to leave in his socks when her old man found out Nigel had been poaching in his pond, oh yes. Chased him down to the pier with a scalping razor ho ho ho. You be careful where you park your Zephyr, my son. Uncle Nobby knows.'

I made a superhuman effort to ignore all of this by focusing on the happy little five-year-old girl holding my hand. She was a sweet thing with white-blond hair, tender cheeks and startling blue eyes. 'Are you going to have a go with the bow and arrow?' I asked her.

She beamed at me and said, 'My dad says bollocks to that.'

Nikki had managed to pacify the silver-haired revolution and the whist drive had been restored to full operational efficiency. From what she told me the grey-haired Whist Liberation Front were ready to hang Nobby by the neck. It wasn't clear what he'd done exactly. I was starting to feel sorry for him. It seemed he had enemies everywhere without knowing how he attracted such odium.

'He gets the blame for everything,' Nikki admitted. 'He seems to set himself up for it.'

'He thinks you and I are an item,' I blurted.

'Chance would be a fine thing,' she said. 'Anyway you're seeing someone else.'

We'd gone up to the beach to have half an hour's peace before our afternoon duties resumed. We sat on the great concave wall with our legs dangling over the grey-white concrete. A light breeze streamed in from seaward. It was a relief because, unless this light wind was a hint of a weather change to come, the heat still showed no sign of breaking. The breeze lifted at her hair.

Nikki turned to me and made a sun-visor of her hand, to look at me. It was stupid because the sun was behind her, and I was the one who was squinting; but she did it anyway. 'I know,' she said.

'Know what?'

'Your little secret.'

'That being?'

'Your little friend.'

I felt as though I had just been given poison to drink. My guts churned.

'Who's my little friend?'

'Oh come on, David.'

'No, you come on. Who's my little friend?'

Nikki dropped her fake visor. She made a little shake of her head. Then she mouthed the name. Or just half the name. Or even just the last syllable. 'Ri.'

'How did you know?'

'Have you ever seen people deliberately not looking at each other?'

She was smart, that Nikki. She was one of those women on whom nothing is lost. She was a much shrewder judge of human psychology than people gave her credit for. Though it was bad that she knew, I had an odd sense, from somewhere nine feet above myself, of staying calm.

'Who else knows?'

'What does it matter?'

'It does matter. Who else knows? I mean who do you know for certain who knows?'

'Calm down, David. If they do know they're really not that interested. Not as interested as you seem to think anyway.'

I nodded. I looked out to sea. I was thinking hard.

'I was more surprised than interested, to be honest.'

'Why do you say that?'

'Well I didn't think she would be your type. She's quite hard-faced. When you get to know her. Oh, am I speaking out of turn now?'

'No,' I said. 'No, you're not.'

'I was a bit taken aback. When I realised, I mean.'

'Right.'

'She just didn't seem to be the sort of woman I would have expected you to go for.'

'What sort of woman would you have expected me to go for?'

'More feminine. More sophisticated, I suppose.'

'More like a dancer?'

'That's the word I was trying to think of,' she said.

'I've been an idiot,' I said.

Along with Gail I was responsible for organising the Glamorous Grandmother competition that afternoon. The previous week when I'd organised the Glamorous Grandmother I'd been an adulterer. Now I was wondering whether it was possible that I was a murderer's accomplice. It hadn't escaped me that maybe Colin had stuck a pig's trotter or two in those bags of meat just to disguise any dismembered human remains. Of course, he might not have done; but all things were possible. I was moving in a world where I didn't know what people were capable of.

I supposed that murderers' accomplices did trivial and quotidian things like anyone else. I mean, murderers peel potatoes and watch quiz shows on the television. But I think it must be quite rare that a murderer's accomplice has to organise a Glamorous Grandmother competition.

And my mind was slipping from the job. I had command of the microphone and before a small audience in the ballroom I had to conduct, in turn, an 'interview' with each of about fifteen ladies of a certain age. I would ask them where they were from and a number of stock questions. One of these questions was to ask the lady what was the best piece of advice she had ever received. Halfway through the show I was about to ask this question to contestant number eight and my mind went blank.

When I say blank, I don't just mean I forgot my words. My mind drained. I stalled. My jaw became paralysed. I was aware of the audience waiting for me. Contestant number eight turned towards me with an expectant expression on her face. Everything went silent. Someone coughed. Then there was a nervous laugh from somewhere. I actually had the microphone held to my own lips, but it was as if time was passing for everyone except me. I couldn't progress time in my own world, and therefore I couldn't speak. A bead of sweat ran down the side of my face. Contestant number eight smiled awkwardly, turned away and gently patted the hair at the nape of her neck, then she looked back at me again. Someone in the audience made a comment.

I saw Gail come towards me, her eyes huge. She gently took the microphone from my fingers. 'There's been a bit of a bug going round the staff,' she said into the microphone, 'and I think David's got it.' There was a murmur of sympathy from the audience. 'He doesn't like giving up but if we can get him to sit down for a minute then I'll carry on.'

I took the cue. I patted my stomach a little theatrically perhaps, but enough to confirm for the audience that what she said was true. I made my way out of the ballroom and went to the gents, where I stood at the sink throwing cold water on my face.

I quickly pulled myself together and went back into the ballroom, ready to reclaim the microphone but Gail indicated to me that she was fine. Pretty soon we had a winner: a sixty-three-year-old school-dinner lady from

Mansfield who was not only a grandmother but a great grandmother. And a big round of applause please.

After the show I cleared the gear away with Gail so that the afternoon tea-dancing could start. I apologised to Gail for making a hash of the show.

'We've all dried on stage,' she said. 'It happens.'

'You were brilliant. Thanks for giving me a way out.'

'You're sweet!' she said.

Sweet, I thought. But was that all that had happened? I'd dried? Got stage fright? It felt like much more. It felt like something terrible was coming to get me. Some spirit of nemesis. We cleared away to leave the floor ready for the afternoon tea-dance and as I made my out I saw one of the barmen pointing in my direction. He was directing towards me a man in a scruffy beige suit. The man made his way to me across the ballroom floor, passing between campers who had commenced a slow foxtrot.

'David Barwise?' said the man. He had sandy hair and freckles, and a sad-looking face. His suit was crumpled and his collar was a little grubby. He had an offbeat air about him. He stared out at the world like a herring on a fishmonger's slab.

'Yes.'

'Could we sit down somewhere and have a chat? I'm Detective Constable Willis.'

'Of course,' I said. 'What's it about?'

He put a finger to his ear to suggest the ballroom music was making it difficult for him to hear, and he gestured that we go out into the lobby. There we found a couple of hard chairs and sat down. He pulled a small notebook out of his suit pocket. A pencil was inserted into the metal spring binding the pages of the notebook.

He took the pencil out of the spring and licked the lead tip. Then he leafed through the pages of the notebook, stopping when he appeared to find something interesting. His brow corrugated for a moment. Then he went back to flicking the pages until finally he arrived at a blank page. He laid the notepad on the table and wrote my name at the head of the page. 'It's about Terri Marchant.'

I blinked.

'She's gone missing.'

'Terri the cleaner?' I asked.

'Yes, Terri the cleaner.'

'Well you should ask her husband, Colin.'

'We can't find him.'

'Well, he got fired from here.'

'No he didn't. He got suspended. But he's gone missing, too, and normally that wouldn't be a cause for concern but Terri's brother says she's taken nothing with her. Nothing from the flat she shares with Colin, no money, no clothes. All her things have been left behind. Which is odd. Do you know where she might have gone?'

I kept flashing on the night we had dumped the condemned meat, and the fact that Colin had worn gloves while I hadn't. I wondered if I was being carefully set up. 'Why would I know?'

'Well, you're a friend of theirs. So people tell me.'

'I'm their friend? Who says that?'

'Look, you're a member of the same political party as Colin and Terri, right?'

'You're crazy. They are in the National Front. Or rather he is.'

'Look, I'm not interested in your politics, son. But I'm told you're in the same party.'

'No I'm not! He's like a fascist!'

'I've told you, son. I don't care if you're in the Chairman Mao party. It's of no interest to me.'

'Chairman Mao?' I said. 'I think that's the other end of the spectrum, isn't it?'

'You're not listening to me: I'm not here to talk politics. I just want to ask you if you have any thoughts about where she might be.'

'I haven't the faintest idea.'

'But you went to some meetings with her?'

'No. Who have you been talking to? I went to one. One meeting, but with Colin, not Terri. And I didn't even know what that was.'

'You went to a National Front meeting without knowing what it was?'

'Yes, that's exactly what I'm saying. Exactly.'

He smiled. If you could imagine a dead fish smiling that was how it looked. 'There are some National Front members in the police force. One or two. But I've never been to one of their meetings by accident.'

'Really? Well that's what happened.'

'So you're saying you don't know Terri Marchant.'

'No, I do know her. She used to work here.'

'Still does.'

'Yes. I mean I know her. And I know Colin, her husband. But I'm not his friend. He's a nasty piece of work.'

Willis chewed his thumbnail and stared hard at me for what seemed like a long time. 'Was there anything between you and Terri?'

'Why on earth would you suggest that?'

'Don't get excited.'

'Excited? I'm not excited.'

He smiled. 'Perhaps you have a guilty secret.'

'Is that a joke?'

'You tell me, David. You tell me.'

I was determined not to look away from his beady-eyed gaze. He weakened first. 'Right,' he said, 'is there anyone else I might talk to?'

'There are a couple of lads in the kitchen who were at that meeting you just referred to. Though Terri wasn't there. I don't think she's a party member.'

'She is.' Willis consulted his notebook. 'Pete Williams and Dan Hanson?'

'Yes. That's them.'

'I've already spoken to them. Anyone else?'

I thought about mentioning that Tony was a party member but I guessed Willis already knew that. 'No. What do you think has happened to her?'

Willis got up from the table. 'They had a violent row. After that, no one seems to have seen her, though according to the brother Colin is still around. So we're guessing.'

'Who is the brother?' I asked him. I didn't even know that Terri had a brother. I wondered if that was who had told DC Willis that Terri and I had a relationship. Perhaps Terri had confided in him.

'John Talbot. I think he's another of your blackshirt chums.'

I ignored the jibe. I remembered John Talbot. I'd met him when Colin introduced me to Norman Prosser at the meeting. He was also the man who'd seen me coming out of the pub with Nikki the day we'd gone into town. So that was Terri's brother. It was a tight circle.

A couple of young girls in backless tops and tiny shorts waddled by on high-heeled shoes carrying glasses of lager. Willis watched them go. Then he looked at me. 'You have an easy life,' he said. I didn't know whether it was a description or an instruction.

He nodded, almost microscopically. 'So you had nothing to do with her?'

'Who?'

'Terri.'

'Look,' I said, 'I barely knew her. If I were you I'd be asking myself who exactly suggested that I was her boyfriend when I've had nothing to do with her. Who would want to deflect your interest on to me, I mean. If I were a detective, that's the question I'd be asking myself.'

'I don't know why you're getting steamed up,' DC Willis said. 'I'm just trying to work out what's gone on here, that's all.'

'But you're saying I'm her boyfriend!'

'I'm not saying that at all. I'm just asking a few questions. I'm just looking for help. That's all. You're reacting like someone with a guilty conscience.'

'In that case,' I said, 'it must be possible for people who are not guilty to behave as if they are guilty. Have you thought of that?'

He looked at the page of his notebook on which he had written my name and nothing else. He closed the notebook, inserted the pencil back into the spiral binding and put it in his pocket. Then he stood up. 'I think about it all the time,' he said. 'Thank you for helping me.'

I watched him walk out of the ballroom lobby. I don't know where he went or who he spoke to after me. I stayed in my seat for a while afterwards, trying to think. The slow foxtrot in the ballroom had given way to a rumba.

Early evening I had to supervise the theatre for a screening of *The Sting*, a film with Robert Redford and Paul Newman that had come out a couple of years earlier to great acclaim. But because it was repeated every week I had by now seen it a good few times and it held no surprises.

Distracted, I made my way across the car park to the theatre. I should have been paying more attention to where I was going, but as I passed in front of one of the parked vehicles someone sounded a horn loud enough to make me jump out of the way. It was just Pinky, climbing out of his car with a lot of shopping bags.

'You're in a world of your own,' he said. He came over to me and pulled a carton of No. 6 cigarettes out of one of the bags and shoved it into my hands. 'Here, have one of these. Say nothing. You okay?'

'Sure,' I said. 'Sure.'

'You don't look okay.'

'No, I'm fine. Thanks for these.'

I went off to the cinema and did my usher's job. I sat away to the side of the auditorium, gnawing my hand. The fact is that I'd been trembling since my run-in with the police officer. My guts were in a state of riot. I was falling apart, and I still hadn't a clue about what had happened to Terri.

I knew I needed to get some help.

After the film was over I went to the Tavern singalong bar. It was there that you could find many of the kitchen staff drinking. I found Williams and Hanson, the two skinhead kitchen porters with whom I'd travelled to the

National Front meeting. Williams, the buck-toothed one who'd called me a poof, looked up from his pint and scowled.

I spoke to the other one, Hanson. I handed him the carton of No. 6 cigarettes. 'I came by these but I don't smoke. Split 'em with your mate.'

Williams looked baffled and showed me a bit more of his teeth, but Hanson was very glad to have the ciggies. 'Nice one, mate. Can I get you a pint?'

'Another time. I've got stuff to do.'

'No worries, mate.'

'I wondered if you'd seen Colin or his missus.'

Hanson turned to his pal. 'We ain't, have we? Ain't seen them for a good few days. His pal shook his head. It was clear they knew nothing. 'Been a copper here asking about them.'

'Right,' I said. 'Well, if you see Colin tell him I've got some ciggies for him, will you?' I knew perfectly well they wouldn't see him before I would. 'Or his missus. if you spot her or hear where she might be, give me a shout, will you?'

'No problem, mate.' Then, as I made to leave, Hanson raised a thumb in the air. 'Hey,' he said. 'You're all right, you are. Sound.' Then he turned to Williams. 'He's sound, he is.'

Williams said nothing. He lifted his pint to his lips and took a sip through his prominent teeth.

17

She completely done me in

I told Pinky that I had a doctor's appointment and that I'd need a couple of hours off.

'Haven't got the clap, have you?' Pinky said.

'I don't think so.'

'Joke,' he said. Then he looked away. 'At least I think it was a joke. We'll cover for you. See you later.'

I put my civvies on and took a green double-decker bus into town and visited a doctor's surgery that dealt with temporary workers from the holiday camps. I waited about half an hour in the reception area flicking between copies of *Vogue* and *Practical Wireless* magazines before finding a newspaper. A fourteen-year-old Sikh boy had been killed in a racially motivated attack in the Midlands and one of the senior figures in the National Front had made a statement saying, '*That's one step closer to a better country.*' I was still reading the report when a rather haughty secretary told me to go through to the surgery

A white-haired GP with half-moon specs and a white coat over a tweed jacket grunted that I should take a seat as he finished making notes in his last patient's records. He took so long over it I was able to observe his impressive, large troll-like ears. When he'd finished he sniffed and wheeled his chair round to face me. He said nothing, just peered across the top of his half-moon specs. He also had huge flappy jowls, like a species of bloodhound. I started to tell him that I was having trouble sleeping but he cut across me.

'Which camp are you working at?'

I started telling him and he opened my notes on the desk in front of him. He interrupted me again.

'It says here you're a student. What *kind* of student are you?'

I thought the question sounded hostile. I began to tell him what I was studying at college and he spoke across me for the third time.

'Well,' he said, 'what's your problem?'

I suddenly felt cross with the man. 'You're the doctor,' I said. 'I was hoping you'd be able to tell me.'

'Can't help you unless you tell me what's wrong with you, now can I?'

'I started telling you and you shut me up. Is this your idea of having fun?'

'You've woken up,' he said. 'You've come to life.'

I had a family GP at home. I nearly told this patronising old bastard what a nice, sensitive and compassionate human being my family GP was. Instead I tried again, carefully explaining that I hadn't been sleeping at all well, for some time, and that on some nights I was only getting maybe an hour or two.

'I'm not going to prescribe sleeping pills, if that's what you're thinking, sonny.'

'Did I say I wanted pills? I don't want pills, I want some help.'

His brittle manner seemed to relax. 'I get all sorts of

young men coming from these camps wanting all sorts of pills,' he said. 'Do you use drugs?'

'Emphatically not.' That one occasion in the archery hut might have caused me to blink.

He blinked back at me. 'Drink?'

'Moderately.'

He asked what I meant by that and I told him. He seemed satisfied. He asked if I was getting enough exercise. I described my daily routines and he concluded that wasn't a problem either.

'Are you anxious about anything at the moment?'

'I'm anxious all the time. For no reason.'

'For no reason?'

'I'm generally anxious. But I never used to be.'

'Roll your sleeve up. I'll check your blood pressure.'

Of course I went along with all of this. He told me that my blood pressure was perfectly fine. He looked in my ear with his otoscope and found no signs of anxiety there. He also actually got a hammer and tapped my knee to test my reflexes – something I only thought happened in comedy films. He listened to my breathing with his stethoscope.

'There's nothing obviously amiss,' he said. 'What happens when you try to go to sleep?'

'Nothing. I lie awake for long periods. Then if I fall asleep for a few minutes I get terrible nightmares.'

'Oh? What are the nightmares?'

I heard myself say, 'Things to do with children. And a man in a blue suit. It doesn't make much sense. I feel like I'm seeing ghosts. Obviously there's no such things as ghosts and obviously I know that but they keep coming. Plus I'm having dreams which are much more vivid than ordinary dreams though I expect that has something to do with the fact that I'm not getting enough REM sleep.'

'REM sleep?'

'Yes REM sleep. Rapid Eye Movement sleep. If you don't get REM sleep it sends you crazy and I'm not sleeping so I'm not getting REM sleep and it's vital for survival to the extent that prolonged REM sleep deprivation leads to death in experimental animals. I don't know if they've studied humans, I mean they probably have but I don't know of the conclusions. Of any studies. You probably know all this; you're a doctor.'

The doctor stroked his chin and regarded me steadily. 'Have you done anything you feel guilty about?'

'No.'

'What about your parents?'

'What about them?'

'Do you feel bad about leaving them? About having left them behind?'

'What's it got to do with them?'

'You'd be surprised. Look, it's not my area. I can refer you to a mental health practitioner.'

'Right. You're shuffling me along.'

Now it was his turn to sound cross. 'Look, I'll prescribe some mild sleeping pills. But it's not going to become a habit, so don't think it is. I'll give you four.'

'Four? Four pills?'

He looked over the top of his spectacles at me then scribbled on his pad at super speed before tearing off the top copy. 'Cut out the drink altogether. No coffee either. Take one an hour before bedtime and then go for a walk before turning in. That's what I do when I have trouble sleeping.'

I thanked him and I got up to go. As I was leaving I

heard him say, maybe to me, maybe to the closing door. 'We're all anxious. What is there not to be anxious about?'

I got back in time for lunch at the canteen. Before I went in to eat, one of the campers tugged at my sleeve. He wanted me to line up with his family for a photograph. The man held up his instamatic and I quickly slapped on my happy face for them.

It was one of the features of being a Greencoat. The holidaymakers always wanted you to be photographed with them. I might as well have been dressed up in a cuddly bear suit for all they knew of me. Would my smiling face define the holiday for them? Would I help to fill in a hole in their memories? Even people to whom I'd never spoken pulled me into their snapshots. I often wondered what they would think when they reviewed these photographs, maybe years later. Would they only see the bright smile? Or would they recognise a troubled young man behind it all? But the photograph was a detail in a holiday story, where I was a theatre prop, a bit of scaffolding on the stage. I crossed from my story briefly into theirs and back again.

I joined Nikki and Gail in the canteen queue and we all filed past the hatch to get our steak and kidney pie.

'You all right then?' Nikki said when we sat down. 'Pinky said you had to go to the doctor's.'

'No secrets there then.'

'Have you got the clap?' Gail said.

'What???'

Gail covered her mouth with her fingertips. 'It's what everyone says around here. Whenever you say you're going to the doctor's, I mean.'

'You haven't, have you?' Nikki said.

'No I bloody haven't.'

'So why the doctor's?' said Nikki.

'I can't sleep,' I said.' It's getting me down.'

When Gail rose from the table to get her dessert at the serving hatch, Nikki waited for her to move out of earshot, touched the back of my hand with a long fingernail and said, 'I could make you sleep.'

I didn't know what to say. I think I coloured.

'You sure you're all right?' Nikki said.

'I'm fine,' I insisted.

That afternoon I used the public telephone in the kiosk outside the theatre to phone long-distance. I don't know, maybe it was something the doctor had said about feeling guilty about my parents. I had a pile of coins in my hand ready to force them into the spring-loaded slot whenever the rapid-pip signal demanded to be fed.

'You haven't forgotten us, then,' said my mother.

'Who are you?' I joked feebly.

I answered the usual questions: where I did my shopping, how was I managing with my laundry, did I know that Tesco's had a giant size box of washing powder on offer at half price. I squirted another coin into the trap and then she passed me on to Ken. I asked him how was business and he told me that he'd had to lay off a couple of men who had been with him a long time. I was sympathetic. I knew the men. When a country moves into recession, building is one of the first things to be hit. I expressed the hope that they would find other work and my dad said that they hadn't much chance of that what with all the wogs taking up the jobs.

I admit I over-reacted. I heard myself calling him

some names – interrupted when I had to shove another coin in the box to complete the list I had in store for him – and to his credit he just took it. Somehow we salvaged the conversation and turned it to safe things: football, the drought. He asked me if I needed any money. I told him I was fine.

'Ken, can you put my mum back on the line?'

When she came back on I immediately said, 'Mum, why did my dad come here?'

There was a long silence at the other end. Then she said, 'What is it you think you are doing there, David? What do you think you're doing in that awful place?'

'I'm working,' I said. 'I just want to know why he was here. I have the photograph. I know he was here.'

I heard a muffled conversation at the other end, then Ken spoke again. 'You've upset her, David.'

'Then we're all upset,' I said callously.

'David,' I heard him say, 'David.' But his voice was overridden by rapid pips in my ear. I had some more coins in my hand, but in the few seconds I had before cut-off I said, 'I'm out of change, Ken. Tell Mum I love her.'

'David—'

The line went dead.

As I put the receiver back on its cradle I became aware of another man standing a few paces away, waiting, as I thought, to use the phone after me. I stepped aside so he could get to the kiosk, but he held out an arm to obstruct me. 'Can I have a word?'

I recognised him. It was the man who had nodded to me outside the pub the time I'd spent the day in town with Nikki, after seeing the lion. I'd met him originally, with his head of black hair swept back and fixed in place with Brylcreem, at the National Front meeting. It was John Talbot, the man that DC Willis had revealed was Terri's brother.

'It's about Terri,' the man said.

'Oh yes?'

'You know she's my sister, don't you?' Though this man was taller and rough-featured, there was a resemblance though not one you would have seen if he hadn't mentioned it. 'She's gone missing.'

'Yes, the police came here asking about her.'

'Police,' he spat. 'Useless.'

I nodded.

'Did you tell them anything?'

'Anything? I don't know anything.'

'You don't know anything about what's gone off?'

'Gone off?'

'Yes. Something's gone off.'

'What do you mean?' I said.

'It's not like her. She's left everything. I smell a rat.' He looked at me hard. I had the notion he was saying to me that he was looking at the thing he could smell. I had to summon all my willpower not to look away. 'The only people she had anything to do with here was Colin, and you.'

'Me? Have you spoken to Terri about me?'

He nodded. Then he wagged a finger in my face. 'There's something not right here. Not right.'

I shook my head slightly. I was trying to model my features into an expression of concern and bafflement at the same time.

'You're a friend of Tony's, aren't you?'

'Tony? The Tony here at the camp? The children's entertainer?'

'You know who I mean.'

'Well, yes. I mean, yes, he's a friend.'

He took a step away from me. He was still tapping his finger at the empty air. 'Be assured I'll be back with more questions. Be assured.'

Then he turned and left me.

I was falling apart. Isolated. I had to know that Terri was all right and that Colin hadn't done something terrible. But I was also re-examining my feelings for her. I suspected that she'd misled me about a great many things. She hadn't actually lied outright but by cleverly editing any information she had given me she had painted a partial picture of herself. Colin's story of rescuing her from prostitution didn't match up with hers, and for some reason I believed Colin's version. She hadn't even told me she had a brother. Just as Colin had led me down one garden path, so she had led me down another. The garden of hate and the garden of love; and I found no succour in either.

Meanwhile I had to go round organising these trivial and inconsequential – not to say silly – activities when all the time I felt like some kind of horrific dragnet was closing in. That night I was on the roster to run the lights in the nightclub. Normally I stayed sober while I was still on duty, but drinking took the edge off my anxieties and stopped certain thoughts from bubbling to the surface. There were three acts on that night: Tony put them onstage and took them off while I dealt with the lights. During the first interval I sat on a high stool at the bar with Tony, when Nikki turned up looking like she was dressed for the London Palladium Royal Command Performance.

'Look at that man-trap,' he said, tapping my thigh.

She was stunning. She wore a short black cocktail dress, opaque black tights and black heels. She had a white flower – maybe it was a gardenia or a magnolia – pinned in her hair, which was tied back. I don't think I'd seen her face made-up before that night. So pretty was she that her natural look served her beautifully on most occasions, but here she was looking like a cover girl from a magazine. Heads turned all over the small room. If she saw it, she made out she didn't.

She made a bee-line for Tony and he received her with great theatricality, kissing her on either cheek, hamming it up for the many eyes –male and female – tracking her movements. He loved it. After all, they were celebrities of this tiny holiday camp world. She stepped over to me and gave me a peck on the cheek, drawing me into their aura. I found her a stool and Tony made an extravagant gesture of ordering Sidecar cocktails, a drink I'd never even heard of.

While we fussed around and Tony made sure she got to sit between us, the cocktails arrived in glasses sugar-frosted at the rim and with tiny paper umbrellas. I know it was a small holiday camp on an unfashionable stretch of English coastline but the way people stared at us made me feel like I was in a Hollywood VIP lounge amid star company. Somehow, inside the club we had become spot-lit by the effects of glamour. I don't know what was in the cocktail but I drank it too fast and Tony ordered up another round.

Luca Valletti was topping the bill and after midnight when he came on to do his set I was already feeling a little woozy. I'd noticed that Luca had stayed in his dressing room when he might have been expected to join us out front at least for a few minutes. Tony, whose tongue had also been loosened by the alcohol, or perhaps excited by Nikki's show-stoppingly glamorous appearance, said some unprofessional things about his Italian co-performer. He described him as aloof and stuck-up, whereas I didn't blame him for being distant after the way Colin had roughed him up.

Anyway, I had to stay focused to finish my lighting job. Luca soared through his repertoire and like the pro he was, he gave the audience a few words about what each song meant to him personally. 'It means a few extra quid,' Tony whispered in my ear as he was passing. *My Fair Lady* had recently had a revival and Luca sang 'On the Street Where You Live' but before going into it he affected a cockney accent to repeat a little bit of business from the stage play. It got a laugh anyway. His beautiful tenor lit up the room as he sang some unlikely words about how *she done him in* when she told him of her *father and the gin.*

I managed to operate the lights without mishap, despite being a little tipsy. When it came to his barn-storming 'Autumn Leaves' I opened with green and gold gels, subtly diffused the colours and closed out with red and gold at end. I did it perfectly – to my own relief – but something strange happened on the penultimate line of the lyric. Luca looked at me, poised at the side of the lighting rig. I don't know what he saw. Maybe I was way over-focused on him, trying to make sure that my tipsiness didn't screw up the operation of the gels. Maybe I was staring too plain hard at him. But he failed to hit a note.

I'm not sure whether the audience even noticed. But when you've heard a singer repeat the same song in rehearsals and in performance several times over, you hear it immediately. It didn't matter. The boozy audience rewarded him with rapturous applause. The Italian tenor took his bow, and he left.

Unusually, Luca didn't come over to say goodnight to Tony, Nikki and myself at the bar. Normally, he made a point of thanking me for the lights, and thanking Mike on the piano. Mike the Beatle-haircut pianist came and had a drink with us and when I got a moment I said, 'Did Luca miss a note?'

'Luca never misses a note,' Mike said. Then he arched his eyebrows and put a finger to his lips as if to say shush!

I remembered the sleeping pill I'd got from the doctor. It was a Mandrax. The doctor had told me to take it an hour before turning in to avoid tossing and turning in bed, so I swallowed it discreetly and washed it down with a Sidecar and a glug of Federation ale.

We stumbled out of the club. Mike and Tony said goodnight and they kissed Nikki extravagantly on either cheek, leaving me alone with her.

'Night's young,' she said. 'Shall we go and sit on the beach?'

'It's two in the morning,' I said.

'But it's a beautiful evening. And it's cool and fresh for a change! Don't be a party pooper.'

The fact was I didn't want to go back to my bed. I was still nursing a dread of what nightmares sleep would bring. What's more, Colin never seemed far away. I felt like he was waiting for the moment I dipped below the surface of sleep.

We went up the sea wall. Nikki as usual wanted to go down onto the sand. She took off her sling-back heels and held the straps between her fingers.

'You'll wreck your tights.'

'That's a point,' she said. She dropped her shoes and without taking her eyes from me she hitched up her skirt and slid her tights down her tanned legs, stepping out of them. She opened her handbag, stuffed her tights inside and then laced her elegant fingers through the straps of her shoes. 'Come on.'

We picked our way down through the sand. I was stumbling a bit. We got away from the lights of the camp and settled down near the water's edge. Though it was a balmy night the temperature had cooled by a degree or two, and the sea was in a more aggressive mood. The waves were foaming, and they were rearing and whipping at the shore. Once again I saw that wrinkle of phosphorescence and it made an illusion like white snakes rearing and spitting. It was exciting and alarming and it said that the weather was changing.

I recalled Tony on one of my first days at the camp saying, 'We've had the party and it's time to pay the cabbie.' But the voice I heard in my head was Colin's gravelly cockney accent, not Tony's. I felt woozy.

'You okay?' Nikki said.

'Sure.'

'It's a bit chillier this evening, isn't it?' She wriggled closer to me and when she'd got comfortable she opened the clasp on her handbag and produced a half-pint bottle of vodka. I remember thinking that I'd just taken the Mandrax and that I shouldn't. I was already light headed from the cocktails and beer I'd drunk in the nightclub. But when she unscrewed the cap and offered me the bottle I took a swig anyway.

What happened next?

I lost my soul, that's what happened next.

Imagine a giant advertising billboard with a photograph of what happened next. Now tear off, at random, three tiny fingernail strips, thin fragments and carry them away with you as the rest of the photograph goes dark. Now lay them out on a lawn and try to figure out all the bits that go in between.

That's what I've got. I'm a dog howling at the moon. I'm a lion-tamer trying to control the waves. I'm staring at a little boy who is holding hands with a man in a sparkling blue suit at the water's edge.

I don't know how much of Nikki's vodka I drank but I suspect that I was hell-bent. People say, oh I've no idea how I got so drunk. Really.

But there is a gap in my memory, and then I have my head up inside Nikki's skirt and I am removing her knickers with my teeth. She is laughing. And then I am moving across the sand on all fours, barking like a dog and I look up and I see the moon and I howl. The howl is so fierce it frightens the moon. It goes behind a small cloud. For a moment I am a werewolf, all blood and sinew.

I know there is a big chunk of time missing because in my next torn fragment I am stark naked and standing next to the tide, shouting at the sea. The mood of the sea becomes worse, angrier. The surf boils and the waves whip and slap at the sand and retreat fast. It wants to get me. It wants to strike me, but it is afraid of me. I know it is afraid of me. The sea hisses and a huge wave coils in the air and paws at me but I duck away from its claws. It has become a lion. The sea has become a lion like the one I saw in town. It roars, it hisses, it spits, it growls but it can't come any nearer. It bares its teeth and it arches its back, but I dance backwards as it lashes another watery paw at me and now I know I can control it. I have magical hands. If I raise my right hand in the air a wave moves up, up, higher following the movement of my arm as if on a string until I am ready to slap it down hard. I can do the same with my other hand. I can conduct the sea, like a man with a baton before an orchestra. No. I am a lion-tamer. I have tamed the watery deep. I will put my head in its mouth.

I hear Nikki come up behind me. She's also a little drunk. 'What are you doing?'

There's another breach in time. Now the sea has gone quiet again. It is perfectly calm, like oil. I am standing at the water's edge and I am looking at a man and a boy. They gaze out to sea with eyes of clear-glass. The man's suit is blue and it darts with watery phosphorescence. The suit is beautiful, alive, quivering like the scales of a fish. The man and the boy hold each other's hand. Their faces are dark, but their teeth are blue in the eerie light. Slowly the man begins to dissolve. His form becomes like wet sand and he slowly melts into the sand itself, and the boy starts to cry. The man liquefies in front of me, leaving only an empty suit. His glass-eyes are the last thing to go. The water laps at the empty suit, almost as if feeding on it, until the suit itself is covered by wet sand. The boy lies on the sand, crying, scraping at the residual form with his fingernails.

Nikki is behind me, trying to pull me away. 'David, it's just a log,' she says. 'Just a log.'

I look again and there is no boy. It is indeed just a wooden log, washed up by the tide. But I can't shake the feeling that in another world it really is a heartbroken boy, so I take the log and I tenderly lift it – him – up onto my shoulder. I stagger up the beach, as if I want to take it – him – home with me. I don't know why. But it's too heavy and the rough wood scrapes my naked skin and embeds splinters in me. I let the log fall to the beach.

Then there is a big gap again. A big, deep darkness.

I was woken in the morning by a sharp tug on my cock. I had a horrible thought that Nobby or even Colin had jumped on me but when I fought myself awake I found Nikki astride of me. She took my hard cock out of her mouth and blinked at me.

'Mornin'' she said. Then she parked her long hair behind an ear before licking and sucking me again.

I felt groggy, disoriented and hungover. The pleasure of Nikki playing with me in this way was counteracted by the headache it triggered. I wasn't going to stop her. But anyway I couldn't even speak to protest had I wanted to; bad as I felt about this infidelity to Terri I was unable to resist.

Nikki eased herself up and straddled me, and guiding the shaft of my cock with one hand she sank herself on to me. She gasped. She was a little dry. It took my breath away, and hers too. Her black pupils dilated, searching my own eyes as she lowered herself down the full length of me. She sat back and put her hands on her hips, rocking me right inside her. Then she yelped.

Someone in the next cubicle along banged on the wall and shouted incomprehensible words. Nikki giggled and put her fingers in her mouth to stifle her own cries. Someone was still thumping on the flimsy wall, making it shake. It only made her laugh out loud and fuck me harder.

In all of this I had a sudden flash of the blue phosphorescent light rippling on the waves and of moonlight foaming on the glass bottle of vodka in Nikki's hands. Fragments of the night's events came back to me.

When we were finished she collapsed on me. I lay in a tangle of her raven-black hair. It made me think of the dark woods of fairy-tale; her sweat and the scent of her all over me. As we lay there breathing hard I tried to remember more about the things that happened during the night.

'You okay?' she said in my ear.

'Yeah.'

'Hungover?'

'Very.'

'I thought I was never going to get you back here.'

'Why?'

'Don't you remember any of it?'

'Some.'

She reached over to the cabinet and picked up the small travel clock I kept there. She sighed. 'I've got to get back to my place, somehow in these clothes. What a giveaway. I need to get my Greencoat outfit and get back here for the briefing.' I waited for her to get up. Instead she shimmied her way up my body, pressing her nipples against mine. Then she soul-kissed me.

'Stay here,' I mumbled through mashed lips.

'I don't want to get up, but I have to.' She hauled herself out of bed and found her dress on the floor. She checked herself in the small mirror behind the door.

'Jesus, I'm a wreck. God, I need a shower but I'm not taking one here.'

Well, her hair was a thrilling mess. Her eye make-up was smudged, too. But as she stood there naked, holding her dress in one hand and running her fingers through her dark hair she looked wonderfully happy. Her tawny skin glowed.

'You look beautiful, Nikki.'

She pulled her dress on over her head and wriggled into it and then she climbed into her heels. 'I can't even find my knickers. They're probably still on the beach, you animal. You threw them in the water.'

'I did?'

'Yes. And lots of things beside.'

'Oh?'

'I got a bit scared of you.' She looked at me oddly. 'A tiny bit.'

'What happens now?' I said.

'What happens now?' She held up her left hand. 'You put a ring on this finger, that's what happens now. Joke. No, I've had my way with you and I'm satisfied. It's done. Thanks. Ta-ra and all that. No, I'm still joking! Look at your face!'

What I wanted to ask her was: are we a secret? Are we an item? Are we open to the others? This wasn't just because that had been the absolute pattern with Terri. Even asking seemed such a statement, a declaration. The question itself seemed to contain a promise. She sat on the bed and leaned in for a kiss, slipping her hand under the sheets and running her fingers along my thigh. Then she quickly withdrew. 'No, I have to go. You need to get moving, too. I'll see you at the briefing.'

Nikki went to the door, unlocked it and opened it just a crack. She peered through the gap and then opened it a little further so she could check up and down the corridor. When she decided the coast was clear she blew me a kiss and slipped out, closing the door behind her. Almost instantly I heard another door open and someone else stumble into the corridor. Bad luck. I heard a loud wolf whistle.

I knew her head would be held high. 'Good morning,' I heard her say loudly, in her bold Yorkshire accent. There was an ironic arch to her voice and her heels clicked noisily as she made her way out.

18

Causing no disturbance around the Jack

There was a morose mood amongst the Entertainments staff when I got to the auditorium for the morning briefing. Pinky sat on the piano stool at the edge of the stage with his hands in his pockets and his socked-and-sandaled feet crossed in front of him. The rest of the staff sat in the front row of the auditorium facing him. They had been joined by another figure in a blue blazer who was perhaps responsible for the mood.

It was the office manager – the man with the pencil-thin moustache who had fed breadcrumbs to sparrows on my first day. He also sat in the front row with his legs crossed and with his hands in his lap.

Nobby started on me as soon as I walked in. He'd surpassed himself this morning. He was wearing his striped blazer, apparently without a shirt. His scruffy, grey trainers looked like newsprint dissolving in the rain and in contrast to Pinky he wore no socks at all. 'Christ, look at the state of you! Dragged through a hedge backwards forwards sideways and head over heels or what and—'

'Give it a break, Nobby,' Pinky said sourly. It was the nearest I'd seen Pinky come to introducing a disciplinary measure.

Nobby was about to reply; then thought better of it. 'Anyone seen Nikki?'

Tony looked at me pointedly, folded his arms, then very slowly turned his head one hundred and eighty degrees away from me.

Gail, who shared a room with her, spoke up. 'She'll be on her way. She's a bit off colour this morning.'

Pinky blinked at her.

'Women's problems,' Gail said.

'There's been a few complaints,' Pinky said. He gazed glumly at the carpet and paused so that we could take it all in. He snorted, like an old coal miner putting a pinch of snuff up his nose. 'Things not well organised. Equipment not laid out properly. Chaotic activities. Lack of attention to detail. People—'

The swing doors opened and Nikki bustled in. 'Sorry I'm behind,' she said, taking up a seat next to Tony.

'Here's the hedge,' Nobby said.

Nikki looked at Nobby. 'What?

'People turning up late for programme duties,' Pinky said. Poor Nikki, who was normally never late for anything. 'Certain activities not even being run. Appearance and personal hygiene. Nobby, you talk about other people but look at the state of you. You better get back to your room and get a shirt on. You're not going out like that. Get some clean socks on while you're at it.'

Nobby's jaw went into overdrive. 'Right right right! You boys get me a shirt that fits not a piece of sail cloth or a winding sheet or a three sheets to the wind sheet one that actually fits as per collar size as per described instead of a boy scout's fuckin' jamboree tent and I will—'

'Just get a shirt, Nobby, you're a disgrace,' said Pinky.

'I'll tell you what is a disgrace, shall I? Shall I? Shall I?'

'You know what?' Pinky said. 'You and I, we've reached the end of the road, mate. End of the road.'

'So what you gonna do? Fire me? Eh? Eh? Eh?'

The man in the blue blazer stood up. 'Come and have a word in my office, Nobby.'

Nobby was on his feet. 'You know what you lot are? All of you? Blackshirt fascists. That's what you are, Blackshirts. Sad little Nazi running-dogs. Night of the fuckin' long knives, is it? I'll fuckin' spill the beans. I will, don't you worry.'

'Come and have a word in my office, Nobby. There's no need for all this.'

Nobby turned to us. 'Are any of you gonna speak up for me? Are you? Any of you?'

There was silence.

'There's your answer,' Tony said. 'And to be fair, you've been told about it time and time enough. You've had plenty of warnings, Nobby.'

'Come to my office, Nobby, let's have a talk.'

Nobby stood with his hands on his hips. He turned and looked at me full on. His eyes were wet. Getting no response from me he shuffled to face Nikki. Then Gail. It was a serious situation but there was something comical about him shuffling from one position to another in his filthy, broken trainers, getting in everyone's face. Finally, he stormed out of the theatre, still babbling, followed by the personnel manager.

We all sat in silence for a couple of minutes after he'd gone. Then Pinky got to his feet. 'Well, I don't know about you lot but I've got work to do.'

He left Tony in charge of deploying us. Nobby's responsibilities were reassigned. We were expected to double up. I asked if this was a permanent arrangement or whether Nobby would be replaced.

'I don't think,' Tony said rather sharply, 'that this is the time to be forming a Trade Union, do you?'

I never saw Nobby again after that.

I didn't get to work with Nikki that morning but I did see her for lunch. Gail joined us, and that suppressed the conversation we wanted to have. But when Gail returned her plates at the hatch I said, 'Tony seemed to know already. Nobby certainly knew, too, though I don't know how.'

Nikki's brow wrinkled. 'Would there be any particular reason why it would have to be a big secret?'

The reason was, of course, Terri. I took a big breath. 'No.'

'I mean I'm not proposing to hand out a press-release to everyone, but what we're doing is not illegal or against any rules that I know about.'

'No.'

'If they find out, they find out.'

'Yes.'

'Only I would like to be able to hold your hand occasionally in public.' She touched the back of my wrist. I must have flinched. She took her hand away and sighed. 'You do want to carry on seeing me, don't you?'

'Of course. 'I'm "seeing" you now.'

'You know what I mean.'

The truth was I did want to carry on 'seeing' her. I wanted to see her naked in my arms right then, right at that moment if you want the truth of it. It wasn't that

I had no interest in her. It was just that I felt terrible about how Terri would take this, assuming she was still alive. I felt an obligation to work through this whole thing and find out what had happened. In reality, Nikki was a relief to have around. She brought a lightness of spirit, whereas Terri was a brooding presence. The demons of a bad history weighed down her shoulders, through no fault of her own, it seemed to me. All the madness of what had happened between us was now thrown into stark relief whenever I thought about Terri, and I knew it always would be. If I'd been dragging chains, Nikki had come along and unlocked them.

'I do want to see you Nikki, yes. I want to be with you. I want to pull your skirt off, right now.'

'There are rules against that, I know.'

'Can we just keep it ... low profile? I mean like you say, we don't have to advertise it, do we?'

'Okay. If that's what you want.'

Gail came back to the table. 'What are you two love-birds up to?'

After lunch I made my way to the bowling green, past the fortune-teller's white caravan, to organise the old boys in their games of crown-green bowls. Before the backstage theatre events I'd been learning from the old boys about how to handle the woods and how to use the bias on the bowl to make it run in a curved path. Now that any and every distraction was essential to the balance of my mind I was determined to try to put my mind to it again.

I'd been astonished at how many forms of delivery there were in simply rolling a bowl along the grass to get close to the jack. But then nothing in life seemed simple any more, not even bowling. 'Draw' shots aim at causing no disturbance around the jack. A 'finger peg' is initially aimed to the right of the jack, and curves in to the left. A 'fire' or 'strike' uses speed and force to knock either the jack or a specific bowl out of play. A 'block' shot is deliberately short to stop an opponent's draw shot.

These elderly men were full of cunning. They enjoyed teaching me all their tricks – or had before I'd suddenly lost interest. One of the old fellows, a retired coal miner, hailed me. 'Has 'ta played before?' he said, puffing on his briar tobacco pipe.

'Once or twice,' I said.

Many men of retirement age like to teach young men. They know that this life is fleeting and time is limited. They want to leave something behind. It was hard to keep my mind on draws and blocks, and on finger pegs and fires, but I did my best. The old fellow with the pipe was gently trying to improve my delivery style. He complained that I had no follow-through. And he told me that I should extract every advantage from having bowled the target-jack.

When I said I didn't know what he meant by that he took his pipe out of his mouth and rolled his eyes. 'Tha bowled the jack, so tha knows the weight and length and curve tha wants to bowl t'wood, don't thee? Tha's still got the memory of it in tha body, han't tha?'

I felt a sudden jolt, like when you crack a knuckle, but somewhere in my brain. I stood there thinking about what he'd just said. *You've still got the memory of it in your body, haven't you?* I looked at him like he was a puffing Buddha and he'd just given me a koan to figure out. He was right. Somewhere in my body was the exact memory of the delivery of the jack, and therefore I should be able to summon it to mind and replicate it. Somewhere in my body lay other memories, too.

I was aware that he was waiting for me to make my play. I bowled and got pretty damn close to the jack. The old boy puffed on his pipe, content with me. Then when I bowled my second, I'd lost it again.

Apropos of nothing at all he said, 'Did you know there was a lion in town?'

'Yes, I've seen it.'

He took his pipe out of his mouth again. 'What? Tha saw it?'

'Yes. You can see it every Saturday.'

'What's tha talking about?'

'The lion. They take it for a walk every Saturday.'

'They won't take it for a walk now,' he said. 'They shot it.'

'What? Who shot it?'

'The police. It killed a dog and attacked a little girl. They shot it.'

'When was this?'

'This morning. It had got loose and was causing mayhem in the town.'

I realised we had been talking at cross-purposes. 'Was it a lion from the circus?'

'Well, I daresay it hadn't come from the Town Hall.'

'That's a tragedy,' I said.

'Tha can't have a killer lion on the loose. Imagine that poor little girl!'

'What little girl?'

'The one it attacked.'

'No,' I said. 'I mean you're right.' I picked up a 'wood', weighing the polished resin in my hand.

'Now then,' he said. 'Head down, eyes still. And always follow through.'

19

A bit of street-fighting is in order and would help

I fell in love with Nikki, plain and simple. It may seem unfeeling to say so, but I thought less and less about Terri. Neither had I heard from or seen Colin since the night we'd driven up to the mine shaft at Black Bank. I could only speculate; and, since I didn't like what I speculated, I even stopped doing that.

In some ways I found it easy to blame Terri for what had happened. It was convenient to convince myself that I had been the one seduced. The truth was that with Nikki it was utterly different. I was allowed to display my happiness at being with her instead of creeping around in secrecy, hiding every smile and disguising every remark.

But I wasn't allowed to forget her completely. One early evening I was making my way towards the theatre with a couple of boxes of candy rock in my arms when four men stepped out of the narrow alley between the theatre and the offices. One of the men was Terri's's brother. Williams and Hanson, the two knaves from the kitchen who had been at the National Front meeting were also there. The fourth was a burly figure I'd never seen before. He was kitted out in the orthodox skinhead uniform of Sta-Prest trousers, Doc Martens and braces over a neat, short-sleeved Ben Johnson shirt.

'A word if you don't mind,' said Terri's brother.

None of them were smiling. 'I'll just get rid of these boxes.'

The unknown skinhead stepped behind me.

'We'll just be a minute,' said Talbot. He motioned that I should lead the way down the alley.

I tried to look over my shoulder but the skinhead crowded me. 'What's it about?' I knew it had to be about Terri.

'That's why I want a word.'

The burly skinhead was still breathing on my neck, and I was flanked by Williams and Hanson. Williams had his usual goofy smirk on offer but Hanson, the one to whom I'd given a carton of cigarettes didn't seem to want to make eye contact. My options were limited. I thought I could either walk down the alley under my own steam or get dragged down there. I opted for the former.

When we got behind the buildings I stood with my back to the wall, still holding the two cartons of candy rock. The meaty skinhead folded his arms, pushing his fists behind his biceps as if to make them look bigger.

'What's in the boxes?' said Williams.

'So what's this about?'

Williams reached across and took the lid off the top carton, exposing the cellophane-wrapped gaily-striped sticks of rock.

Terri's brother stepped in between us. 'You're a Leavisite.'

I squinted at him but said nothing. I hadn't a clue what he was talking about. What had this got to do about Terri? The only Leavisites I'd ever heard of were followers of the flowery literary critic F. R. Leavis; I knew in my bones that Terri's brother hadn't got me up against the wall to discuss Literature.

'You're Colin's man, aren't you?'

'In what sense?'

'Don't deny it.'

Hanson piped up for the first time. 'He's sound; I've told you.' He glanced at me and then he looked away. He was embarrassed by all of this; I was grateful I'd bought him with a carton of cigarettes.

Terri's brother held up a large, putty-coloured finger to silence Hanson. 'If I get a scrap of proof of what's gone on: you, Tony, Colin, Broomfield ... all the lot of you. It won't be a little chat next time. Do you understand me?'

I was about to tell him he may just as well have been speaking in Urdu for all the sense I made of it, but given his affiliations I thought better of it. But I couldn't say no I don't understand you, any more than I could implicate myself in all of this by saying yes I understand you, so I remained silent.

After a moment, Williams swatted the cartons out of my hands. The cheerful sticks of rock spilled across the concrete path, many of them breaking in the process. Williams bared his teeth at me, but the burly skinhead closed his eyes. Hanson too turned away in shame.

'Pick the fucking things up and put them back in the box,' Terri's brother said to Williams with barely repressed fury.

I looked hard at Williams. Imagine, I thought, being a person of such low instincts that you are an embarrassment to your fascist friends. Williams slammed the broken kiddie's rock back into the carton. Terri's brother led them away up the alley in single file.

I was still shaking when I dumped the broken rock and went hunting for Tony. He had a show that evening with the rest of the troupe and I was pretty sure I'd find him in his dressing room preparing. I tapped lightly on his door. With Tony you never knew with which voice he would answer. He used to have a ventriloquist act – he was a former vent in stage jargon – with dummies. You might get one of his vent voices. There was a squeaky schoolboy and a crusty old drunk and other things. This evening I got squeaky schoolboy. I pushed the door open.

Tony was at his mirror and he was blacking up. There was part of the show where he and another singer painted their faces and wore straw boaters and sang Al Jolson songs.

'Come in,' he said, still in his squeaky schoolboy voice, 'sit down if you can find a seat.'

There was a stool. I had to move his boater and hang it on a hook before sitting down. 'What's a Leavisite?'

Tony widened his eyes and leaned towards the mirror, gently stroking black over his right eyelid. Then he did the other eyelid. Finally he said, 'Who have you been talking to then?'

'I've been reading.'

'Reading what?'

'Pamphlets.'

Tony sighed and stared at his black self in the mirror. 'Leavis wants to take the party in one direction. Others don't.'

'Is there any need to go into such fine detail?'

Tony turned on his rotating stool. 'That's one thing this place has taught you: withering sarcasm. Good.

223

All right then. Leavis wants a more popular front. Recruit the shire Tories who are our natural friends; pull in a few MPs, members of the Monday Club who want supported repatriation; bring in more of the working classes, because they're the ones who are going to get rained on over the next few years. Who speaks for them? The fucking Labour Party led by privately educated baby-faces fresh out of Oxford and Cambridge? You're a working-class lad, are you happy with that?

'It's wide open. But to do that we have to distance the party from the Paki-bashers and the idiots who still think Adolf Hitler was a jolly good chap. We'll fight the elections. Exploit the media and go with the democratic process.'

'And you agree with that way forward?'

'Broadly.'

'You're a Leavisite?'

'Yes. I think if we don't go that way, the Tories will outflank us at the next election. They'll lurch to the right, steal our clothes and we'll lose our momentum.'

'And the other mob?'

'The other mob want to recruit more soldiers from the football terraces. Get a bit of streetfighting going with the coons and the commies.'

'Rivers of blood?'

'Now as a scholar, David, you should know Enoch Powell never used that phrase. What he did say was "like the Roman, I seem to see the River Tiber foaming with much blood". He was quoting Virgil.'

'But it's blackshirts against brownshirts, right? Who's going to win?'

He started to sponge his face again. 'Can't say. By

which I mean I don't know. But if we lose, the Tories win. Whose side are you on, David?'

'Where did Colin and Terri stand in all of this?'

'You have been talking to someone, haven't you?'

'I'm interested.'

'Colin's with us. It's getting a bit tasty. The other day at a meeting in London, some idiot threw a punch at Leavis. Which was a very silly thing to do.'

'Why?'

'Leavis has a lot of loyal supporters and minders. Like Colin. And Colin threw a few punches back. So now he's got people after him and he's gone to ground.'

'Was Terri with him when all this kicked off?'

'As far as I know.'

'Is she in danger?'

Tony threw his sponge down in irritation. 'What do you think we are, son? The mafia? We're not uncivilised people despite what all those pot-smoking lefty university lecturers have been telling you. Though I will say that there are a few freelancers in the party who were very cross with Colin; and these types are not always easy to control. What the hell is it to you anyway?'

'Since I went to that meeting I've been interested.'

Tony laughed. 'Don't bullshit me, son. If you were interested you wouldn't be getting your leg over a Paki—'

'She's lovely,' I said flatly. 'And her mother is from Guyana, which is about as geographically distant from Pakistan as you can get.'

'Can't you find yourself a nice white girl?'

At the time it didn't seem odd to me that a man with a blacked-up face was asking me this question.

'By the way,' Tony said. 'One of your long-haired

gits. Eric Clapton. You like that sort of thing, don't you?'

Clapton was a guitar-hero of mine. He played black man's music, rocked up for a white audience. He was the sort of figure I looked up to. 'Yes.'

'He's one of us.'

'I don't believe it.'

Tony reached for a newspaper, flipped a couple of pages and folded the paper neatly before handing it to me to read. The report stated that Eric Clapton had treated his audience in Birmingham to a five-minute foul-mouthed tirade saying that 'wogs' and 'coons' should be thrown out of the country. I put the paper down and looked hard at the man in the make-up.

'And that David Bowie: he said, "Britain is ready for a fascist leader." Though we wouldn't have the fucking poof in the Party.'

I handed the newspaper back to Tony. I had no words left. Nothing. I turned to go.

'It's coming,' Tony said. 'People are waking up. People are choosing sides, David.'

I closed the door behind me. But behind it I heard him add, in his ventriloquist schoolboy voice, 'Whose side are you on, David?'

20

Yet there is one who seems to have prior knowledge

I had another dream about the fortune-teller machine on the pier. The glass was still smashed in the dream. In the dream there was the head of a live woman instead of the manikin. But her face was badly made-up: lipstick was smeared all over her pancaked face and black mascara streamed from her eyes. It was horrific. She delivered a card from her mouth instead of the slot. I couldn't read the card because the words had been smudged by her saliva.

Without telling Nikki, I took a green double-decker into town and went onto the pier. I was utterly carried away with the idea that I would find the glass in the machine broken, and that my dream was going to be somehow prophetic. Of course the glass was intact when I got there. I didn't know whether to feel disappointed or relieved as I stood for a while at the end of the pier looking out to sea. A lonely gull bobbed out there on the swell. I knew where Colin and Terri lived. They had a small apartment in a street just behind the sea front. Terri had told me the address. I didn't want to go there. I didn't know how Colin would react. But I had to find out what I could about Terri.

Colin was supposed to be lying low in London, but

if I bumped into him I would say that I'd come because the police had been up at the resort asking questions. It seemed plausible, except for the fact that he'd never told me where he lived. I would lie and say I found out from someone in the wages office.

They rented the ground floor of a house next to a second-hand car lot on Beresford Road. I lurked around, making out I was looking at the Ford Anglias and the Toyotas until a salesman came out. Then I took a breath and walked right up to the front door of the house and pressed the bell.

The bell was actually a buzzer and the button vibrated under my finger. I swear that a bell or a buzzer ringing in an empty flat makes a different sound. I waited but no-one came. I rang again. I rang a third time but this time I held the letter-flap open with my fingers and peered through the flap, listening hard, trying to detect movement inside. Anyone inside was keeping very still.

I went round to the back of the house. The curtains were partly drawn. The sun was so strong I had to shield the glass with my hand to see through, but inside I could see a very tidy lounge. There was a low coffee table with a clean ashtray, a pack of No. 6 cigarettes and a plastic cigarette lighter all placed in meticulous order, almost as if someone had primed for a session of viewing the television across the room. An indoor aerial sat atop the television set.

Perhaps I'd expected evidence of slothful or chaotic living, but it was all so neat. On the mantelpiece was a gilt-framed wedding photo of Colin and Terri. Colin looked young, handsome and smart in his wedding suit. Terri looked deliriously happy. At the other end of the mantelpiece was one of those lacy flamenco dolls – with a mantilla shawl and fan – that people that brought back from their holidays in Spain.

I moved to the next window, making a visor of my hand so that I could peer through the glass. This was the bedroom. There was a blue camberwick cover over the bed. I could see a dressing table and its mirror was hung with necklaces and bead chains. In an alcove a pole had been affixed so that clothes could be hung. I saw a black dress hanging there – the black dress Terri had worn the night she appeared in the Slowboat, the night she had set me on fire. There were four or five other pretty dresses: in gold lame; and blue satin; and red cotton; and black and white polka-dot. Not exactly the purdah garments she'd complained to me that Colin kept her in.

There was nothing else to see. I don't know what I'd expected. Signs of a struggle perhaps? There was nothing like that. I left, and I took a bus back to the resort.

It was as if I'd had an appointment with Madame Rosa from the very first day I'd arrived at the holiday camp. The little white-painted caravan with its sign-board tucked away between the crown-bowling green and the office block had left its door open to me almost every day. After my fruitless visit to Colin and Terri's apartment I spiralled in towards her like water sucked down the plug-hole of a bath. I took the two steps up to the caravan and held the sides of the door as if I was making a last desperate grab for the side of the bath. Then in I went.

'I was just boiling the kettle for a cup of tea,' she said, 'and I suppose you want one.'

'Yes. Please.'

She pointed at a sofa seat and I sat down as she

poured water into a pot, stirred the tea with a spoon and covered the pot with a knitted cosy. She opened a cupboard over her head and took down two bone china cups and saucers. 'You've been avoiding me,' she said.

'How did you know?'

Behind her was a table draped in heavy lace and in the middle of the table was a small crystal sphere. I suppose if I'd ever thought about fortune-tellers' crystal balls I imagined them to be about the size of a large grapefruit, but this one on the table was about half the size of a billiard ball. The glass – or crystal or whatever it was – was a gluey grey consistency. Nothing swirled within. It was rather unimpressive.

She saw me looking at it. 'I don't need that to know you've been avoiding me.'

She was a big woman with large hips and in her floral print skirt she took up a lot of space in the tiny caravan. She had a bandana-type scarf tied over her hair. Her face was quite heavily made-up, with an exaggerated cupid's bow painted on her mouth in scarlet lipstick. Her eyes, scanning me now, were the colour of light oak.

'You all come to see me, eventually.'

'Really?'

'The staff. Ninety-five per cent of you. Not everyone wants it known that they come and see me. But you all come. Shall I tell you how I know you've been avoiding me?'

'Go on.'

'Every time I've seen you walk past my caravan you've taken a little step to the side. As if you didn't want to come too near.' She giggled. 'As if you might fall in.'

'You're observant.'

'Observant?' She looked out of the window at

someone hurrying past. 'How do you think I do what I do if I'm not observant?'

I nodded at the crystal ball on the table. She snorted derision. 'Milk and sugar?'

'Milk with no sugar, please. Your name isn't really Rosa, is it?'

'It is actually. What's on your mind?'

'Do I pay you now or afterwards?'

'You can pay me now or you can me afterwards, my darling. You can pay me whenever you like. You can pay me next week. Just so long as you pay me.'

The caravan door was propped open. I wondered if she closed it to signify that a 'reading' was in session. I pulled some notes out of my pocket and put them on the table. She fussed around with the teapot and filled the bone-china cups. I helped myself to milk. I glanced at the crystal ball again.

Something had alighted on it. It was a ladybird. Since the bug invasion had come and gone I'd only seen one or two. Now here was one of them settled on the perfect curve of the sphere and it seemed to perch not on the glass but on the arc of the light itself.

Rosa lifted the crystal from the table and held it in front of her eyes. She seemed not to notice the ladybird. For a millionth of a second I hallucinated that the pupils of her eyes flared scarlet with black dots; but like a lot of things, I knew it was in my head. 'You know who Billy Butlin is?' she said. There was a rival Butlin's camp just a little way along the beach. 'When Billy Butlin was a little boy travelling with his mother on the show circuit he threw that crystal ball at my grandmother. She picked it up off the grass and looked into it and predicted he was going to get a good spanking, which was what he got. He never did see how the two things were connected.' She put the crystal ball back down on the table. The ladybird had flown. 'You're wondering when the reading starts, aren't you?'

'Yes, I am as it happens.'

'Already done.'

'What?'

'You've already been read.'

'You're joking.'

'Drink your tea. Tony says you're a bright lad. I don't think so.'

'Oh?'

'Look, if you want me to peer into that glass ball I'll do it. If you want me to read the lines on your hand I'll do that as well. That's all theatre. But you're not a civilian. You're in the business.'

'So what have I paid for?'

'You've paid for the reading. And I said it's done. I read you the moment you stepped in here.'

I couldn't tell if she was pulling my leg or, worse, just taking me for a fool.

'The first one, she's bad news. She's already put a mark on you. The other one, the one you've got now, I like her much better. You can make each other happy. You've got a good chance. That what you wanted to know?'

I thought for a moment. On the one hand yes, I wanted to know about Terri; but I also wanted to if she were safe. 'I'm worried about her welfare.'

'Who?'

'The first one. As you called her.'

'I can't tell you things like that. Only things directly to do with you. If I knew everything I'd have won the pools by now, my darling.'

I must have looked a little blank.

'There is another thing bothering you. Something much more serious. But you're hiding that even from yourself.'

'Am I?'

'Oh yes. Too dark for me to see. That's why I'm going to send you to see someone else. She's much better than me. She doesn't like doing it and she'll take no payment. But if you say I sent you, she'll see you all right. Now drink your tea and tell me about the people you come from.'

I walked away from Rosa's tiny caravan not quite sure if I'd been fleeced or whether she was one of the cleverest women on the planet. On the face of it I think I got just as much useful advice from the coin-operated machine on the pier. 'Choose your future wisely.' Had that cup of tea just cost me £4.50? I was in no position to ask her any direct question. Perhaps I should have asked her if Enoch Powell was right in his *Rivers Of Blood* speech. But of course the future depends on who you ask, and what people want it to be. To the Enoch Powell question Tony would say yes. Nikki would say I love you, let's have multi-racial babies.

Then it occurred to me, with forehead-slapping stupidity, that I'd let Rosa mesmerise me with tea and talk. She even had the honesty to tell me that everything she said she could have observed from the window of her caravan. She saw everyone come and go. Just a little intuition could put most of it together. And yet she seemed to see.

She told me she would arrange for me to see this other person. She would send a message when this other person was ready.

233

21

The question of who pays is easily settled

At last the weather broke. One day the temperature suddenly swooped downwards and the flags on the white painted poles outside the camp gates started flapping with a kind of angry excitement. The rain came. Undramatic, heavy, relentless. It wasn't fun for those holidaymakers late in the season who wanted the hot weather to continue, but I found myself walking out in it in my white shirt and trousers. I was supposed to referee a kids' football game when the rain came. The boys ran like hell to get out of it but I stood alone in the middle of the football field and I let it soak me and it felt good. The ground was hard as bone and at first the rainwater lay in great sheets. Then it found its way between the cracks and fissures in the dry earth and slowly began to saturate the soil. I remember that it rained morning, noon and night.

I got out of the rabbit hutch staff accommodation. Nikki found a little flat above a shop that sold postcards and plastic buckets and spades and rubber rings. We moved our stuff in together. It was good to get off the camp every night so that we could rediscover who we were before we'd arrived there. With the rain coming down we spent all our free time there. I even managed to get Nikki interested in books. She read Erich Segal's *Love Story* and *Carrie* by Stephen King and *Fahrenheit 451* by Ray Bradbury.

One day when the rain had stopped I passed by the reception and Edna, the sweet lady who worked there, came running out to say that I had visitors.

'Who is it?' I asked.

'They're waiting in here.' Edna beckoned me back to the reception desk and I followed her indoors. Two plastic chairs had been drawn up by the desk and there, waiting patiently, were my mother and my stepfather. On seeing me they both stood up.

'Here he is!' my mum half shouted, flinging her arms around me and kissing me.

Ken was all smiles, too. 'Look at you,' he said. 'Striped blazer and everything.' He turned to Edna. 'He looks the part! Doesn't he look the part?'

They were all smiles. It was in neither's nature to reveal to Edna or anyone else any of the tensions behind the fact that I was working there. So our reunion was a moment of laughter and high spirits.

Edna smiled. 'We're proud of him,' she said. 'We're all proud of him here.'

'I'll have to get one of those striped blazers myself,' Ken said. 'They're quite the thing.'

'You'll have to lose a few pounds first!' my mother said, laughing.

'It's okay, they have slightly bigger ones,' I joked. 'We can get you fixed up.'

'What's he saying about me!' shouted Ken, his eyes bulging. He laughed. My mum laughed. Edna laughed. I went along with this jollity, but it was almost unbearable.

Having taken me by surprise Ken said he wanted to take me to lunch, and did I know anywhere. I knew we could get something at The Dunes pub around the corner so I suggested that. I'd already arranged to have lunch with Nikki so I told them.

They exchanged a look.

'No, that's fine,' said Ken. 'We'd love to meet her.'

'Yes,' my mum said a little too quickly. 'We'd like to meet your girl, wouldn't we?'

We had to wait for about ten minutes before Nikki was through with her activities in the ballroom. I asked my parents to wait as I went off to get her. I wanted to cushion Nikki a little.

'Really? They're here? Now?'

'Yes. In reception.'

'Okay. Let's do it.'

I needn't have worried about Nikki. She took charge. It was as if she'd been through this ritual many times before. She utterly charmed them. She asked if they'd come far and how was their journey; she smiled and laughed at their jovial comments and paid great attention to my mother's words.

'We thought we'd go for lunch,' Ken said.

'Great idea,' Nikki said. 'I'll just go and freshen up. Mrs Barwise, do you need the loo?'

'You have to call me Jean,' my mum said, happily following Nikki to the ladies' room.

After they'd gone Ken took me aggressively by the elbow. 'She's stunning!' he said. 'Where the heck did you find that one?'

'She works here.'

'Well, she's got good taste. And so do you. You lucky sod.'

'I'm surprised to see you here, Dad.'

'Look, son, it's your mother. You know what she's like. She worries about you.'

'I'm completely fine. What is there to be worried about?'

'Nothing by the look of you!'

Pinky came by, carrying some cartons of Players No. 6. I introduced the two men. They were of a similar generation and they exchanged a few pleasant words. Pinky made my cheeks burn by saying what a good chap I was and how well I'd fitted in, and then went on his way.

'It's just that,' Ken said, 'your mum was a bit taken aback by that phone call the other day.'

'What?'

Ken looked at me hard and for the first time I thought I saw hatred in his eyes. No, it wasn't exactly hatred: it was betrayal, and confusion, and the look of a man who had decided he'd had enough. It was like he'd tried hard with me all my life to get me to trust him, to give him a fair chance, and now he was ready to give up. He was probably right. I would never trust him. He was wasting his time.

Before he could say anything Nikki and my mum re-appeared. My mum was giggling. Nikki winked at me.

I'll say one thing for Ken: he was a good actor. 'Come on then, ladies.' He rubbed his hands. 'Anyone hungry?'

'Me me me,' said Nikki.

'Me me me too,' went my mum.

So this jolly group of us left the camp and headed round to The Dunes. The infamous Skegness breeze had picked up and we braced against it. Ken wore a trilby, which he pressed to his head as we walked. My mum had tied a floral headscarf round her tight perm. Nikki's hair whipped in the wind.

The Dunes was busy and the only table free happened to be the one I'd sat at with Colin the time he'd brought me there. Nikki was terrific again. 'Pull that chair up for your mum, David; it's more comfortable. I'll get the drinks.'

'You will not,' said Ken, standing up.

'Sit down and talk to your son! You haven't seen him in a while.'

He looked flustered. He took his wallet out of his pocket and found a large banknote. 'Well, you can get them but I'm paying.'

Nikki accepted the banknote. 'And what's everyone eating?'

With Nikki away at the bar my dad said, 'She's lovely.' He was clearly smitten.

My mum took off her headscarf. 'She's quite a bit older than you, isn't she?'

I looked out of the window. I wondered if it might rain again.

'Well I'm older than you!' Ken said to her. 'What difference does that make?

Mum sniffed and affected to look critically at the upholstery and the curtains in the pub.

'What do they pay you here, then?' Ken wanted to know.

I didn't name a figure but I told him that you had to take into account that you got lodgings and three meals per day in with your wages. Then Nikki came back with a tray of drinks. She took them off the tray and placed them in front of us. 'Babycham for mother. Pint

238

of bitter apiece for the boys. And half a lager for little me.' She leaned the tray on the floor against her chair and sat down. Then she picked up her lager. 'Cheers.'

'Cheers,' said Ken.

'Good health,' said Mum. 'Isn't this nice?'

We talked about the hot weather and the drought conditions, and how it had been here, and how it had been at home. Ken made a joke to Nikki about saving water by taking a bath with a friend. We discussed the ladybird invasion, which obviously hadn't been as intense at home as it had here on the coast. They were amazed to hear about it. I was surprised how light Ken could be in different company. I was seeing a different side to him. My mother meanwhile stroked her throat and looked around the pub a lot. Her smile seemed to ache by contrast to his.

Our meals arrived. Chicken-in-a-basket with chips. Gammon and pineapple. 'Have you been to university, Nikki?' my mum asked, apropos of nothing.

'No. Not bright enough.'

'Me neither,' said Ken. 'And it hasn't stopped me putting away a bob or two.'

'Ken!' said mum.

'Well,' he said genially, 'there are all these students out of work. Graduates, stacking shelves in the super-markets. What's the point?'

'But education is a great thing, isn't it, Ken?' Nikki said. Searching him with her dark brown eyes. When she said that I thought: I want to marry you.

'Of course it is; of course it is. But there have to be jobs at the end of it.'

'What will you do, Nikki?' asked my mum. 'Now that the season has nearly ended.'

The three of us had Black Forest gateau for dessert while Ken smoked a cigarette. The conversation stalled and there was the sound of forks on plates and crumbs of cake being scraped together. When we'd finished, Nikki got up to go to the ladies' room and when she'd gone my mother suggested we go outside.

'What for?' I said.

'You'll stay here with Nikki, won't you, Ken?'

'What's this about?'

'I'll buy her another drink,' Ken said. 'Don't you worry. I'll keep her company.'

'Can we step outside, David?' My mum looked at me, pleading.

Mum put her coat back on again, and her headscarf, and out we went into the stiff breeze. We walked away from the pub, but slowly, the way people do when they have no direction in mind. She linked her arm in mine. The fine sand blew across the path under our feet. 'Why did you come here, David?'

'To work, obviously.'

'I know that. But why here? Why this place?'

'I heard there was a job going, that's all.'

She looked at me with sadness. I noticed for the first time that her eyeballs were slightly jaundiced at the sockets. 'I don't know how much you know and how much you don't.'

'You're talking in riddles, Mum.'

We made it onto the promenade. The wind was gusting out there. The sea looked choppy. Maybe a squall was coming in. The gulls were all floating in a tight colony on the bobbing grey tide. 'You were three years old, David. He'd brought you here. He hadn't told anyone.'

'Who? My Dad?'

'Yes, your father. Your natural father. He kidnapped you away, you see. He brought you here. I didn't know where you were. I was going out of my mind. The police got dragged in. Everything. We'd broken up, your dad and I. I wasn't happy. He was a difficult man.

'At first I thought that by coming here you were punishing me. Punishing me and Ken. Making a big point. Because that's what you do, David. You don't say what you're thinking. You just do things. But now I know you weren't. Weren't making a point, I mean. I really believe you don't know about this place.

'We should have talked about it. All those years when you were growing up, we should have told you. But we felt so bad, David. You have to be easy on us. We felt so deep down bad. Because Ken and I had got together and that seemed to be the thing that drove him over the edge.

'This is where they found you David. On the pier. This is where it happened.'

I stopped dead. 'Where what happened?'

And she told me what she knew.

She opened her handbag and she pulled out a small leather wallet. 'He abandoned you, David. He left you wandering alone on the pier. Three years old, and he left you. You were holding this wallet, which he must have given you. There wasn't much in it. A few pound notes. The photograph which you took from me. Some bus tickets. The police took you in. Then his body was washed up. I'd reported you missing. Ken and I came to collect you and I had to go and identify him. I should have told you all this before. I tried to, many times. But I couldn't.'

And then she cried. The wind gusted around us, blowing sand at us, gritty sand that blew in our faces and stung. I tried to comfort my mother as the wind gusted and dropped, gusted and dropped; but I was numb, and all I could think of was that east coast advertising slogan: it's so bracing.

Before leaving, Mum and Ken made Nikki promise that she'd come with me to visit them at home. We waved them away. When they'd gone I ventilated a huge sigh.

'You all right?' said Nikki.

We'd got duties to attend to. Nikki was in the Slowboat and I was due in the Games Room. 'I'll tell you later,' I said.

Nikki scuttled ahead and as I walked back across the car park I was intercepted by Rosa, who called me from her caravan. 'She's ready to see you,' she said. 'Any time this afternoon.'

I managed to steer the table-tennis and snooker through to their respective finals. I wrote down the names of the winners. I told them stage jokes. *With the right amount of training and practice ... you might just be able to hit that ball.* Eventually I made my way to the path between the offices and the bowling green. My appointment was with Dot, the grizzled ogre of the steam-cave that was the laundry room.

I had to wait in line behind a couple of the cleaning staff who were sorting and folding white sheets. There was some kind of dispute. Clouds of steam settled on Dot's shoulders as she demanded to know why they needed extra sheets when they'd already been issued. The argument went on for some time. I shuffled my feet nervously.

242

Finally it was resolved. Without acknowledging my presence Dot moved a pile of sheets from the counter to the deeper recesses of her lair. From the back a strip light flickered on and off at irregular intervals. At last, and with no gesture or word of recognition she said, 'I don't like doing it; but if it's to be done let's get on.'

'You're Rosa's sister?' I said.

'Twin. Pull up that chair.'

It seemed astonishing to me. They hardly looked alike. Rosa was buxom with ample, swinging hips whereas Dot was rake-thin. I pulled up the chair and Dot was pulling up one for herself when another cleaner poked her head round the door.

'Shall I come back later?' asked the cleaner. 'I see you've got a *young man* in here with you, Dot.'

Dot got up, waddled to the door and closed it sharply, almost in the woman's face. She dropped a latch. 'I can't be doing with foolishness,' she said, motioning that I should sit down. I took it as a warning.

She pulled her own chair up opposite mine and sat down. Our knees were almost touching. 'What is it, then?' she asked.

'Well, Rosa said I should see you.'

'We know that. What do you want?'

I must have looked vacant.

'I don't do mumbo-jumbo,' Dot said sharply. 'There's no fortunes to be seen or told. You have to tell me what it is, and I see what I can do for you.'

I glanced round the gloomy laundry cavern. Clouds of steam were still thinning under the ceiling and the light in the back of the chamber was flickering. Dot had her eye fixed on me. Her thin bleached grey hair seemed almost like a hood. I took a deep breath and told her everything my mother had told me at lunchtime.

'I see. And what else?'

I said that was it.

'You're holding something back.'

I thought about it for a second, and then I told her about my dreams and hallucinations and the boy and the man in the blue suit.

'Give me your hands,' Dot said firmly.

I gave her my hands and she held them in each of hers. Her own hands were surprisingly warm and soft but her knuckles were big and chafed, and it was at her knuckle bones that she seemed to look rather than at me. 'Oh I see. There we are. Oh dear. Oh no. Oh dear. There we are. That's the way. Poor duckie. That's the way.

'I feel very nervous. I feel it all the time. Like something bad is going to happen.'

I was about say something bland but she carried on speaking in a way as if I wasn't even in the room there with her.

'I feel very small,' she said, 'and very lonely and I think that all the trouble may be because of something that I have done, though I don't know what it is. I'm too small to know these things. I love him, but I feel something bad is going to happen.

'There's a moon,' she said, 'very very bright over the water. There's a movement at the water's edge. I see it. Two figures, where the waves are foaming. They're holding hands, these two, and looking out across the sea. What are they looking for? What do they want?

'I'm going to the sea wall. I'm going to see what they want, these two. I'm walking the promenade for a short way and – here we are – the concrete steps down on to the beach. I can smell salt and sea-gas. They've moved on, these two, but there they are, still silhouetted in the moonlight. Look at them holding hands. So tightly! So tender!'

I was still holding Dot's hands, or rather she was holding mine. Her eyes were half-closed as she said all this. The extraordinary thing was how clearly I could visualise everything she said.

She went on. 'It's a boy and a man, isn't it? A boy and a man. That's strange: their eyes are like clear glass. I see moonlight – or is it the phosphorescence in the water – reflecting where their eyes should be? It's strange. I'm going to hurry a little. Catch up with them. Oh, but the sand, you see, the sand is sucking me down, slowing me. I can't catch up. They're going towards the town. I've got to hurry to keep up with them.

'Look. Look. We've come to the pier.'

'We've come to the pier,' I heard myself say.

I looked around and I was there, at the water's edge. I seemed to have arrived there in mere moments. Dot's voice had gone and I inhaled the brine and heard the lap of the water and felt the soft sand under my feet.

I followed the man and the boy to the pier, and there was a boat drawn up at the water's edge. The man looked around him nervously as if he didn't want to be seen. He still wore his blue suit and it too foamed with gentle phosphorescent light, like it was made of water. Eels of blue light swam and sparkled in the threads of its fabric. It was beautiful. He took the boy by the hand, and together they walked into the water and climbed into the boat.

As the man pushed off with the oars I ran and caught

up. I hurried into the water, splashing and soaking my shoes and my trousers and I climbed into the boat beside them. The boy smiled at me briefly but the man didn't so much as acknowledge me.

The man rowed steadily. The bright moon shone on his face and for the first time I was able to see him clearly. He no longer had eyes of clear glass. Now he wore spectacles. The boy too: now instead of eyes of glass he had ordinary wide, trusting eyes of nut-brown. Though I had an aching dread inside me, I sat in the boat quietly as we moved deeper out to sea. We cast a moon-shadow on the calm water behind us.

The little boy watched me carefully. He turned sharply to look at his father, then back to me. It was as if he was asking one of us for an explanation about the presence of the other. I tried to speak, but some paralysis had me by the throat and I struggled for the faculty of words. Still the man showed no interest in me as he rowed steadily.

About two hundred yards out to sea the man stopped rowing and shipped oars. He looked back at the shore and decided to take off his shoes and socks. Then he stripped off his jacket and his shirt and trousers. He wore swimming trunks underneath.

At last I overcame my paralysis and managed to speak. 'Isn't it cold for that?' I said. The balmy nights had given way to chilly evenings and even though I was fully dressed I was shivering and wet from the knees down.

The man looked at me and in a voice that I knew he said, 'No-one will bother us here.'

I looked for the boy, but he had gone. The man reached for some ropes that were lying in the bottom of the boat. The ropes were secured to heavy iron weights, not unlike those weights that braced the flats backstage of the theatre. He made certain that the weights were properly secured to the ropes and then he tied one of the ropes tightly around his leg just above the ankle.

He took another rope and a weight and he looped it around my ankle and knotted it tightly.

'What's that for, daddy?' I said. My voice was tiny, child-like.

'No-one will find us, even if they're looking for us.'

A surge of panic and self-preservation shot through me. Moonlight reflected in the glass of the man's spectacles, preventing me from seeing his eyes. I looked for the little boy again. I was scared. I thought he must have fallen over the side of the boat.

'Just you and me together and all the time in the world,' said the man.

The man was my father. I didn't know what he was doing but I trusted him.

He glanced back at the shore, as if expecting or perhaps hoping that someone would come after us. I looked over the side of the boat at the dark water. I didn't like it at all. It looked cold. 'I'm frightened.'

'No need to be frightened, David.'

I opened my mouth again to say Can We Go Back but something silvery and red flew into my mouth. It flew into my throat and I spluttered. Then the thing was on my tongue and I spat it out into my hand. It was a ladybird. It righted itself and crawled into the centre of the palm of my hand, where it stayed. Here we were in the middle of the night and a ladybird, painted by moonlight, had flown into my mouth.

I showed it to my father. I said very clearly, but in my deep adult voice, 'I've come here from another time.'

He seemed thunderstruck, hunched forward in the boat staring at the tiny creature in my hand.

But it was as if I couldn't remember what I'd just said to him. That is, I knew as myself, as the older David exactly what I'd just said. But as the little boy I couldn't remember.

I held the ladybird in the palm of my hand up to the light of the moon. The great strontium-white ball of the moon seemed to expand massively in the sky. I blew on my hand and the ladybird, silhouetted, expanded its wings and flew in a dizzy pattern across the face of the moon before disappearing into the blackness.

'Can we go back?' I said. 'I'm frightened.'

My father seemed crestfallen, beaten. His brow was creased. In a kind of daze he gathered the oars and he dipped them in the water. He turned the boat around and steadily but firmly rowed the boat back to the shore. I sat opposite him and he didn't take his eyes off me, not for a single stroke.

When we reached the shore he untied the rope from around my ankle, then from his. He put his trousers and his jacket back on and lifted me out of the boat to carry me onto the sand. After setting me down he took my hand and we walked to the pier.

The light changed and it was instantly daytime; the sun was shining, gulls were calling and wheeling in the blue sky and the pier was busy with people and music and with gaiety. We walked together to the end of the pier. 'I'm leaving you here, David,' he said. He took his wallet out of his pocket and he pressed it into my hand. 'Someone will come for you. Wait here.'

I watched him walk away, along the boardwalk of the pier. He didn't look back at me. I could see him through the cross-hatch of railings as he got down onto the sand again, making his way back to the boat. He pushed the boat back into the water, climbed in and heaved on the oars, rowing steadily out to sea all over again. The tiny boat became a dot out at sea and seemed to become still. I watched it lift and fall on the swell for a long time.

Eventually I became distracted by some music playing on the pier. I moved between the people. I found a penny on the boardwalk and I tried to put it into a machine, but I couldn't reach. A young couple saw me and laughed. The young woman lifted me up so I could reach the coin slot, but then the young man said, 'Oh, a penny won't do it for Madame Zora.'

He found the right coin and Madam Zora began to whirr and click and go through her routine but I kicked away from the young couple and ran down the pier, following my father. I ran onto the sand shouting his name. I think I knew he was never going to come back.

'It's my daddy!' I shouted. 'It's my daddy!'

In an instant I was crying and screaming and there was no-one to hear me. I wanted someone to help me. The sun was high and hot in the sky as I ran over the sand. I slipped and I fell. The loose sand scraped my face; it seemed not to want to let me get help for my daddy. I fell again and scrambled along the beach, screaming for him to come back.

But there was no-one there. I couldn't even see the boat out on the distant swell of the water. Tears stung my ears. I couldn't breathe. The beach had become a vast and hostile wilderness. No-one came. 'It's my daddy!' I screamed, and the sea just groaned and shifted its obstinate and infinite weight. 'It's my daddy.'

I sat down on the beach and I sobbed, gulping, trying to breathe.

Then I saw the young woman from the pier rushing towards me. She put her hand on my shoulder. 'Who are you with?' she asked me. 'Tell me who you are with?' Then she took both of my hands.

'Hush! Hush!' she said. 'Here you are! Here you are!' And the person holding my hands was no longer a young woman on the pier, but Dot, in the laundry room. 'Hush now. Here you are.'

'It's my daddy,' I cried to her.

I cried openly and unashamedly before this hardened old woman as she sat quietly and held my hands. Finally she got up and she found me a clean handkerchief and told me to blow my nose. 'Don't worry, I've seen a lot of tears,' she said. 'A lot of tears.'

When I'd recovered enough, Dot said, 'Are you all right? I've got a lot of work to get on with, duckie.'

'Yes.'

'It's hard, isn't it?'

'Yes.'

'It's hard for a lot of people. You know that.'

'Yes.'

'Anyway, at least we know who they are, don't we?'

I said, 'But why are they haunting me?'

'Oh no duckie,' she said. 'No no no. They're not haunting you. You're haunting them. They don't want to be here.'

'But—'

'It's not your father; it's what he was. That boy isn't you; it's what you *were*. Leave them alone. Why don't you leave them alone?'

My eyes wanted to fill with tears all over again. I managed to stop it. Someone tapped on the door. She ignored it.

'He was very, very confused,' she said.

'Yeh.'

'He wasn't much older than you are now.'

'No.'

'You can't hate him.'

'No. I don't.'

'You have to forgive him. That's important.'

I nodded.

'You have to forgive him. I pull the stopper out. That's all I do.'

I stood up. 'I'm ready to go. Thank you.'

She got up stiffly, pressing a hand to her arthritic hip, and moved to the door, where she lifted the latch. I thanked her a second time and made to go outside. 'Hold on a moment,' she said, 'there's something else.'

'What's that?'

'I've had some new shirts and trousers in as will fit you now.'

22

Oh there will be time for sweet wine

Can someone hold your hand and make lost memories come tumbling down? Nikki and I fell asleep that night drugged with sex and folded in each other's love. But new forces were dragging me back. I had a dream that looped horribly. It played over and over. If I woke and went back to sleep it would start again. It was just a dream of being in a small boat out at sea, but a hole had appeared in the boat. Instead of water running in, grains of the boat were running *out* and into the water like sand running in an inverted egg-timer. At first the grains appeared not to move at all, then a hole collapsed in the boat and the grains appeared to run faster, running towards some groaning terror that would cause me to wake up.

I spent the next day curled up in bed like a foetus. Nikki went into work and told them I had a stomach bug. In breaks between activities she came back to the flat above the bucket-and-spade shop and fed me soup or got into bed with me and made me talk about these things.

'I can see why your mother never wanted you to come here,' she said. 'But you must have known. You must have known that this is where it all happened.'

'I was three years old. I didn't know anything.' Perhaps that wasn't entirely true. Clearly some dark and secret place inside me knew everything perfectly. But those events had accreted a shell and burrowed under sand to be covered with water. Not everyone with lost memories can swim their way back to remembering. The muscle will perish; the shell will be picked clean; the waves will break the shell and pound it into sand.

I didn't blame my mother or Ken, even though they should have spoken to me about these things. They were already busy blaming themselves. They simply could not bear to prise open the subject.

After the events I have described, other memories came tumbling back to me. I remember being at home and playing in the front garden. The wooden gate opened and there was my natural father in a smart, blue suit. I hadn't seen him for some weeks and when I ran to him he swept me up in his arms. I loved him and I'd missed him. I didn't know why he'd been away so long.

He was wearing spectacles. I hadn't seen him wear them before and I didn't like it. He seemed not to be quite like my father. But then he looked up the path and asked me if I wanted to go to the seaside. I said yes. He put me in his car and he drove us to the seaside. He hadn't told my mother. He hadn't told anyone. When we got to the seaside we were hiding out while he made his plans.

Nikki encouraged me to go back into work the next day. Even though I was in a fragile state I was mindlessly efficient. I smiled when I needed to smile. It can be done, and is done often. I sometimes think that half of humanity is smiling across a profound agony. Nikki

253

and I were in every sense professional. We didn't tell anyone about what had happened.

One evening Nikki was dancing in the Variety show at the theatre while I was calling the giant bingo session in the Slowboat. Between intoning Two Little Ducks or Kelly's Eye Number One into the microphone I medicated myself with beer and stood at the bar, chatting to Eric the Brummie drummer. Someone tapped me on the shoulder.

I turned round and I almost dropped my stein of beer. 'Awright?'

I felt the blood drain from my face, and then rush back again. 'Colin. How are you?'

'I'm all right. You?'

I stared at him as if he were the ghost of Macbeth. 'Can I get you a drink?'

'Just the one. I'm not staying. I'm up for poker night. Last time.'

I moved over to the bar and ordered a pint of Federation Ale for him. I was afraid of my hands shaking again, just as they had when he'd taken me for a beer at The Dunes. I took a breath, composed myself and carried his beer over to a table. He joined me, but he kept looking out of the corner of his eye, as if he was scanning the room for someone.

'Is Terri up here with you?' I asked.

'Na.' He took a sip of beer and the foam printed a moustache on his upper lip.

'Where is she?'

'Dunno.'

We sat in silence for a minute. He scanned the room

constantly. Then he volunteered some information. 'I took her off to Marbella after last I seen you.'

'Marbella.'

'Yeh. It's in Spain.'

I wanted to say I knew where Marbella was but I thought better of it.

'Thought that would suit her. We used to go there in the old days. We was alright for a while. Then she ran away.'

'Ran away where?'

'I've a good idea.'

'Oh?'

'With someone from 'ere.'

'I don't believe it,' I said.

His eyes flared open and he tipped back his head. I saw the back of his upper fillings. 'I nearly catched her at it. In that feater over there.'

'What, *this* theatre?' I was incredulous for him.

'I followed her in one day. It wasn't that Italian cos he was 'aving a smoke with Pinky. When I gets in there she's in the dark with that scrote, your mate.'

'My mate?'

'That fuckin' soft Mancunian. Whatsisname?'

'Nobby? Are you sure?'

'He was wearing that kit like you wear.'

'But are you certain it was him?'

'Less it was you, or that prat with the wig.' He flashed me a half-smile. 'Na, it was him all right. I know cos he disappeared off the scene straight after.'

'I don't know, Colin,' I said helpfully. 'Nobby? It doesn't add up. He's not her type.'

'Her type? Anyone with a hard cock is her type. Maybe I'll go up to Manchester. See if I can't find 'em both.'

It occurred to me that Colin might just do that. I don't know what it was about Nobby but he always fitted the bill. I suddenly felt emboldened. 'Colin. Why do this to yourself? Sometimes you have to let it go. Walk away.'

He sniffed. 'Listen to you. Givin' the advice out now, aincha?'

'I didn't mean to –'

'It's alright, son. I've heard it. It's alright.'

It was impossible to tell if he was lying about Terri's fate. I tried to look deep into his eyes. It was like looking down a mine shaft.

He drained his beer glass and stood up. 'Might see you here next season, then?'

I got up off my stool. He dug his hands in his pockets, almost as if to tell me that he didn't want any handshake ritual. 'Might well do, Colin. Might well do.'

He nodded briefly, turned and left. It wasn't until he'd passed through the doors that I let out a big sigh.

I rejoined Eric the drummer at the bar. He was chatting with one of the bar staff and, when the barman moved across to serve someone, Eric said to me, 'I didn't know he was a friend of yours.'

'No,' I said.

The Saturdays came and went, the sea turned the grey of gun metal and the infamous and bracing east coast wind grew squally and bitter. Most people had gone back to work and for the last couple of weeks the resort was populated by special groups: disabled people, children from care homes and the like. It was actually more fun to work with these groups but the numbers of holidaymakers were already well down on the peak season and I was aware that many of the staff had already left.

The performers were signed off and a rudimentary programme was offered for the rump of the season. A goodbye party was held for the theatre people. Luca Valletti made a brief appearance. He arrived late, had one drink and then went round solemnly but punctiliously shaking hands with everyone equally.

When he came to me he blinked, smiled and offered his hand. 'I wish you every success with your studies.'

'Thank you, Luca. I learned a lot from you.'

He blinked and regarded me rather strangely, I thought. Then he offered me almost a bow and moved on to the next person.

Nikki, meanwhile, was already thinking about her next job. She had an audition in Coventry for a part in a Christmas pantomime production. Puss in Boots, where the chorus line wore leather boots up to the top of their thighs. I saw her off at the train station and went to meet her when she came back. She didn't know whether she'd got the part or not. We avoided discussing the future.

In the final week we had a party of disabled children from a special home and Nikki, Gail and I threw ourselves into designing a fresh programme suitable for kids in wheelchairs. Even Tony – yes, Tony the fascist – got enthusiastic about whether we could make it all accessible and high energy, so that we could give the kids our very best.

And then it was all over. I said goodbye to Pinky and he made me promise that I would come back the following year. 'Your face fits,' he said.

Tony shook my hand manfully and apologised for

not being able to knock some political sense into me. He pointed at me with a big tanned and nicotine-stained index finger. 'Don't let them commie professors fill your head with nonsense, mind you. And don't forget about us.'

They were all wonderful with the sweet wine.

I talked Nikki into shacking up with me in Nottingham. We scoured the local newspaper and we found another flat together near the town centre of Nottingham. We bought paint and freshened the place up and she gave it some feminine touches. We were playing at being a couple. One day she came home with a little gift for me.

'What is it?'

'Open it.'

I unwrapped some tissue paper and I found it was a heavy glass paperweight. The glass was red with black spots and bifurcated to look like the carapace of a ladybird.

'It's to remind you. Of the summer.'

I weighed it in my hand. 'It's lovely.'

'It's for your studies.'

Perhaps I looked confused. I don't know what type of student Nikki thought I was: maybe she had a notion of me at a big desk with a brass telescope and a silver engraved pen and a huge blotter, with a pile of maps and scrolls.

'It's a silly present, isn't it?' she said, suddenly losing confidence.

'No it's not. It's beautiful.'

'Silly.'

'I'll treasure it.' I weighed it in my hand for her to see. 'Really.'

Nikki was entertained and amused at being part of the student scene. She met my friends, and we drank in the union bar. We even sneaked her into a few lectures, completely unnoticed, just so she could get a sense of what we did. She was three or four years older than my contemporaries and though she never criticised them I could tell that their immaturity bored her. Nonetheless she became excited by the lectures; she always wanted to discuss what she'd heard; in fact she was more interested in learning than ninety per cent of the student population. She hungered for learning.

She almost fell over backwards when I explained that it cost nothing to be a student at university; that the government paid all fees and awarded a grant to students so that they could live and study in reasonable comfort; that education was a right to be claimed. No-one had ever told her. We found out that she could apply as a Mature Student on reduced qualifications, and she immediately prepared to take an extra couple of O level examinations in order to matriculate the following year.

One rainy, misty Thursday evening we were on our way to the Old Angel Inn to meet with some friends. We would always walk the short distance into town from the flat, and on the way we passed by a small theatre, a place that staged both amateur theatre and irregular concerts. One night you might see a rock band and another night a comedy act. Billboards outside the theatre advertised these various shows and one particular billboard proclaimed 'for one night only' a performance of 'A Selection of Songs from *My Fair Lady*'.

The billboard caught Nikki's eye. I was still walking

when she summoned me back. The billboard indicated that this was the public's *last chance* to catch this *amazing show* before it went on an *international tour*. 'What?'

'Look at the photos,' she said.

I saw it at once. In the photograph his appearance hadn't changed at all, but his name had. He was no longer called Luca Valletti. His new stage name was Dante Senatore. His duet partner was Shelly Diamante. To be precise she was billed as Shelly 'The Nightingale' Diamante. I don't think I would have recognised her from her photograph: it was a very professional and air-brushed Terri who gazed out with tender eyes from the billboard as she leaned her head against the breast of Dante Senatore's tuxedo. Her hair had been restyled and her lips were painted with luscious red lipstick. She no longer looked like someone who mopped the floor after hours.

I remembered Pinky's words, about whether telling someone they have a nice voice constitutes making a pass. *Sometimes it does and sometimes it doesn't.*

We were way too early for the show but Nikki suggested we find out what time they finished, and that we come by and say hello. I was reluctant, but she said it would be fun to surprise them. We went inside and asked at the box office about what time the performance ended.

After that we went on our way to The Angel Inn, where we drank with friends until about ten o'clock. I was comfortable and I didn't want to go, but Nikki was determined. She persuaded me that it would be rude not to say hello. When we got to the theatre people were already spilling out of the doors, turning up their collars. Knowing that Luca's professional habit was to get out quickly, I thought we might have left it too late. Nikki dived inside and asked someone where the stage door was. It was at the side of the building.

'Should we send a note? Say we're here?'

'No!' Nikki said. 'It will be more fun if we don't.'

I really wasn't sure about that.

Soon enough the stage door opened to reveal a rectangle of yellow light. The figures of a man and a woman carrying large prop bags and with polythene-wrapped stage costumes over their arms emerged into the shadows. As they joined the illuminated main street in front of the doors of the theatre we were able to intercept them

'Luca!' Nikki said. 'And Terri!'

They were both paralysed by our sudden appearance. Their eyes flared wide in the light from the streetlamp. Traces of stage make-up remained at the corners of their eyes. They looked pale, ghosts of the people I'd known at the holiday resort.

Terri looked at me without a trace of expression.

'Don't you remember us?' Nikki said cheerfully.

Terri was the one who recovered first. I could almost feel the engine of her brain turning. 'Nikki and David!' she said. 'Look, it's Nikki and David! From the resort,' she added, as if she needed to prompt Luca into re-membering who we were.

Luca was still floundering. 'Yes of course! How amazing to see you! Simply amazing!'

I intuited all the thoughts processing in Terri's mind. She stepped forward so that she could kiss me. She stood on tiptoe to reach me; a gesture that still burned.

'What a coincidence to see you both here!' I said.

'Yes,' he said, 'a coincidence.'

'Actually,' I said, 'we passed the billboard earlier. Nikki was the one who recognised you!'

They both looked at me, smiling, as if I were telling a truly fascinating story.

The hiatus was embarrassing so I said to Luca, 'But you changed your name.'

Nikki said, 'It's just showbiz, David!'

Luca said, 'Yes I changed my name. A different show. A new start, you know?' He put his hand in his pocket and fumbled with some loose change, then he bought out a set of car keys.

I stepped over to the billboard and examined the picture. I looked back at Terri, and then back at the picture. 'It's fantastic! I mean, we all said you should be on stage.'

'We formed a duet,' she said unnecessarily.

'What, after you left? You formed a duet?' I had Terri on the rack, and I wasn't going to stop. You see, in that moment I understood with shining clarity that Luca and I had both been her lovers at the same time. I suspect Luca might have guessed, too. It meant of course that Colin's initial suspicions were confirmed after all.

Luca looked up the street and then back at me with the same fixed smile. He wasn't saying much at all. He shook the car keys in his hand.

'So is this where you are a student?' Terri asked me, swinging the spotlight in another direction. 'What about you, Nikki? What are you up to these days?'

'I'm applying to University, aren't I, David? I'm going to be a stoooooooodent!!'

Terri smiled the long, long smile of wonder and dismay.

'*Autumn Leaves*, that was my favourite.' I said to Luca. 'I really used to enjoy doing all that. And of course it's autumn now, isn't it?'

'I never found such a good lights man since,' he said chivalrously. His jaw, too, must have ached from smiling. 'Look, lovely people, I'm very sorry but we have to slip away to a party.'

'A party!' Nikki said

"Well, you could come, couldn't they, Terri? Except that it's a family thing, you know, and I don't think it's appropriate.'

'No, that wouldn't work, would it?' I said. 'A pity.'

'Why don't you give us your telephone number?' Luca said. 'Then we could call you. Have a coffee somewhere. Coffee and a nice cake.'

'I don't have a telephone number. Student, you see. Always broke. You know how it is.'

Terri opened her handbag, struggling with the polythene-wrapped stage dress over her arm, and produced a pen. 'Let me give you our number, then.'

There was a wonderful moment when we thought we hadn't got a scrap of paper between the four of us on which to write. Then Terri went back into her handbag and found a bus ticket. We had a laugh about that – writing on a bus ticket. How funny. On the reverse of the ticket she very carefully wrote out a phone number, and she handed it to Nikki rather than to me.

After that, Luca held out a hand that wanted shaking. 'Goodbye for now,' he said and we shook hands. Terri stepped forward to kiss me again, and Luca kissed Nikki.

We watched them go. They passed before the yellow lights of the small theatre and I watched them, Terri with her quick, almost angry little steps and Luca striding to keep up with her.

'That was hard work for some reason,' Nikki said as we walked away in a different direction.

'It was.'

'I don't think they were all that pleased to see us.'

'No. I don't think they were.'

Nikki turned her collar up to the damp air and linked her arm in mine. In the mist and damp air of Nottingham town she was so beautiful.

Nikki got the pantomime job in Coventry. I helped her with her O levels in the meantime. We were ecstatically happy. Over the Christmas holidays we stayed with Mum and Ken. They treated Nikki to the best china and silverware and Ken told stories that even I hadn't heard. I think Ken had fallen for her.

College life restored equilibrium to our days. There was the routine of lectures, seminars, coffee bars and the union bar. Nikki got bits of work here and there, but she loved being a student even if we were broke a lot of the time. She changed the way she dressed and wore a duffel coat and a long, winding college scarf. We joined the Anti-Nazi League and sent Tony a badge. We never heard back from him.

The National Front meanwhile turned inward on itself, dissolving in bitter faction and violence as they disagreed on ways to make the country Great again. There were court cases, scandals, violence. Some of those leading figures are still around. There were no rivers of blood in the following years, and of course certain people were rather disappointed about that.

In the spring we got a letter from Pinky asking if we wanted to work for him again the following summer.

One night in April I was roused from sleep in the small hours by a tapping on the window. For a split-second I thought it was going to be Colin; or perhaps the boy on the beach, all over again, because the boy never completely went away. But it was only a friend, a fellow student who had locked himself out of his student lodge and wanted to sleep on our floor.

Whether it's Madame Rosa, or her sister Dot in the steam laundry, or the mechanical slot machine on the pier: the advice comes down to the same thing. The future will be what we choose it to be, just so long as we carefully engineer the present. As for the past, it moves like sand under your feet. These things happened a long time ago, yet remain luminous in my mind. As I write this I have resting on a pile of papers on my desk a glass paperweight. Scarlet with black spots, it is designed to look like a beautiful ladybird.

ACKNOWLEDGEMENTS

The wonderful American writer Jeffrey Ford deserves a special mention for encouraging me to write this novel after I'd explained the colourful institution of the British holiday camp to him over a beer. I also thank my wife Sue, who is my first reader and an indomitable critic; my loyal agent Luigi Bonomi; and my incredibly supportive editor Simon Spanton. I'd also like to thank Jon Weir and Charlie Panayiotou at Gollancz, as well as Colin Murray.

I worked on different holiday camps all those years ago and I must say that my fellow workers were generally much kinder than some of the characters in this novel. I hope that in the unlikely event of any of them reading this book that they don't feel betrayed by what is mostly fictional. Meanwhile the 1976 heat wave and the swarm of ladybirds are exactly as I remember them and the political mood of the time was volatile. I'm very glad that the dire predictions of some political commentators of the time did not come to pass.